The Missing Marquess of Althorn

The Lost Lords
Book Three

Chasity Bowlin

DRAGONBLADE
PUBLISHING, INC.

Dedication

As always, to my wonderful husband for always being supportive and for telling me every day that I am loved and appreciated.

I'd also like to take a moment to thank Violetta Rand for reaching out to me about the wonderful opportunity with Dragonblade Publishing and I'd like thank Kathryn Le Veque at Dragonblade Publishing for taking a chance on me and Scott Moreland for tolerating my irregular spacing, inconsistent capitalization and spelling that sometimes looks like it belongs on a poorly-written ransom note.

Thank you all for helping me to produce books that I am incredibly proud of and that have renewed my faith in the publishing world.

Books from Dragonblade Publishing

Knights of Honor Series by Alexa Aston
Word of Honor
Marked By Honor
Code of Honor
Journey to Honor
Heart of Honor
Bold in Honor

Legends of Love Series by Avril Borthiry
The Wishing Well
Isolated Hearts
Sentinel

The Lost Lords Series by Chasity Bowlin
The Lost Lord of Castle Black
The Vanishing of Lord Vale
The Missing Marquess of Althorn

By Elizabeth Ellen Carter
Captive of the Corsairs, *Heart of the Corsairs Series*
Revenge of the Corsairs, *Heart of the Corsairs Series*
Dark Heart

Knight Everlasting Series by Cassidy Cayman
Endearing
Enchanted

Midnight Meetings Series by Gina Conkle
Meet a Rogue at Midnight, book 4

Second Chance Series by Jessica Jefferson
Second Chance Marquess

Table of Contents

It was an arranged marriage neither wanted... and a love neither one expected.

Betrothed to Marcus Balfour, the Marquess of Althorn, since infancy, the entirety of Miss Jane Barrett's life has been planned for her by others. Through an overheard argument, Jane discovers at a very tender age that her betrothed is opposed to the match. The knowledge wounds her deeply and sews the first seeds of rebellion in her. Rather than marry her, the marquess joins the army but disappears in one of the war's bloodiest battles. Jane is left in a state of limbo—betrothed to a man who never wanted her and who is most likely dead, but still not free to pursue love elsewhere.

Marcus' objections to the marriage were less about the bride than the immorally young age of the bride at which their greedy and meddling fathers wished to force the match. While fighting for king and country, Marcus is confronted with the knowledge that there is a traitor in their midst, a man far closer to him than he might wish to admit. But he is captured, imprisoned, tortured, and left to rot for years until he can make his way back home to take up his rightful place as the Elsingham heir... and as a husband to Jane Barrett.

The years that have passed have eradicated any reservations about marriage to his betrothed, at least on his part. No man looking at her would ever mistake her for a child. More surprising is the attraction that he feels for her instantaneously and his determination to make her his, whatever the cost. It appears, however, that his bride to be will require some convincing.

As Marcus sets out to woo her, to prove that there is the possibility for something far more than a simple contract between them, danger lurks at every turn. The enemies who robbed him of years of his life by handing him over to the French is close at hand... and has their eye on Jane and her fortune, as well.

Prologue

London, 1806

MARCUS BALFOUR, MARQUESS of Althorn and heir to the Duke of Elsingham, stared at his father in growing horror. His betrothal had always been a sore subject between them. The duke was from a different generation, a time when arranged marriages for the sake of furthering finances or social gain were the norm. He had never been able to understand Marcus' reticence when it came to marrying the young woman he'd been affianced to while still too young to understand the meaning of the word marriage, much less the reasons for which it should be undertaken. Marcus hardly considered himself to be a romantic, yet the notion of marrying solely for the benefit of the family coffers left him cold and uneasy. That was bad enough, but what his father was asking now was beyond even that.

"I refuse," Marcus stated firmly. His tone was emphatic. For once, when it came to the subject of Miss Jane Barrett, he intended to stand up for himself entirely. In this instance, it wasn't only for himself but for her as well. At one and twenty, he was still far too young to be married. She was just shy of fourteen if he remembered correctly, and still looked very much like a child. The last time he'd seen her, only the summer before, she'd been playing with dolls. The very idea of marrying a girl so young turned his stomach. While there were men who would not balk at such a thing and who were, in fact, more attracted to younger girls and the younger the better, he was not one of them.

"You cannot refuse. Mr. Barrett and I have discussed it at length in letters! We both feel it has been delayed too long already!"

"How can it be delayed too long when the girl is not even out of the school room? She is too young to be married. For that matter, I am too young to be married!" Marcus demanded of his father. "You are wrong. Both of you are wrong. This is archaic and I will not be a part of it!"

His father waved his hand dismissively. "Girls are fine to be married so young! They don't have the same sort of needs that men do that require living a bit before settling into marriage! The younger you marry, the more likely you are to have many healthy children to carry on the family line."

"Sons," Marcus corrected. "You could not care less whether or not we have healthy children... only healthy sons to carry on the name. Your morals may permit it, but mine will not! I will not force myself on a child for the sake of conception and the continuation of our apparently corrupt line!"

The older man ran his hands through his hair in frustration and spoke from between clenched teeth, his anger evident in every gesture. "I'm not happy about it either, really. This girl has no rank and only the most limited of connections socially. She's barely considered gentry! But needs must, my son! Financially, we had no other choice but to agree to the match. It is to our benefit to keep Barrett happy!"

"You had no other choice, Father!" Marcus had rarely openly defied his father. He'd certainly never raised his voice at the man. Yet they were shouting, the both of them. "I have choices and I will not be forced to wed a child!"

The duke sighed heavily and settled into his chair. "It's Barrett who is pushing for the marriage. He wants the girl out of his home so that he can wed again. Apparently, his bride-to-be is less than pleased at the notion of having a nearly grown stepdaughter in the house. She feels that the servants will be divided in their loyalty to her if they are still pandering—her words, mind you! I have it in a direct quote from Barrett himself—to her predecessor. If you don't wish to consummate the marriage until she is older, fine. Wed her, set her up in a house in the country and continue sewing your wild oats in the city. Discreetly, of course," the duke suggested. "There's no reason marriage should interfere with your living your life just as you please. In truth, we'd have more readily available funds and you could, if you chose, live it up quite right!"

Marcus couldn't believe what he was hearing. He had no particular affection for Jane Barrett. In truth, they hardly knew one another beyond exchanging greetings when both families were gathered in the same location, but that didn't mean he lacked a certain degree of sympathy for her. A more unpleasant, cold-hearted and tight-fisted man than William Barrett he'd never encountered. It was evident in the way he treated the girl that he harbored no great affection for his daughter. As for their impending marriage, she was locked into the same contract he was by their managing parents, and by virtue of being female, had even fewer options available to her. "Lock her away to rusticate in the country? Marry her and abandon her immediately? Is no one else capable of seeing just how grossly unfair this is to Miss Barrett?"

The duke made a pshawing sound. "Since when did you care so much for her feelings? Normally, you can't even be bothered with her!"

"Because she's a child!" Marcus protested. "I know nothing about children, much less one that I find myself betrothed to! I will not do it. I will not be some monster who weds a child bride and then locks her away somewhere while I rut my way through society."

"This isn't some ridiculous novel by that Radcliffe woman!" the duke snapped. "This is about our lands, Marcus, our tenants and all those who depend upon us for their livelihoods. Can you imagine the shame if we were to begin selling off parcels of it? All of society would know that we are in dun territory!"

"Where we've landed precisely because you and your own father chose to marry unwisely and then philander your way through the *ton*!" Marcus retorted hotly. It was a well-known fact that his grandfather had married a penniless woman for love. That love had faded quickly in the face of his infidelity and gambling, but the pennilessness had remained a constant thorn in his grandparents' tumultuous marriage. She'd left him eventually, and her children as well, and fled to Spain with her lover. As far as scandals went, even fifty years on, it was still whispered about. His own father was no better, having married a woman with a small annuity and then living in excess of it as if he'd filled the family coffers to overflowing. With his mother gone, then his stepmother having sought an early grave via laudanum, ostensibly by accident, and now a new stepmother on the horizon, one with apparently very outlandish taste, their financial ruin was a forgone conclusion.

"I tell you, we've no choice!" his father snapped. "Barrett is threatening to have the contract dissolved if we do not come up to snuff, Marcus. He feels the girl is of a marriageable age and as he is her father, we've no right to gainsay him. Do I need to remind you what the financial situation of this family was before we made the agreement with him? If we have to pay back what has already been given much less forfeit the windfall that is due us upon the marriage and again with the birth of an heir, then we'll all be in the Fleet together!"

Marcus rose to his feet. "I will not force some terrified child to the altar. I've consented to wed her, committed myself to it, and I shall do so when she is of an appropriate age. Not before!"

"You will do as you are told!" the old man shouted, a vein protruding in his forehead as his face purpled with rage.

Marcus' own anger had reached the boiling point, as well. The unfairness of it all, of having his life mapped out for him by a man who couldn't have cared less for him, to essentially be bartered off—a title with a pulse for a pot of money—sickened him. That was bad enough, but to expect him to force a girl still in the schoolroom to marry was beyond villainy.

"This entire debacle is repulsive! I will not marry her. The thought of it is positively repugnant and I will not be a part of it!" Marcus' voice had risen with indignation and fury at the injustice of at all. He turned on his heel and strode toward the door of the old man's study, ready to march out of the house in a storm of righteousness. But when he opened the study door and stepped into the hall, he found himself staring into the round, youthful face of his betrothed. She appeared stricken—pale and wide-eyed with trembling lips.

One awful thought circled in his brain as he looked at her. *What had she heard?*

"Miss Barrett—" Marcus stopped short. There was little he could say to mitigate the damage already wrought.

"Lord Althorn," she said quietly, "My apologies for arriving earlier than anticipated. The roads were far better than anyone could have imagined. How terribly inconvenient it must be for you."

It was obvious from her expression and from the chilled tone of her voice that she'd heard what he'd said, or at least some small and very damning portion of it. Any attempt to rectify the matter would likely only make it worse. What could he say to her after all? "Forgive me, but I must go. I cannot stay."

"To do so would no doubt be utterly repugnant, would it not?" Her reply was uttered softly, her voice presenting as far more womanly than the rest of her. With her round face and pudgy figure, she looked exactly as a young girl should, except for her eyes. They were not only wise beyond her years, but also haunted. The pale blue held a wealth of sadness and quiet resolve. Whatever her life was at home, it was not easy. Her father was a difficult man in the best of circumstances and Marcus doubted very seriously that he offered Miss Barrett anything resembling affection. "I release you of the only duties I have the authority to bid you freedom from. Any social obligation to tend to me as your guest, Althorn, may be considered discharged. You should carry on as if I weren't even here."

Marcus flinched. She was wise, insightful and had a pointed wit that struck with surgical precision. "What you heard—it is not what you think, Miss Barrett. Trust me when I say that my refusal to meet my father's wishes today is in both our best interests."

She dropped her gaze to the floor, but her tone when she spoke did not match the subservience of her pose. It was cool and sharp. "I have never labored under the assumption, Lord Althorn, that what I wanted or what was in my best interests was pertinent to the situation. It is a hallmark of your elevated station by virtue or your sex and title that you are permitted to question authority and challenge the status quo. I cannot."

Those were the most words she'd ever spoken to him, he realized. He'd had to insult her, albeit unintentionally, and strike her to her very soul with humiliation before she'd ever been bothered to acknowledge him.

Marcus stepped forward until they were standing only a few feet apart. "I am not attempting to renege on the arrangement between our families. But I will not wed you when you are still a child. I would never forgive myself for it."

She looked up at him then and her gaze pierced him, seeming to see right through to the heart of him. It was as if she could see every flaw inside him. It was not the first time she had looked at him thusly, and if they were ever to wed as their families had long since agreed, it would likely not be the last. "I understand that my appearance is not pleasing to you. I understand why you think me a child, Lord Althorn. Yet, you are the one standing in your father's study, stamping your feet and demanding to have your own way in things. I agree that the existing arrangement demands we marry when I am still too young in years to be a bride. I would also posit that you will still be too lacking in maturity at that time to be a husband."

There was no argument against that as it was both true and not. Still, he'd managed to wound not only her feelings but also her pride. She'd earned a bit of indulgence if she wanted a pound of flesh from him. "I have some things that require my immediate attendance, Miss Barrett. Excuse me. Whatever you heard here today, I promise it is not what you think. And whatever comes, it has to do with doing what is right, and not avoiding our shared destiny."

With that, he turned on his heel and left, knowing that he would not be returning any time soon.

JANE WATCHED HER betrothed hasten from his father's home. He left so quickly that the door didn't even latch properly behind him. The wind caught it, whipping it open again. The butler immediately set it right, but the damage was done. The wake of Lord Althorn's departure and the subsequent rush of cool air that had entered had ruffled the vase of flowers on the hall table, sending petals and leaves cascading down onto the inlaid tabletop. Jane watched them fall and felt a strange kinship to those poor flowers. She felt as if many of her own petals had been sacrificed in their bloodless but still damaging exchange.

There had never been any false hope for her that theirs would be a love match. In fact, she had never anticipated that her betrothed would have any wish to marry her. It had been drilled into her almost since birth that her father had used his money to procure a match for her that would result in position and social cache for him. She was the sacrificial goat that would bring him into the highest reaches of society where he longed to be. What it might do for her or to her was entirely incidental. Of course, it was one thing to accept that her betrothed might be less than eager. It was another entirely to face the knowledge that he not only wasn't eager, but was, in fact, completely unwilling. It scalded her already singed pride, adding greater insult upon preexisting injury.

Repugnant, he'd said. That word wounded her to the quick. Her looks had never been remarkable. At best, she'd been called pretty by those who were feeling charitable, but never beautiful. Her figure remained stubbornly trapped in childhood. Round faced, flat chested, with no waistline in sight, she looked closer to girlhood than womanhood though the opposite should have been true. At nearly fourteen, other girls her age were beginning to wear their hair up and dress in lovely gowns. She still had braids and looked like a child. Was it any wonder he was so repulsed by the idea of marrying her?

It was of no consequence that she'd harbored the most tender of feelings for him, even if she hadn't expected them to be returned. She couldn't allow it to be. Handsome as he was, as charming as she'd seen him be with other people while always being stiff and formal with her, she'd only ever felt shy and embarrassed in his presence. Now, only the embarrassment remained. Humiliation, she corrected. He loathed her and the idea of being wed to her left him utterly repulsed. What on earth was she to do with herself in such a circumstance? She could not wed him, not knowing that.

At least hearing his awful admission had freed her from the painful worship she'd harbored of him. He hadn't simply fallen from the pedestal she'd had him upon, but leapt from it with abandon. The shyness that had always kept her frozen in his presence had vanished in the face of that and she'd finally managed to speak coherently, if rather scathingly, to him.

Her father entered then, the butler closing the door softly behind him. He frowned when he saw her, but that was his typical response whenever she was in his line of sight. Immediately averting his gaze and addressing the butler as if she were not even present, he demanded, "Was that Althorn leaving?"

Riggs, the duke's staunch and loyal butler nodded. "Yes, Mr. Barrett, sir. Lord Althorn had to depart somewhat hastily."

Her father turned his cold, sharp gaze on her. "Did you speak to him?"

"We spoke, Father," she answered evenly, not revealing the unpleasant nature of the exchange.

"About what?" he snapped. "Answer me, girl! I'm tired of this nonsense!"

"I believe," she offered hesitantly, "that the Marquess of Althorn is not pleased at the prospect of our coming marriage. It is my understanding that he and the duke have disagreed quite vehemently about it. Perhaps the duke will be able to provide more insight."

Her father looked at her with disdain. "Can't say I blame the boy. You've done little enough to make yourself even remotely palatable to the opposite sex."

"What should I have done then? Painted myself like a harlot?" she asked. Normally, she would never have spoken disrespectfully to him. But it was a rare day to have her heart broken and her lingering pride crushed in one fell swoop.

Her father said nothing, just turned and walked away. It was not an uncommon occurrence. He despised her and always had. Jane glanced over to the butler whose normally stern expression had softened into something akin to pity.

Holding her tears of humiliation at bay, Jane kept her voice calm and composed as she said, "I believe I will sit in the garden for a while, Riggs, if anyone should ask for me." *If anyone could be bothered to care.*

"Certainly, Miss Barrett," he said. "I will see to it they are informed if anyone should ask."

Jane turned then and headed toward the doors at the back of the corridor that would lead outside into the small garden that butted against the mews. No bigger than her own bedchamber, the tall hedges still offered more privacy than she typically found inside the house. Her father would badger her at the behest of her soon-to-be stepmother. The duke would be all that was polite, but he was so stiff it was never pleasant to be in his company.

Instead, she utilized the only escape that was available to her. Despite the cold, despite the burning pain that had blossomed in her chest and the withering of her paltry confidence in the face of Marcus Balfour's clear displeasure at their match, she retreated into a world where it didn't matter that she was plain. It didn't matter in the least that she was still as flat chested as a boy. She lost herself within the pages of a novel.

Chapter One

Eight Years Later

JANE SMILED POLITELY at the Duchess of Elsingham as the sherry was poured. Dinner was shaping up to be another disaster in what had been a long list of disasters besetting their annual visit to the Duke of Elsingham and his wife. Each year, it became more and more difficult to get through the weeks without everyone in the house succumbing to fits of either the vapors or ill tempers, depending upon one's proclivities.

"It is so lovely of you all to come and visit us here," the duchess said, gulping her sherry more than sipping it. "Ever since the Battle of Corunna and poor Marcus' disappearance, our society is so limited. No one quite knows what to do with us! Are we in mourning? Are we not? Is it within the bounds of propriety to invite us to dinners but not to musicales? I find it so tiresome to sit in the house and look at the same walls day in and day out! At least dear Charles made it home safely. Just imagine how awful it would have been had we lost them both to Bonaparte? How I despise that awful war! It's done terrible things to society!"

The duchess paused in her diatribe long enough to cast a sympathetic glance toward Jane. "But it must be so much worse for you, my dear! To have your betrothed simply missing... your life perpetually in a state of limbo when you ought to be well married and setting up house with children of your own! You are not getting any younger either! Time does slip away so quickly!"

Jane's only response was a tighter smile and a raised eyebrow. She was one and twenty, hardly in her dotage. Of course, as there was no end in sight to her strange period of half-mourning, that offered no comfort at all. She'd spent the last five years wearing nothing but drab gray or black. Their visits to town were infrequent and the stodgy country society near their home would never dream of inviting someone in mourning into their midst. Sadly, the dismal company of the Duke and Duchess of Elsingham was the closest thing to social interaction she could lay claim to.

Dull, dreary and always disappointing, it was hardly something to be anticipated, as they were trapped in the same state of limbo she was. Of course, she couldn't blame society hostesses for their reticence in including them. What were they to say? What were their other guests to say? *I'm terribly sorry your betrothed would rather run off to war than marry you. I'm terribly sorry your family had the misfortune to post the banns before he left and now you're stuck in matrimonial purgatory. I'm terribly sorry that your betrothed, who couldn't stand the sight of you, has been missing for five years and your life is in stasis because of it.*

Upon further examination, Jane decided that it was simply better for everyone involved if she had limited social engagements and fewer opportunities to be insulted or reminded of how poorly her life was playing out. Of course, as she would rather spend her days with fictional characters than real ones, that really was not such a terrible thing. And if the Duchess of Elsingham wished to continue harping upon it, Jane intended to make certain that the woman's sherry glass was refilled liberally and frequently so that the conversation might be shortened. If, Jane thought, she could get the duchess deep enough into her cups, she could call an early night for herself and retreat to her room and the trials of Lady Gray. That book had her in fits!

"It does, indeed. More sherry, your grace?" Jane asked softly.

The woman's eyes brightened. "Yes, yes indeed!"

The Duchess of Elsingham was not all that much older than Jane herself. Just shy of thirty, she'd married the Duke of Elsingham and become stepmother to Jane's betrothed only days before he left to join the fighting on the Peninsula. It always grated when the woman, who had not had children herself, reminded her that her own precious child bearing years were slipping away. Of course, she was still preferable to Jane's own stepmother.

Mrs. Barrett, as she insisted upon being addressed even by Jane herself, was the very devil. Luckily, she had not yet come down. The woman was perpetually late, more so because she liked to make an entrance than because she poorly managed her time. She'd, no doubt, be wearing one of her new gowns, brightly colored and prettily trimmed. It was that, even more than her difficult personality and questionable character, which prompted the current intensity of Jane's dislike of her at the moment. She resented the woman's freedom and her seeming imperviousness to William Barrett's foul moods and fouler temper.

As a footman refilled her grace's glass, Jane asked the question that propriety demanded of her. "Has there been any word from the investigators yet or the war office on Lord Althorn's whereabouts?"

The duchess shook her head sadly. It was an expression she adopted routinely when anyone asked about the fate of her stepson. She had taken to the roll of martyr with aplomb from the very moment of Marcus' disappearance on the field of battle. No one had ever looked so fashionably grim in their mourning clothes as the lovely Duchess of Elsingham.

Jane had the sneaking suspicion that because black was so flattering to the woman's cool blonde beauty, it was she and not the duke that delayed in having the Marquess of Althorn declared dead. It allowed her to draw out the period of mourning for ages longer.

"No, my dear. None at all. I fear we may never know what fate has befallen poor Marcus. So young and so handsome," the duchess mused. "What a shame for Alfred! His only son and heir gone without a word of explanation! The poor dear... his health is failing him so dreadfully. He has been all that is kind and gracious to me. Why, I could not ask for a better husband! He says nothing of what I spend. He is content to entertain himself and does not require that I dance attendance upon him at all times. Why the thought of—well, not to be indelicate, Miss Barrett, but the rules of etiquette are quite muddied on this subject. Alfred is significantly my elder and, as such, will likely precede me in death. I will, of course, mourn him terribly."

"Your grace, I cannot help but feel a question is buried somewhere within that soliloquy," Jane said, hoping to hasten the woman to the point. She had found that the duchess frequently took a meandering route to the heart of any conversation.

The duchess smiled and looked coquettishly at Jane through her lashes. The woman flirted shamelessly with everyone regardless of age, gender, or infirmity. It occurred to Jane that the woman was so spoiled by her own beauty she had never thought to explore anything else she might have to offer in life beyond a pretty face and a charming smile. Age would be a cruel comeuppance.

After a deliberately dramatic pause, the duchess continued, "I cannot help but wonder if I would be thought badly of if I did not continue to mourn Marcus once Alfred is gone. Would it be very gauche of me to pack away anything resembling black bombazine after a suitable period has expired?"

"I don't think so," Jane said. "You hardly knew Marcus, after all. It would be quite unfair for society to expect you to mourn him as you would a son when I do believe he is, in fact, your senior by at least two years."

Her grace sat back in her chair and beamed with a beatific smile. "I will continue to wear black on occasion, I think. It does look very lovely on me... and it camouflages any number of sins, particularly related to cook's lemon cakes. I haven't worn satin in ages. Do you not miss it, Miss Barrett? Opening your wardrobe and seeing an array of lovely colors spread out for your choosing?"

There had never been an array of colors in her wardrobe. Her father had always been quite the skinflint with her. As he'd already secured a husband for her, it would have been, in his words, a waste of funds to try and make her a silk purse from a sad, little sow's ear. She'd had only a handful of gowns and they'd been worn only in society. At home, she'd worn simple day dresses of rough fabrics that would have easily seen her pass for a scullery maid.

"I don't suppose I should speak of such things to you," the duchess said, clucking her tongue sadly. "My poor dear! Unless Alfred relents and has Marcus declared dead, or if Charles can do so if my poor Alfred does pass, why you might never wed! You will be stuck mourning for a man who might have been your husband for the rest of your life. I do believe that might be the most tragic fate I could imagine."

Jane nodded noncommittally. Had it not been for her father's insistence that the banns be posted so early, right after Lord Althorn had left for the army and never returned, she'd have been free to marry as she chose with the belief that Lord Althorn was dead. Of course, it had been a strategic move on her father's part. Announcing the betrothal had given him entree into the society that he craved. The connection to a dukedom had elevated his status just as he'd hoped. And her reluctant marquess had been conveniently absent to protest.

She was forever trapped and her own father had done that to her with his obsessive greed for a title. As it was, her grace was undoubtedly correct. With Althorn simply vanished, and no word of where he might be, dead or alive, there was no path open to her to move forward other than spinsterhood. Not that she wished for one, she reminded herself. Marriage was a fantasy best saved for pretty young girls with no notion of how cruel and unfeeling men could be. She was simply biding her time until her next birthday and the small settlement her grandfather had left for her would allow her to finally escape her father.

The duchess sipped her sherry. "Perhaps by next season we might slide ever so slightly into half-mourning? Perhaps dip our toes in the water by adding some lavender or lilac touches to these drab widow's weeds, no? We could still go to some parties, just nothing too grand or gay. Surely, no one would frown upon that after so many years?"

The door opened and the butler entered, pausing with his toes directly even with the door. "The honorable Mr. Charles Balfour, your grace," he intoned with all the gravitas of one announcing the Prince

Regent himself.

Charles entered immediately after him, his dark hair dusted with snow and a too-bright smile on his lips. He might have been handsome had his nose been a tad shorter and less hawkish, and had there not been a coldness about him that even the brightest of smiles could not truly hide.

"Well this is a pleasant surprise! I had not realized you had come to visit, Miss Barrett!"

The sentiment was offered with a false warmth that always made Jane uneasy. While a small part of her was flattered by his attention, her discomfort far outweighed it. Lovely compliments from a tainted source certainly lost some of their luster.

"Mr. Balfour," she said, inclining her head. Being in his company grated on her nerves. "I cannot imagine how you would find it surprising. We are here for two weeks following Christmas every year, are we not?"

He laughed, though there was an ugly gleam in his eyes at her slight rebuke. "What a wit you are, Miss Barrett! I find it quite difficult to equate the shy little girl you once were to the beautiful and witty woman before me. I daresay, you have come into full blossom."

"My father is closeted in the library with the duke. I have no doubt their conversation would prove much more edifying to you than the humdrum gossip that her grace and I are indulging in," she suggested gently.

His smile stretched into what could only be described as a predatory grin. "On the contrary! I'd much prefer to stay here. And if your conversation may be lacking in edification, I will still have a far superior panorama to console me, will I not? I daresay, the two loveliest ladies in all of London are before me!"

"Only in London?" the duchess questioned. "Surely in all of England at the very least!"

The door opened again and, once more, the butler stepped inside, toes even with the doorframe and his posture completely stiff. "Dinner is served, your grace," he intoned, dry as the dust that was never

.ced to settle anywhere in the house.

The Duchess of Elsingham nodded in acknowledgement and then .ooked to Mr. Balfour for his escort.

Charles smiled again, this time with a predatory quality. "Forgive me, your grace, but if I may… I'd like a private word with Miss Barrett before going in to dinner."

The duchess appeared quite put out, her chin inching upward and her back stiffening like a cat's. She was clearly offended that any man would choose to spend time with Jane rather than her. It was a stark reminder that while the Duchess of Elsingham could occasionally be pleasant company, they were not truly allies. Jane had no allies in that house and it was to her benefit to remember that always.

"Certainly, Charles," she replied. While her words were congenial, her tone was anything but. It was quite evident that the slight had been noted and would not be easily forgiven. The duchess glanced at Jane, eyeing her figure and then her face before turning away dismissively. "I will leave you to your conversation. It is a certainty, of course, that nothing inappropriate would ever occur."

Charles leaned in and kissed the duchess' cheek. It was a gesture that was far too familiar. "I promise to make it up to you."

The duchess smiled again and whacked his arm flirtatiously with her fan. She giggled and then cooed, "Yes, you will, you silly man!"

A feeling of dread had washed through Jane the moment Charles Balfour arrived. Watching the interplay between him and the duchess, earlier suspicions about the nature of their relationship reared their ugly head again. But more terrifying still was whatever it was that he wished to speak to her about. Anything he desired to say to her that required privacy was obviously nothing she would wish to hear. On that score, she was certain.

Helpless, Jane watched the Duchess of Elsingham sail from the room in a cascade of graceful black skirts. Her grace had been correct on one count. With her perfect, blonde beauty she wore the color well, whereas Jane always thought she herself looked like a sad but very plump crow. Even given the strange and quite charged exchange that had just occurred, Jane had to admire the woman's stunning beauty with no small degree of envy.

When the door closed behind her, Charles looked back at Jane with that same smile. It made him resemble the confidence men who hawked elixirs which they claimed could fix every ailment from gout to a man's loss of vigor, whatever that was. In reality, those elixirs only succeeded in making the unwary buyer poorer and too foxed to care. "My dearest, Miss Barrett—Jane—you must know why I've asked to speak with you privately."

Jane rose from her chair, feeling very much at a disadvantage. He towered over her regardless, but at least on her feet she felt marginally better about the situation. "No, *Mr. Balfour*," she stressed the formal address, hoping against hope that he'd take her meaning. "I cannot fathom that there would ever be any need for us to speak privately, for any reason."

"Jane," he continued, and his expression was both overly earnest and incredibly determined. It was a dangerous combination. "You must understand that over the years of our acquaintance, I have developed a deep and abiding admiration for you."

"Our acquaintance has been just that, Mr. Balfour. We see one another socially perhaps a handful of times each year. It is hardly of any significance," Jane insisted.

"Dare I confess it?" He continued as if she hadn't spoken and, in truth, he was so doggedly focused on his own ends it was possible he had not heard.

"No. Do not dare. Do not confess anything, Mr. Balfour," she said with greater force, her voice rising with panic.

"Jane," he continued, blissfully ignorant or deliberately obtuse regarding the terror he had invoked. "While you are certainly not a fashionable choice and your appearance is not that which would inspire great sonnets to your beauty, during our acquaintance, I have come to see that your beauty shines from within!"

Jane's lips parted in stunned offense. Panic gave way to umbrage. She gaped at him like a fish for several seconds as the magnitude of the insult sank in. Had he truly just said he wished to marry her because he'd known her long enough to overlook how unattractive he found her? He had! The pompous, puffed up idiot had, in fact, addressed how singularly unappealing he found her in his marriage proposal! His ineptitude would have been laughable had it not been so insulting. Only moments earlier, he'd been lauding her beauty. How quickly he had forgotten!

"I understand that you are still entangled with this kerfuffle of my cousin's disappearance and that you are not free to wed... but as the heir presumptive, there is every possibility that your father might be amenable to extending or modifying the existing contracts so they would be inclusive of my offer for your hand," he continued, his tone conciliatory.

Jane shook her head. "There is no offer, Mr. Balfour. There can be no offer! I am betrothed to your cousin—"

"Who is dead!" He stated it with a firmness that was somewhat surprising given that he had also been at the Battle of Corunna and had been unable to offer any information as to Marcus' whereabouts or condition. More concerning was the complete and utter lack of feeling the sentiment appeared to invoke in him. They'd never been close, as she understood it, but they were family, after all.

"Who is missing," she fired back quickly. "Missing and presumed possibly—maybe—could be dead, but not definitively dead. Certainly not so dead that I would feel compelled to throw off the marriage contracts that have been signed, the past reading of the banns and the scandal that would ensue were I to trade one member of your family for another! No, sir. Such an offer is beyond scandalous and it would be best for both of us to simply go on as if it never happened," she stated firmly. It wasn't really beyond scandalous. People did it all the time in slightly altered circumstances. But she was seizing upon any excuse she could to avoid a fate she deemed far worse than either spinsterhood or death.

The truth was, Jane realized, that being betrothed to a man who was not present and was most likely not alive, had given her a certain amount of freedom. It wasn't as much as if she'd been married and then subsequently widowed. Regardless, it wasn't something she wished to give up just yet. That small taste of freedom had given her a yearning for more and she'd made plans accordingly. They most certainly did not include being wed to a man of Charles Balfour's ilk.

Certainly being in mourning for as long as she had been did require some sacrifice. She didn't miss the parties and the balls. Wearing black and gray all the time was a bit of a set down but, in truth, it was a small price to pay. She was largely left alone with her books and her writing. Giving that up to marry a popinjay who was so utterly puffed up with his own importance—well, it would not and could not happen.

"Surely you are not seriously rejecting my offer, Miss Barrett? You only need time—"

"I am quite serious, Mr. Balfour," she replied evenly. "Time is not and will not be a factor in my decision."

"Even if Marcus is declared dead at some point, your marriage settlement and your father's extensive fortune will not be enough to have suitor's knocking down your door!" he snapped. "You haven't the sense to recognize a decent offer when presented with one!"

"I've not yet been presented with a decent offer," she replied quietly.

He drew back as if struck and, in some ways, Jane supposed she had struck the man. It didn't matter that he'd all but called her ugly and offered up his willingness to look past it because she was a good person. That didn't even brook commenting upon. But she'd refused him for sound and viable reasons that anyone else in society would champion, and he was insulted by it.

Rallying, he smoothed the front of his waistcoat and schooled his features into a neutral expression. It still reminded her of drawings she'd seen of crocodiles. The teeth might be concealed, but they still posed a very real threat. "I see, Miss Barrett. Perhaps, I have been overzealous in my pursuit of you and we've gotten off on the wrong foot. I understand that women prefer to be wooed slowly. I shall endeavor to move at far less frantic pace over the course of the remaining season as I attempt to sway your affections and secure your hand."

Jane blinked in surprise. Surely not, she thought to herself. Surely, a man of reasonable intelligence was not so foolish as to think a grown woman did not know her own mind when refusing his courtship. "Let me affirm for you, Mr. Balfour, I am not open to courtship or being wooed. Not by you and not by any man. I am betrothed to your cousin. If he should ever happen to be returned to us, I will honor that agreement between our families but I will seek no other offers and I will accept no other offers... specifically, I will never accept yours. Is that quite clear?"

His expression altered, shifted into something dark and even threatening. For a moment, it looked as if he might actually strike her. In the end, he stepped back, smoothed his hands over his hair and stated bitterly, "He's not coming back! He's dead and rotting in a Spanish grave... or are you too addlebrained to realize that?"

Jane had stepped back as well. Instinctively, her hand had searched for a weapon, landing upon the neck of a priceless antique case. She drew in a deep and steadying breath, but kept her hand there, ready to strike back if it should prove necessary. She'd actually been afraid of him. It wasn't simply her nerves or her overactive imagination. For that brief moment in time, Charles Balfour had dropped his mask and shown her a glimpse of all the nastiness that lurked beneath his well-polished surface.

Jane tried to retain a mask of poise and civility, and forced herself to let go of her makeshift weapon, her hands now resting at her sides. She clutched her skirts to hide their trembling. It was a better option than braining him. While the duchess was kind to her, Jane would never presume to say the woman was fond of her. Breaking an expensive vase against his impossibly hard head would likely strain the relationship. "I have refused you as kindly and firmly as I can, Mr. Balfour, and have done so in a manner that leaves you without question that my refusal would stand independently of your cousin's return or continued absence. I believe I will beg off dinner and dine in my chambers. I bid you good evening, sir."

"Don't bother. I'll not be insulted further by sitting at the dinner table and taking the scraps tossed my way while everyone bemoans the absence of a dead man who never deserved any of it to begin with!" he snapped at her as he turned on his heel and exited the room.

Left alone, Jane exhaled so forcefully that it left her quite dizzy. So much so that she had to grasp the back of the chair nearest her as she struggled to make sense of all that had occurred. She'd been aware of Mr. Balfour's changed feelings for her. *No*, she corrected. It was not that his feelings had changed, only that his intentions had. It was quite obvious that he believed taking on the abandoned fiancée of his late cousin would be a strategic maneuver on his part to further cement his claim to the titles and whatever inheritance was also intended for him.

She simply had not expected him to act so soon or to be quite so fervent and intractable in his offer. Was he in dun territory and trying to get his hands on her marriage portion to save himself? It was a likely explanation as she knew he liked the cards far better than they liked him. Whether she wished to wed him or not, it was much more palatable to believe that his offer was not entirely related to what he thought marriage to her might gain him financially. But her own vanity did allow her to deny the voice of reason or logic. His motives, beyond a doubt, were purely mercenary. That didn't mean she hadn't bruised his pride with her refusal. Whether he truly wanted her or not, he'd fully expected that she would want him. Disabusing him of that notion could have consequences.

When she'd regained her equilibrium to some degree, Jane stepped out of the drawing room and into the foyer. Her foot was on the bottom step of the grand staircase as she prepared to retreat to her room. The knock that sounded at the door filled her with dread. Had Charles returned to further press his suit or to hurl more insults at her head? Glancing over her shoulder, Jane watched with trepidation as Riggs opened the door and a man stepped inside.

Swathed in a dark and heavy cloak with triple capes, it was difficult to tell much about him at first. The coat was of good quality and very new from the looks of it as he stepped deeper into the more brightly illuminated hall and out of the shadows of the doorway. There was something familiar about him, about the way he moved. When he removed his tall beaver hat and passed it to the butler, even Riggs appeared taken aback.

A ringing began in Jane's ears as she watched him. It couldn't possibly be, she thought. The light struck his dark hair and she could see the shimmering blue undertones in the deep black strands. She'd known only one man in her life to have hair that black, like ink spilled on parchment.

"Althorn?" she uttered the word on the merest whisper of breath. It was enough. He turned to face her, but he did not smile. Instead, he looked at her levelly, his expression guarded in a face much leaner and harder than she recalled.

"Miss Barrett," he offered. "It seems you've quite grown up since last we met."

She would have to be married. It was that thought, more than the man standing before her that prompted the very first swoon of Jane's heretofore completely practical life. The breath whooshed from her body and the room seemed to spin about before her eyes. The floor was rushing up to meet her as the darkness closed in about her.

⚜

MARCUS BALFOUR, MARQUESS of Althorn, heir to the Duke of Elsingham and a long list of other lesser titles, had fought his way back from the brink of death. He'd survived battles, injury, disease that had wiped out entire regiments, capture and torture at the hands of the enemy, and even five long years of hard, back-breaking labor in an island prison off the coast of Spain. But walking the city streets of London, navigating the polite society that had once been his home, those things struck fear in his heart like nothing else.

It was that fear which had prompted him to hide out, to seek refuge in the less than stellar accommodations of the Thorn and Thistle Inn. While he hadn't intended to remain there forever, he'd hoped for a slightly longer reprieve to gain his bearings and decide how best to proceed with resuming his rightful place.

Back on English soil, he'd sought out one of the only allies on whom he could fully depend. Lord Highcliff had been a friend since they were boys at school. He was also one of the few men who knew precisely what sort of duties Marcus had undertaken while in service to the Crown. Highcliff still worked in secret, moving through the highest echelons of society and ferreting out those whose loyalties might be divided.

Not content to simply be a foot soldier, Marcus had worked in intelligence, providing false information to the French and ferrying back any tidbit he'd learned while in their midst. It had been danger-ous work and Marcus had thrived on that. *Until Corunna.* Everything had gone wrong, from the moment he encountered his cousin in the small city to the second when he'd looked up and seen Charles' face as he was being dragged away by French soldiers.

For a brief moment, he'd felt relief thinking that rescue would not be far off. But time had made both a liar and a fool of him. Charles had watched him being carted away. If what Highcliff had said was true, Charles had kept that information to himself in the years since, effectively leaving Marcus for dead.

So his return was a cautious one. He'd taken several days' time to gauge the temperature of the waters that awaited him and to discover just what had been done in his absence. It had been something of a relief to discover that his family had at least waited and not already petitioned the House of Lords to have him declared dead. That would have added yet another layer of complication to the Gordian knot that required unraveling.

During his brief stay at the Thorn and Thistle Inn, far from anyone who had expectations of him, he'd been slowly working his way around to returning to the family fold. A late night stroll to his father's home had ultimately made the decision for him. Marcus had watched

Charles enter and then watched him leave. Cold fury had washed through him as he thought of that bastard taking his comfort in the house that was to be his after Charles had watched him being carted off to prison and an unknown fate.

But now, as he stood on the threshold of the life he'd left behind, ready to take up his rightful place as the heir apparent to the Duke of Elsingham, Marcus found that he was nervous. Far more so than he'd anticipated, in fact. It might well have been the bad terms on which they'd parted. It could have been that despite their parting, he didn't anticipate that anything about his situation would have changed in spite of the fact that he had—very much so. The things he'd endured and the things he'd seen had eradicated the privileged and spoiled boy he'd once been so completely that it hardly seemed possible he would ever be able to fully assimilate to that life again.

Nothing could have made that more apparent than coming face to face with the girl he'd run from. But she was not a girl anymore. While she'd been little more than a child at his departure, the voluptuous figure so flatteringly displayed by the cut of her drab, gray gown was a stark reminder of just how long he had been gone. From the horrified expression on her lovely face, it was very apparent that she had neither forgotten nor forgiven their last meeting.

"Althorn?" The incredulity of her voice as his name whispered from her parted lips was to be expected, of course.

What did one say to a woman after so long? And she was a woman now. That was unfailingly clear. Whatever changes nature had wrought on her in the eight years he had been absent had marked her very sex very clearly. Ample curves and a face, that while not beautiful in the classical sense, was still quite arresting, made it almost impossible to reconcile the girl he'd known with the woman who now stood before him. But if his shock at seeing her so grown up was impossible to process, then what could she possible be feeling at seeing him very much alive? What on earth could he say to her when he'd left her to face the disapproval of their managing families while he'd run to another continent to escape their machinations? Nothing, he decided.

Addressing that at all would be a terrible strategical error. Instead, he attempted to be flippant.

"Miss Barrett, it seems you've quite grown up since last we met."

Her response was not at all what he'd anticipated. Marcus watched with dawning horror as her gaze went blank and she began to sink slowly to the floor. He rushed forward, managing to catch her just before her head struck the marble floor.

He winced as the muscles of his leg protested the added weight of another body. It had taken months of constant effort to rebuild his strength, to avoid walking with a limp for the remainder of his life. Even with that, it still pained him and likely always would.

"Riggs, would you have a footman carry Miss Barrett back into the drawing room?"

The butler was still standing there, his normally stoic face ashen. Reminded of his duties, he issued a curt nod. "Certainly, sir—my lord—Lord Althorn."

The man was so agitated he couldn't even fathom how to address him, Marcus thought bitterly. Immediately, a footman rushed forward and lifted Miss Barrett into his arms. Marcus straightened, winced as the muscles in his thigh contracted again, cramping to the point of agony. Willing the affected tissue to relax, he massaged the knotted muscles there with his hand until, at last, he could risk taking a step forward. The bullet he'd taken in his leg during their escape continued to provide many lingering reminders of the injury it had wrought.

The doors to the dining room opened and his stepmother emerged, followed by Mr. Barrett and a woman he did not recognize. He did not see his father.

His stepmother stopped mid-stride, stumbling as she gaped at him. "I don't understand! Marcus! We thought you were dead!"

Hoped, he realized. She'd never had much use for him. Dead, he would have at least garnered her sympathy and attention. "Well, I am clearly very much alive. Your grief, Stepmother, was for naught. Where is Father?"

It was Mr. Barrett who spoke. "You've been gone for many years,

Lord Althorn. Your father's health has been deteriorating for most of them."

The stab of grief was unexpected. He loved his father. It would take a monster to have no affection for one's own parent, but it was much stronger than he'd anticipated given the contentious nature of their relationship. "Is my father dead then?"

"No. He is not deceased," Mr. Barrett answered, "But he is quite changed. He had a fit of the brain nearly two years ago and has had some difficulty speaking since that time. He suffers with palsy and is unable to walk. I'm sorry, my lord. We had no way of keeping you appraised of his condition."

There was a note of reprisal there, as if it had somehow been Marcus' choice. He frowned at that, at all that it implied of just who was in charge now given his father's ill health. "They were not amenable to the sending and receiving of letters in the prison where I was held, Mr. Barrett. You'll forgive me for being unable to inform you of my direction, I hope. Now, if it is of interest to you, your daughter has fainted. I can't be entirely certain, but given what I recall of Miss Barrett's characters, that seems somewhat unusual."

The woman who was unknown to him stepped forward. "I will check in on her, my darling." The statement lacked anything resembling warmth or concern as she sailed past her husband toward the drawing room where Miss Barrett had been taken to recover.

Marcus shouldn't have found it surprising that Mr. Barrett was remarried. His desire to do so had been one of the compelling reasons he'd put forth for pushing up the date of the wedding between Marcus and Miss Barrett, after all. What was it that his father had said all those long years ago? That her new stepmother didn't wish to share a roof with her predecessor? Well, he'd certainly managed to muck up her plans.

"Perhaps we should all retreat to the drawing room," Marcus suggested. "I'm certain that once she awakens, Miss Barrett will have many questions just as all of you will and I would prefer to answer all of them at once if possible."

Chapter Two

J ANE SLOWLY BECAME aware of the low hum of numerous whispered conversations about her. Memory seeped in—Charles' proposal and Marcus' return. Oh, dear. Her lashes fluttered for a moment and then she managed, at last, to open her eyes. She started to sit up, but the duchess laid a warning hand on her shoulder.

"Not too fast, my dear. It would be a pity for you to swoon again when we've all been waiting to hear what dear Marcus has to say!" The admonishment was uttered in a tone that was all friendliness and warmth, yet still managed to make Jane feel like a slugabed for having had the audacity to faint and inconvenience everyone.

Still, Jane moved cautiously into an upright position. Everyone was gathered. Marcus was in the room and the duke sat near his son in his wheeled Bath chair. Her own father and stepmother were present and, naturally, the Duchess of Elsingham was there, enjoying her moment at center stage, as always.

"You're really here," she murmured. "You've come back!"

"I have," he concurred. "I did not stay away so long by choice. I was nearly killed and I've been held prisoner for the past five years. You do understand that?"

"I do. But I also understand that you very much left by choice," Jane reminded him. "It has been eight years, in fact, since you left. More than five since we've even heard from you. That is not an easy absence to simply ignore. Many things have changed, my lord."

He cocked an eyebrow at her. "And many remain the same," he uttered smoothly, "such as our betrothal. I understand, of course, that you may wish to have the banns posted again. It will suffice as an announcement of my safe return and will cement for anyone going forward, including my cousin, Charles, that we are as betrothed now as we ever were. I understand from Riggs that he offered for you just before I arrived."

How dare he! Gone for so many years, having left because he so despised the thought of their betrothal, only to return and protest as if he had the right to jealousy! Jane rose to her feet, her blood all but boiling with indignation. "So you're to play dog in the manger now?" Her tone of voice shifted as she laid out his transgressions, from incredulous to strident. "You left me here while you ran away from home like a spoiled child, joined the army, and nearly got yourself killed. You did succeed in getting yourself captured—all simply to avoid being married to me. Now, you've returned and because Charles had the audacity to ask for my hand, you want to be possessive and claim me as if you suddenly have the right?"

"I don't have to claim you. You're already mine," he insisted. "We've been betrothed since you were an infant! Please tell me that you aren't actually considering an offer from that worthless dandy?"

The other occupants of the room took up the battle then. Her father and the duke began yelling back and forth, Mrs. Barrett glared daggers at the lot of them. Only the duchess was unaffected. She looked from one person to another with a gleam in her eyes as if savoring the excitement.

Ignoring the others and focusing only on Althorn, Jane said, "How do you know he's a dandy? You haven't seen him in years!" Of course, she had no interest in Charles' offer and had already informed him thusly, but she was deeply and bitterly resentful of Althorn's assumption that he could simply waltz in and behave in such a high-handed manner with her. She wasn't a shy little girl any more, desperate for him to show her even a shred of affection. If he thought to cow her or control her then he was terribly mistaken.

"He was always a dandy. I doubt it's changed!" His reply was just as cross as hers. They'd been in one another's presence for less than a quarter hour based on the mantel clock and they were already at one another's throats. "There are things about him that you cannot possibly know but that make him a most unsuitable choice for you!"

Jane continued on, oblivious to the back and forth swiveling of heads as everyone in the room watched them argue. "Why on earth should it matter to you if I am considering his offer? If you'd wanted to marry me at all you wouldn't have run off to shoot guns with all the other little boys!" As soon as she'd said it, Jane clapped her hand over her mouth.

It was a terrible thing to have said. The war had been brutal and bloody, robbing many of their lives, their limbs and their spirit. Hadn't she seen them when she volunteered at the church to feed the poor? Soldiers with terrible scars and haunted eyes lined up for soup and old bread because the country they had served had failed them so miserably upon their return. Even worse than those soldiers were the widows and orphans who arrived, just as haunted and destitute. To make light of what anyone had suffered there, even the man before her, was unforgivable.

Althorn drew himself up to his full and rather impressive height. His eyes flashed with anger and every muscle in his chiseled face was taut with anger. "I'll grant that I might have been a boy when I left, but it takes little enough time on the front lines of a bloody and gruesome war to become a man. As I said at our last meeting, my reasons for leaving that day are not what you believe them to be! Regardless, they should not be discussed here in front of everyone else."

The duchess blinked at them. "Well, don't stop now. Dear heavens! This is more entertainment than I've had in years! Why on earth they feel the theater is an inappropriate activity for those in mourning I cannot begin to fathom. Certainly comedies should be avoided, but a nice tragedy could be enjoyed without appearing to be too gay, could it not? Perhaps you should take this particular act to Drury Lane?"

Jane clamped her lips firmly closed. In one instance, he had been correct. This was not a conversation they should be having in front of others. Her behavior was abominable, but then his wasn't much better. They were bickering like school children. Of course, everyone else in the room was behaving like children as well.

"Walk with me," he suggested.

"Where?" she asked. It didn't matter. It wasn't really in her best interest to refuse him. She could see her father glaring at her from across the way and her stepmother counting all the various ways in which she'd been unpleasant and undermined her. She'd no doubt hear from both of them later. By agreeing to speak with him privately, she was at least giving the illusion of being somewhat agreeable.

"Just in the garden... we can speak privately there," he said.

"If you'll ring for the maid, she can bring my pelisse," Jane said.

The duchess laughed. "Oh darling girl! Why bother? She's right outside the door along with every other servant in this house. Sarah," she called out, "Go and fetch Miss Barrett's cloak for her!"

Immediately, the sound of footsteps could be heard outside the door as the maid left to do her bidding.

Gossip. How Jane despised gossip! Even if it had earned a tidy sum of money for her. Perhaps, it was best to say she despised being the butt of gossip. In the immediate aftermath of his presumed death, she and Althorn, in absentia, had been the subject of countless rumors and stories. Now they would be at the center of them again. And she would have to return to society. The respite provided by her period of mourning for him was over. She'd have to face the lot of them. *If they ever find out who you are and what you've done you will pay dearly.*

That thought echoed in Jane's mind and brought forth a whole new wave of panic. How could one person's life become so inordinately complicated in the span of a single evening? A missing bridegroom returned, another would-be bridegroom running off in a snit, and a secret career that was both scandalous and lucrative and that would embroil the very elite family she was to marry into in a scandal that would set the *ton* on its ears—it was no wonder she'd fainted for the first time in her life.

The maid appeared with her pelisse and, once it was donned, Jane permitted Lord Althorn to take her arm and lead her through the corridor to the doors that opened onto the terrace at the back of the house and the small garden beyond.

Outside, the cool night air settled around them. It eased the burn in her cheeks from both her own embarrassment and her anger. It wasn't simply that he'd been gone; it was that gut-wrenching scene which had occurred immediately prior to his departure. She'd never forget the humiliation she'd felt that day at hearing him describe the idea of marriage to her as repugnant. Even now, it threatened to swamp her.

"Where have you been for so long?" Jane asked the question in an attempt to establish some sort of normality in an otherwise abnormal situation. How did one comport oneself in such a muddle?

"There was a small island off the coast of Spain that was controlled by the French. As I said, I was imprisoned there for several years," he answered evenly.

Imprisoned. He'd said it dispassionately, as if it didn't conjure up horrific images. "Well, it sounds positively hellish."

He ducked his head, his lips quirking slightly. "You do not mince words, Miss Barrett. Not at our last meeting and not at this one either. It was hellish. We were treated very poorly initially. Eventually, it got better."

"And they let you go?" This man was very different from the stiff and priggish boy she remembered. But then, she supposed fighting in a war, being captured and held as a prisoner for years and whatever else he might have gone through would be enough to significantly change a man.

"No, Miss Barrett. I escaped," he said softly.

"Was it dashing? Worthy of a penny novel?" The moment she uttered the question, she wished she could draw it back. If she wished to be circumspect, she was doing a poor job of it, indeed.

"Hardly that," he said dismissively. "As the war progressed, fewer guards were stationed at the prison. They were all called off to serve in other capacities. Finally, it reached a point where only two fat old men who preferred wine to work were left to monitor the lot of us. We overtook them, and sailed to shore in Portugal in a leaking boat that reeked of rotted fish and unwashed men. It was not dashing or heroic. It was dirty, smelly, difficult and altogether anticlimactic after years of imprisonment."

"I wouldn't say so," she protested. "You faced the threat of death if you were caught. And I don't understand why you would have been imprisoned in such a way, at all! It was my understanding that the French allowed officers to live in towns on a sort of parole! It seems very unfair that you were treated so differently."

"When I was captured, I was not dressed as an officer. I was working in intelligence at that point," he admitted after a long and thoughtful pause. "I was taken for an enlisted man and, given the information that I had, it was best for all concerned that my captors continue believing it. By the time the information was no longer valuable and I could profess my true identity, no one believed me. They all assumed I was claiming a different rank simply to get out of the hard labor that was part of my sentence."

"But you're here now... in England. You did not return to your unit!"

"I was injured during our escape," he explained. "When we arrived in Portugal, we reported to the nearest British contingent. I was treated, relieved of duty and put on the first English naval vessel headed home."

Jane allowed that to sink in. While she did, she made a study of him. From the elegant cut of his coat, the perfectly-fitted waistcoat and trousers and a pair of boots that possessed a high shine and new soles. It was a puzzle to her how he might have procured such clothing if he'd only just arrived.

"That is English tailoring, my lord," she said, pointing to his coat and the part of the tale he'd presented which bothered her the most. "It was made for you and you alone. Which means you did not just return to England. You have been here, in London most likely, long enough to have a custom suit of clothing made for you. And yet, you

32

waited until tonight to make your presence known. Why?"

He looked away then. His profile was different, she thought. Sharper, his nose slightly misshapen from having been broken. There were other small differences that could easily be accounted for simply by the nature of maturity and the violence he'd suffered while fighting in the war. But those differences, along with his changed demeanor, might be enough. A plan started to form in her mind.

"To put it simply," he replied, "I wasn't sure if I should come back and if I should, how. What does one say after such a long absence and such certainty of death?"

"A letter warning of your arrival might have been a good starting point," she chided. "Why not write us before leaving Portugal? Why not give us some indication that you were still amongst the living?"

As it was quite clear from the set of his jaw that he did not intend to expand upon his answer to her question, Jane continued. It stung regardless. Even now, eight years later, was the idea of returning to the life that had been planned for them that repellant to him? It wasn't as if she wanted to marry him at all, really. But it was a blow to her pride to think that he still dreaded the prospect so intensely he'd sacrifice his own identity to avoid it. Finally, he offered, "The letter and I would have arrived at the same time and likely on the same ship."

That might well be the truth, but it was obvious to her that it was not his only reason. He was lying for some reason and she would not be satisfied until she knew why.

"You look very different. I'm not even sure you are Marcus Balfour." She certainly didn't want him to be. It symbolized the end of her freedom. "What are your titles?"

He turned to her then, a smirk on his lips. With an imperiously arched brow, he asked, "Do you want all seventeen of them?"

That was a gesture she recognized, effectively quelling her doubts. But she would brazen it out regardless. She hadn't truly doubted his identity, but then her doubt or belief was not the most important factor. Her freedom would rest on her being able to make others question just enough to delay the wedding. It was in her benefit to prolong the inevitable as long as possible. She was six months shy of her birthday. Six months away from the inheritance left by her grandfather that her own father could not touch. Six months to freedom from every man and managing relative in her life. "At least a few of them, I would think... for the sake of authenticity."

"Obviously, I will one day be the Duke of Elsingham. Currently I am the Marquess of Althorn. I am also Lord Helingford, Lord Avondale, and a few others. There is an endless string of them, Miss Barrett, and I can recite them all if you like, but I hardly see the point. I am who I say that I am, and our situation has not changed since I left... even if we may have."

"Your situation is unchanged," she snapped. "Mine is changed greatly. I'm capable of supporting myself now and can live independently of all the people trying to manage my life for their own gain! Independently!"

He went very still. "Support yourself how precisely? To my knowledge there are only a certain number of occupations open to a young woman of your standing... and none of them are reputable. What have you been up to in my absence, Miss Barrett?"

Jane could have struck him. If she'd thought slapping his face would have served any purpose other than to hurt her own hand, she might have done so. "You've no wish to marry me. That was true eight years ago and it is still true today. So don't pretend to be concerned for my welfare, the state of my virtue, or my reputation. If you'd had a care for any of those things you wouldn't have abandoned me when you did and proclaimed to the world that you'd rather lose your life at the barrel of a French gun than to wed me!"

She wasn't going to tell him about her publishing career. Her credits to date might have been nothing more than nasty little pamphlets filled with rehashed society gossip that she got second hand through the servants, but they were hers nonetheless. Published under a nom de plume, they had earned a nice little income for her. It wasn't enough to live on in the style she was currently accustomed to but it gave her a sense of pride in having her own money, even if it was languishing in a bank under a false and masculine name. It was her emergency fund, in case her father had ever gotten it into his head to marry her off to someone else rather than wait for the unlikely return of the man before her. She'd have run then, and hidden until she could claim her inheritance. Would it last her six months without having to exist in absolute penury? Probably not, she thought grimly. But there were worse things than simple and temporary poverty.

MARCUS FROWNED. THIS was more than wounded pride from his ill-timed and misconstrued statements all those years ago. He found himself presented with, possibly, the rarest creature of all—a woman with no wish to marry. It wasn't exactly unheard of but for a woman in Miss Barrett's position it was very unusual. At least he could be certain that she wouldn't marry Charles. He'd have to proceed cautiously on that front.

Curious at her clear desire to pursue spinsterhood, he asked, "I must ask, Miss Barrett, is it the state of marriage you are averse to... or me?"

Her chin came up and her gaze was steady and unflinching as she said, "Are they not one and the same for me, my lord? Never in all of my life have I been able to entertain the notion of being married to any man other than you. And as your desires clearly ran in a very different direction, even prior to your unwilling absence, I had to assume that we would not have a happy union. Therefore it has not been something to look forward to or pin one's hopes and joy upon."

"There are things about that last day before I left that I regret," he said softly. "Among them are the rather cowardly manner in which I fled my familial duties and also that I wounded your feelings in the process. What you heard, Miss Barrett, was not a reflection on your person or on the idea of someday being wed to you. I was, however, adamantly opposed to the idea of marrying when you were little more than a child."

"We were to be wed when I was sixteen, my lord," she protested. "And while I realize that is still younger than most gently-bred girls marry today, it's hardly unheard of."

She didn't know, Marcus realized. Somehow, no one had ever bothered to inform her that the already hastened timeline of their union was to have been hastened yet again. "Indeed, while sixteen is troublesome to me, it was not our impending marriage in two years that forced me to flee. Your father, and I apologize as it seems you are unaware of this, was pressuring mine to have us wed immediately... when you were not even yet fourteen, I believe."

Miss Barrett blinked at him for several seconds. "Surely, you misunderstood. As unfeeling as my father may appear at times, even he would not stoop so low!"

"I did not misunderstand, Miss Barrett. I apologize for revealing this information to you in such a manner. I had thought you aware of the circumstances... My father made it clear to me that the change in the original plan from eighteen to sixteen and then from sixteen to fourteen was a reflection of your stepmother's hesitance in marrying into a household where her predecessor still resided."

"Her predecessor!" Miss Barrett uttered the word with contempt. "I was a child attempting to run a household that would be challenging even to the most experienced of chatelaines. The servants ignored me half the time and blatantly disobeyed the other half! I would have welcomed her into that house if only to have the assistance and someone to—"

She had stopped abruptly and turned away from him, staring out into the nearly barren garden beyond.

"Someone to what, Miss Barrett?"

"Someone to talk to I suppose. Father was gone so very much and I was very alone at that time. I have learned since to enjoy the solitude and to make good use of it," she replied stiffly.

Marcus knew something of solitude. He'd had many solitary hours in his cell on that small island to reflect on his actions, on what had been asked of him and to see the uselessness of his life beforehand. He had many regrets, amongst them all the time he'd wasted on idle pursuits and things that brought no meaning to his existence.

"My methods of avoiding your father's request were questionable, Miss Barrett. But I assure that my motives were not," he uttered in complete earnestness. "Those things you heard me say were only a reflection of my unwillingness to marry you at such a tender and inappropriate age. Nothing more."

"That changes nothing," she said. "Regardless of your reasons for protest—and under the circumstances those very hurtful things I heard are certainly mitigated—I am not that same desperate young girl you left behind. I find I am quite content to remain unmarried. I had grown to embrace the idea of it. And now, on a whim—your whim—my life turns once more."

Marcus considered his answer carefully. "Miss Barrett, to simply renege on this contract will amount to financial ruin for my family. All I ask is that you give me time to court you and to attempt to establish a relationship between us that has nothing to do with that infernal contract, our meddling fathers or our very muddied past. Let us get to know one another before we make any hasty decisions."

His strategy had been sound in making her an offer that he knew she would not be able to refuse. Marcus watched her struggle with that, wrestling to find some way around it. He could see the moment of capitulation on her face before she even opened her mouth to speak.

"It isn't as if I have the option to reject such a request, now is it?" The admission was uttered grudgingly without anything resembling graciousness. In fact, she was quite curt. "Very well, my lord, I consent to your courtship. I only feel it sporting to warn you that I am unlikely to be swayed."

Marcus smiled. If he'd learned one thing during his time in that French prison it was exactly how hard he was willing to fight to keep what was his. "And I feel it only to sporting to warn you, Miss Barrett, I am unlikely to give up."

Chapter Three

GIVEN THE EXCITEMENT of the evening and the unusual turn of events that had occurred, supper was served on trays as everyone retreated to their rooms. For Marcus, he had retreated to the study where his father waited for him.

The old man was stooped in his chair and aged far more than a mere eight years ought to have wrought upon him. Haggard, weak and rail thin, he looked to be near death and a far cry from the vigorous man Marcus had quarreled so heatedly with.

"You've come back," the old man said, his voice low and quavering. His lips did not move as much as they ought to have and the words were garbled, though still audible.

"It was not my wish to stay away so long. I had not intended to be captured," Marcus said, striving for a lighter tone. There were elements to his long disappearance that could not yet be revealed. There was too much at stake.

Marcus took a moment and studied the old man, noting every change in his appearance. It hurt him to see his father so. It was a stark depiction of the fragility and finite nature of life. It was also a stinging reminder that he did not have long to try and make things right, or as right as they might ever be.

"Your willfulness did this," the old man mumbled. "You left, and I had to try to save face... we were barely keeping the creditors at bay. And then this... my own body betrayed me. You'll make it right!"

Marcus didn't protest. "If Miss Barrett agrees, I will honor the arrangement between our families. If she does not, I will not force her."

"Bah! You will do as you are told," he snapped and banged his fist against the wooden arm of his wheeled chair. "Finally! Why you can't be as obedient and eager to save this family and our good name as your cousin, Charles, I will never understand!"

Some things had not changed at all while he had been gone it seemed. His father's temperament was as ill as ever and his tyrannical demands remained the same. The same tired and repetitive comparisons to his worthless cousin continued. If only they knew, Marcus thought. The urge to blurt out the truth, that Charles had betrayed him for his own selfish ends was there, but it was too damaging.

He would not utter something that could ultimately hurt the future of the Elsingham estates. Marcus could not afford to have the same hotheaded response to those things that he once did. There was no driving need to test the boundaries or have his father concede defeat. He was no longer desperate for the old man's approval and attention. Prison had taught him many things, and one of them was to choose his battles well. Fighting the old man would only end poorly. And as they were both in agreement on his course of action, it was easy enough to yield to some degree. "Yes. I will. Not because you demand it of me but because I committed myself to do so years earlier and now her age is no longer an impediment."

"And if she's unwilling? What then? We can't repay the debt!" The old man snapped the words out with ferocity that was not at all impeded by his drawn mouth. "You're as worthless as you ever were to me!"

Marcus let the hurt wash through him, settling deep. But on the surface, at least, he remained calm. "I will do everything in my power to ensure that does not happen, short of violating my own ethics."

"We can't afford your ethics! Your damned stepmother is going to break me... one new gown after another even when she's been told no. And now you're back and she'll want more new gowns as the mourning rags won't do! It would have been better if you had stayed gone and I'd had you declared dead in the House of Lords!"

It was not unexpected. He'd harbored no great illusions that his father would be overjoyed at his return. But he'd thought, or hoped at the very least, that there might be some relief. It had been a foolish hope it would seem. "I see. I'm glad to see that you're so overjoyed and happy at my safe return, Father. It means the world to me."

"I'm happy that the contract will be honored and that we can live as we were meant to all along instead of pinching every pence like a shopkeeper!" his father groused. "If you were a good son, you'd never have gone at all!"

Marcus rose. "And if you'd been a better father, I wouldn't have had to. We all have things to regret in this. I won't add more to it. Good evening, sir. I shall retire, assuming that there is a room for me here."

"It'll be yours one day whether I like it or not," the duke said with a shrug that lifted only his right shoulder, the left remaining paralyzed at his side. "I'll not raise a scandal by having you tossed out into the cold now."

"At least your priorities are in order then," Marcus said and rose to his feet. "By all means, let's avoid a scandal."

Exiting the library, he climbed the stairs and headed in the direction of his old suite. The maids were airing it out, having made the bed up with fresh linens. Water for washing was being kept warm for him on the hearth and a supper tray had been laid on a table nearby. As he entered the chamber, two maids were there.

"You may go," he said. He wanted to be alone with his own thoughts and even the presence of servants was too much.

"Should we turn down your bed, my lord?"

"I can manage. It's fine." He gestured toward the door and the two maids rushed out giggling and whispering under their breaths.

Alone once more, he removed his coat and jerked at the knots of his neckcloth. After so long in the rags that were all that remained of his uniform and then the simple clothing he'd procured for the journey home, the trappings of his old life felt stifling in so many ways.

In prison, working like any common laborer, back-breaking hours hauling rock and dirt with the hot sun beating down on him, all he'd thought about was returning home. His survival had been fueled by only two things, revenge and reclaiming what was his. He would make Charles pay for his part in sending him to that hellhole. But it had been the idea of retreating once more into the isolated luxury of the upper classes that allowed him to cling to hope in those early days. The idea of sleeping in soft beds draped with clean linens, of eating rich foods and washing them down with only the best of wines had become more and more distant until those things seemed more fantasy than memory.

"I do not belong here anymore," he whispered aloud to the empty room. But if not there, where? He was not a common laborer though his hands would belie that at present. But he wasn't the same spoiled aristocrat he'd once been. He was lost in some netherworld between the two. Somehow, he'd have to make that work, to carve out a place for himself in a world that now seemed rather useless and silly and amongst people who seemed the same. Regardless of what his fate might hold, he would not allow Charles to claim the dukedom.

Miss Barrett was an intriguing aberration though. And she had a secret. He would find out what it was. He would also find out what Charles was up to. His cousin had never been the trustworthy sort and his proposal to Miss Barrett smacked of desperation. While Marcus found her wholly appealing, she was not the sort of woman that Charles typically gravitated to. She didn't simper and flirt. She was too smart, too inquisitive, and too much of a handful for him.

Lifting the cover from his supper tray, Marcus took in the assortment of food, the freshly baked bread and then examined the bottle of wine sent to accompany it. There were pleasant aspects of his return, regardless of his less than warm welcome by all parties involved.

IN HER CHAMBER, Jane sat at her desk with her supper tray untouched before the fireplace. How could she eat at such a time? Her entire future was hanging in the balance, and she still had a deadline to meet.

Withdrawing a blank sheet of foolscap from her writing desk, she decided that the very least she could do was to announce her betrothed's return in her latest pamphlet. The news would be well received by many and it was just the kind of story that her readers wanted—the contentious homecoming, the less than willing bride. She would use her own life in those short booklets for a change instead of simply relaying gossip about everyone else's.

Althorn's return would be the scandal of scandals. Everyone would talk about it and everyone, from the highest to the low, would be fascinated by it. And if she were to include in the column that there were questions as to whether or not he was truly who he claimed to be, it would buy her the necessary time. She didn't trust his offer of six months. She didn't really trust anyone. If what he'd said tonight about her father was true, her lack of trust in men was well founded.

Her maid entered and took one look at her ink-stained hands and sighed heavily. "Where are your writing gloves, miss?"

"They're not writing gloves. They're more akin to never write again gloves. I've tried... it's all just illegible scratching when I wear them. We'll just scrub extra hard in the morning to get rid of all the ink stains."

"Miss, there's only so much I can do," the maid said.

"Sarah," she began, having eschewed the tradition of calling one's lady's maid by their last name. As the girl worked in the kitchens when they were back home at Oakhaven, it only complicated matters to change the rules midstream. It was only when they came to town that her father, to keep up appearances, assigned her such duties. "If I can get this column written and to the printer by tomorrow, I can have the story of his return out to the public in greater detail than any of the news sheets. That means I will sell more copies and can request a higher wage! And when I leave Oakhaven, you can come with me. I'll have enough money to hire you on as my housekeeper. It won't be grand, but you won't have to work yourself to the bone like you do for Father and Mrs. Barrett."

"I suppose you can wear gloves when with company tomorrow," the maid said softly.

Jane glowered at her. "If you're only here to scold, then you can leave!"

"He was very handsome," the maid said quietly as she began tidying up the room. "Very handsome. I couldn't help but notice that when I brought your pelisse earlier."

"He's handsome... and arrogant, high-handed, rude, demanding, utterly conceited and full of himself," Jane said, continuing to write. The man was as insufferable as he'd ever been, but she was far less inclined to tolerate it in her current state.

"You gathered all that in the short conversation you had in the garden, did you?" Sarah asked with her tongue in cheek.

Jane looked up and gave the maid a warning glare. "No, I reaffirmed that opinion, formed all those years ago during our short conversation in the garden. He is as he always was. But I am not."

"That's not what the servants say. They've all remarked on just how different he is."

Jane put her quill down. "If you had gossip you should have told me that first! It might change the entire tone of what I'm working on. It is really him, isn't it?"

Sarah looked at her in shock. "Well, no one said it wasn't, miss."

"Drat! Of course they're all certain it's him. Why would they question it when he will likely be the one who pays their wages later on?" Jane murmured under her breath. Never mind that he looked every inch the part and had the same mannerisms. Never mind that there was a perfectly reasonable explanation for every slight alteration to his appearance that could be attributed easily to the passage of time and the endurance of hardship. She was grasping at straws and she knew it.

"What was that, miss?" Sarah asked, eyeing her worriedly.

"How is it that he's changed according to them?" Jane replied, not acknowledging or explaining her previous statement.

"The under butler was assigned to be his valet, but he declined. He said he could manage to dress without aid. And he does everything for himself. He turned down his own bed, dismissing the maids before they could!"

"That's hardly noteworthy." Jane couldn't keep the disappointment from her voice. She'd hoped for something more significant to support her claims.

"For a gentleman, an aristocrat no less, to decline a valet? I wonder if he was injured and is trying to conceal his scars?" Sarah mused. She uttered the questions with wistful dreaminess. "He must have been so brave."

"Perhaps it isn't the presence of a scar... it could be the absence? If he's not Althorn, but an imposter, then he wouldn't have the same marks on his body. A valet, or a servant who had been with the family for so long would know that! Maybe he really isn't Althorn? But how to prove it?" Jane was muttering to herself, spinning plots as if she wrote gothic novels instead of gossip rags.

Sarah shook her head. "There would be no way to prove it. But if you could make other people doubt it, then perhaps he would have to prove it himself. Are you certain you wish to do this, miss? I think it might not go well for you if you do. Your father will be furious. Your stepmother will be more unpleasant than usual. And, well, it isn't my place to say it, but are you certain marriage to such a man would be so bad?"

"So bad? It would. Of course, it would! I don't want to be married. I want to be free!" Jane insisted. Freedom for women was, of course, a relative thing. She'd never be truly free but she might have the liberty of at least making her own choices in some aspects of her life.

"But he said you could call off the wedding! Isn't it a bit dishonest to sabotage him so?"

It was, but Jane was desperate. "I'll do whatever is necessary. I'm not letting any man dictate my life ever again. Father has done enough. I won't trade one jailer for another!"

Sarah sighed heavily as she stepped behind Jane and began taking the pins from her hair. "Yes, miss. I only hope you don't come to regret it. There's something to be said for having the love of a man in your life."

Jane looked down at the words on the page. "Love has no part in this particular play, Sarah. It's all about money and has been from the start. I'd rather be alone than with someone who required compensation to be with me."

The opinionated maid had no response to that. She worked in silence, brushing and then braiding Jane's hair before saying goodnight.

Alone, Jane returned to her writing. She was sealing her fate in essence, creating a rumor that he was not truly the Missing Marquess as the scandal sheets had dubbed him. It was life or death, she reasoned. To her mind, being trapped in a miserable and loveless union with a man who would attempt to rule her every thought and action was a kind of death. The slow loss of one's self to another was something she never wanted to experience it. Her mother, in the few memories that remained of her, had been a ghost of a woman. Bullied and downtrodden, browbeaten by her husband so often that she barely uttered a whimper of protest at anything—Jane would not let her own fate mirror her mother's.

CHARLES ENTERED HIS suite of rooms and, still in a fit of temper, slammed the door behind him with such force it rattled the windows. It reverberated so fiercely that empty wine bottles toppled from the table and tumbled to the thinly carpeted floor. He was living in poverty, subsisting on table scraps. After all that he'd done to ensure his future, he was still living on the fringes of the world that should have been his.

He'd stopped at a hell on the way home, lost more markers that he lacked the funds to cover and consumed copious amounts of brandy that he could not pay for. No doubt, there would be a stern talking to from his uncle in the near future. How dare that little cow dismiss his offer as if it had no merit?

The woman on the bed was draped in silk woven so finely it was transparent. She rolled to her side, propped her head on one hand and allowed the other one to rest on her hip, highlighting the exaggerated curve of her waist. "What a tear you're in!"

"That pie-faced cow turned me down," he all but shouted as he paced the room. "Stated quite firmly that she had no desire to be married to me regardless of my cousin's fate and that nothing I could say or do would sway her."

The woman smiled at him and patted the bed. "Come sit here with me, darling. She's not even a woman... upon my word, she was born a dried up old spinster! I still can't believe you offered for her! We discussed this!"

"What has that got to do with anything?" he snapped, even as he settled onto the edge of the bed. She rose on her knees behind him. Her hands moved to his neck, massaging the knotted muscles there with a precision that had his eyes closing and his lips parted on a groan before she even replied. "I've no choice in the matter... the money lenders are breathing down my neck and your blasted husband keeps the purse strings tied up so tightly I'm lucky to see a guinea!"

Cassandra, the Duchess of Elsingham, pouted at her lover and her nephew-by-marriage. "I know he's a tight-fisted miser... but we have bigger issues to deal with."

"I should have seduced her," he said. "If I'd ruined her entirely, then she'd have no choice but to marry me, would she? Course, I'd have had to drink a gallon of brandy beforehand. Plainest chit I've ever seen!"

"That plain chit's father was willing to settle a hundred thousand pounds on the occasion of her marriage with additional funds to follow with the birth of each child," she reminded him gently. "I daresay that even if her face wilted your manhood, those banknotes would rally it quickly enough."

"How on earth am I supposed to seduce her, my love? When all I can think of is you... no other woman could compare," he said quietly.

"But we cannot live on love," she whispered, soothing the sting of the reply with a soft nip at his earlobe. "And now, we won't have to."

"I don't understand," Charles muttered. "Did he die? Did the old bastard cock up his toes? I'll petition the House tomorrow to have my cousin declared dead!"

She laughed. "No, my darling. Your uncle, the duke, is still very much alive... but he won't be for long. As for your not having to marry Jane Barrett, the pie-faced cow... someone else will marry her for you. Marcus has returned."

Panic hit him, socking him squarely in the gut and making it difficult to even draw breath. That couldn't have happened. It wasn't possible.

"Think of the life we'll have once they're both gone! We'll live in the lap of luxury with all of her lovely money. The finest parties, every sensual delight known to man at our fingertips. He'll bring her to heel, add her little fortune to the family coffers, and then they shall both meet with a rather tragic and unfortunate demise."

"God, but I love you," he said. Her wickedness, concealed by her pretty face and her often mindless rambling, was the truth of her and that was the part that he savored, that was reserved solely for him.

She made a face. "It'll be such a tragedy when they meet their untimely ends... reunited at last, and then taken from this world far too soon. We have to give them enough time to consummate the marriage, but not so much that there might be an heir."

He clasped her hands and brought them to his lips. "I will shower you with jewels. You'll never want for anything... and you'll never again be obliged to let any man touch you but me."

"You've worked so hard for this, my darling... when I think of the danger you faced at Corunna and what might have happened if you'd been caught! The dukedom will be yours... no matter the cost," she said softly. And she would be his duchess.

"It'll be a scandal when we marry," he said.

"If there is one thing I've learned, my darling, society loves a scandal. We'll be celebrated as the greatest of romances by them before the ink has even dried on the register. People already feel sorry for me because I'm married to such an old, ugly and impotent man. Little do they know, my maid's herbs are the cause of his impotence," she said with a laugh.

"Then keep her herbs well away from me," he said, pushing her back onto the bed. "How did you get away tonight?"

"The same way I always do," she said. "I gave him a little extra laudanum and then took the carriage. No one dares question me... you know that."

He dipped his head and sucked lightly at the skin of her breast, just above her nipple. Only when he'd left a slight mark there, did he draw back. He pressed his fingertips to the mark, tracing it softly. "And do you explain such things to your helpful maid? Does she wonder at giving your husband a potion to make him impotent when she sees my marks upon your perfect skin?"

Cassandra reached for his cravat, untying the knot with skilled fingers. "She dares not. I'd have her tossed out without a reference and she knows it well enough. Trust me, my love, all will work in our favor or feel the consequences of crossing us!"

As excited by her viciousness as her beauty, Charles was done with talking.

Chapter Four

WHEN MARCUS ENTERED the breakfast room the following morning, he was tensed as if for battle. It was as likely an occurrence as anything would be given how unwelcome his return had been. His father's behavior he understood. The old man had never been warm or particularly affectionate. Any hopes or disappointments he felt in that reunion were of his own making.

Miss Barrett he understood, as well, to a degree. Given his explanation the night before, he hoped that she would be in a more hospitable frame of mind but he wasn't counting on it. She had a deep aversion to being married, not just to him, but to any man he believed. Still, none of it made for a pleasant homecoming.

Crossing to the sideboard, he filled his plate liberally with eggs, potatoes, bacon and Cumberland sausage as well as a generous portion of bread. The sight of it and the glorious scent of it all was enough to make him weep with joy. If there was one true blessing in being returned to the family fold it was that the food would be utterly divine. He'd fantasized about food just as often during his imprisonment as he had about the glorious company of women.

Taking his feast back to the table, he seated himself and poured a cup of tea, a luxury he hadn't missed nearly as much as the food. It was still a pleasant reminder of all the comforts London and his home had to offer.

"Do you really mean to eat all of that?"

The question had come from behind him. Miss Barrett moved like a cat it seemed. Marcus turned to look at her over his shoulder. "Every single, solitary bite of it... and I shall enjoy each morsel with hedonistic pleasure."

She made a slight sound of disapproval that he chose to ignore. Watching her, he noted how gingerly she filled her plate, only a single bite or two of only a few foods.

"One has to wonder why you even bother to have the meal at that point," he said.

Her cheeks turned a rather charming shade of pink. "I enjoy a good meal but, like everything else in life, one should indulge with moderation."

"I would hardly call breakfast an indulgence," Marcus replied, bemused by her stuffy, staid and well-rehearsed answer. "Tell me truthfully, why such a ridiculously small portion?"

"Very well," she snapped, placing her fork with a slight clink on the edge of the plate. "If you must know, my stepmother has pointed out to me that I have grown plumper than my current gowns permit and she refuses to allow my father to purchase new gowns for me when the fault lies entirely upon my own doorstep. My lack of self-control and love of cakes has made me quite fat, according to her."

Marcus laughed. In the face of such utter idiocy, it was all that he could do.

"I'm certainly happy to have amused you, my lord. Now that my humiliation is complete, I shall return to my room," she said as she rose from her chair, clearly offended.

Sobering, he studied her expression and found it to be entirely earnest. Her stepmother might have voiced the opinion, but Miss Barrett believed it entirely. Rising to his feet, he commanded, "Sit down. You aren't going anywhere."

Miss Barrett blinked at him in surprise. Then her lips firmed in a clearly displeased line. "I am not a servant to be ordered about, my lord."

"No," he said. "In this instance, I will be your servant." With that, Marcus crossed to the sideboard and filled a plate generously with helpings of each of the items prepared. Returning to the table, he placed it before her. "Eat what you like. She has no power in this house. If you want new gowns, you'll have new gowns."

"You do not understand the dynamics of this household... she will make my life, and everyone else's, quite miserable!" Miss Barrett insisted. "She's like a viper. Constantly slithering about, ready to strike without warning."

Marcus glanced back at her, taking stock of every curve. Some might have called her plump. But for himself, he'd barely managed to drag his gaze from the lush bounty of her breasts or the delightful sway of her hips beneath her skirts. Not that she would welcome such a blatantly inappropriate comment even if it was intended to be complimentary. Instead, he offered vague and far too faint praise. "There is nothing wrong with your figure. Nothing at all. I daresay, it is precisely the sort of figure that I myself, and most of the men of my acquaintance, find very pleasing."

She blushed furiously. "Thank you, my lord, but pleasing you or any other man is not of great importance to me—keeping the peace is!"

"Miss Barrett, I starved for the first six months in that prison. I ate things to survive that I cannot even bear to recall. With the bounty of a beautiful meal spread before us, it is painful for me to watch a person deprive themselves for such a silly reason," he explained. "It would do much for my peace of mind to see you eat a meal and take joy in it."

She said nothing for the longest time. "I am sorry for what you endured, my lord," she finally managed. "But if I do not do as she wishes—"

"She will not turn you over her knee, Miss Barrett. She will not order your father to beat you. And she doesn't have to starve you since you are apparently willing to do so yourself at her direction. No. She can only run roughshod over you if you allow her to. At this juncture, everyone in this house wants us to be married except for you. You may not realize it, but that actually puts you in a position of power. Use it to your advantage."

Marcus walked away then, returning to his own seat and the plate of food he was determined to enjoy with fervor.

"It's too much food," she said. "I could never eat all of it."

"Then eat what you like of it. You're not a child to be instructed to clean your plate," he replied. "You will not be bullied in this house."

Miss Barrett stared at him, her expression a study in confusion. "You have never been kind to me before. I cannot understand why you are doing so now."

That gave him pause. Had he truly been so wrapped up in his own life before that he had been cruel? No, he had not. He had largely ignored her though and, perhaps, to a young and impressionable child that was much the same. Had her life been so completely devoid of kindness that his current behavior could be considered such? "Was I so very unkind then?"

She looked down at her plate. "Not unkind. But cold. Very cold and very distant. Your dislike was never voiced, not until that last day, but it was implied at our every meeting."

Marcus considered his answer carefully. "I suppose my actions could have been interpreted thusly. The simple truth is, Miss Barrett, I had no idea how to behave in the presence of a young girl. You were to be my wife, according to everyone else, and yet you were not old enough to be courted, not old enough to share common interests with me. I had no notion of what I ought to say to you then. The entire thing was deucedly awkward."

"You certainly seem to have recovered from that, my lord. You've been saying a great many things since your return," she pointed out.

Marcus took a bite of the rich, buttery eggs and let the flavor explode on his tongue. By God, he'd missed good English fare. With that bite completed and the pleasant sensation of fullness beginning to settle in his belly, he sat back in his chair and met her gaze levelly. "So I have. The reasons for my previous reticence have become a moot point as you are now definitely a woman grown and certainly old enough to be courted."

"And is that what breakfast was? Filling my plate and telling me to stand up for myself? Is that courtship?" she demanded.

He smiled. "It isn't a romantic gesture, I grant you. Perhaps, I'll get you chocolates and a posy later."

IT WAS A romantic gesture. Perhaps not in the traditional sense, but it felt quite heroic and romantic to her. She'd never had someone stand up for her, to have someone be willing to openly defy her vicious stepmother on her behalf—yes, it was romantic. It was also guilt inducing. She felt the faint stirrings of it inside her—the awful sinking, wrenching feeling of remorse at all the insidious things she'd written the night before. Dishonesty, in spite of the secretive nature of her trade, did not sit well with her.

"I suppose I'll need a new wardrobe at any rate. I can hardly continue to be seen in mourning now that you're returned. Whatever would people think?" Her teasing tone belied her inner turmoil. It was a defensive gesture. The conversation might have appeared superficial to most, but it scratched at much deeper issues. It also tugged at her conscience. She'd remained at her small desk late into the night, finishing the damning and damnable column for her publisher. Just before entering the breakfast room, she had sent one of the kitchen lads to deliver her latest masterpiece to the man in question. Guilt and shame were sinking their teeth and claws into her deeper with every passing second.

Jane tamped those feelings down, ignoring them willfully. Her course was set. In the five years since he'd been reported missing, she'd not just accustomed herself to the idea of not being married or beholden to any man, she'd come to relish the day when she had true freedom through the annuity that had been left to her. Simply because he appeared to be much changed from before and to be cut from very different cloth than her father was no reason to alter her plan. She would stick to it and ignore any lingering scruples that might interfere. It was the only way to hold on to and possible even expand the small amount of freedom she'd managed to carve out for herself.

"I suppose you will," he agreed. "Before you undertake your massive shopping expedition, perhaps you'd join me for a drive in the park?"

"The park?" Sitting in an open carriage with him, tooling through Hyde Park for all of society to see was not simply an announcement of his return. It was an announcement that their engagement would continue as planned.

"That is part of courtship still, is it not?" he asked, his voice pitched low and the teasing tone reflected in the twinkling of his dark eyes.

It was most assuredly a rite of courtship and she had agreed, at least at face value, to allow him to court her. There was no graceful way to refuse and no good reason to do so unless she were to admit that she had no intention of being honorable in their agreement. "Indeed, it is. Are you quite certain you wish to announce your return with such a public outing to start?"

He chuckled at that. "My dear, Miss Barrett, the servants in this house have told the servants next door already. And they have told the servants two houses down. Before we even sat down to breakfast, I daresay word had already reached Regent Street."

Of course, it had. The speedy gossip of servants was primarily how she earned her modest living, after all. He clouded her thinking. Having him home, having their betrothal looming over her once more rather than simply the specter of impending spinsterhood left her feeling unsettled. It had nothing to do with the fact that he had possibly grown even more attractive in the years since he'd left. It certainly had nothing to do with the more tender feelings she'd had for him as a young girl until, with a few careless words, he'd crushed her fragile heart and even more fragile ego.

"Certainly," she agreed. "Gossip flows swiftly and typically gains embellishment with every retelling."

He didn't smile, but his lips did lift slightly at one corner. It was an all too appealing expression on his too-handsome features. She could not and would not allow herself to soften toward him. The tender-hearted young girl with her heart on her sleeve was no more, and she would not allow any lingering remnants of her painful tendre for him to muddle her current thinking. Her plan remained and she would hold fast to it. No man would have dominion over her ever again. Once she managed to shake off the yoke of her father, she'd never give up her independence no matter how handsome the man asking might be.

"Is half past eleven convenient for you?" he queried.

No. It was not convenient. Nothing about their current situation was convenient for her. But as she had no other engagement to use as an excuse to beg off, she nodded. "Certainly. I shall meet you in the drawing room, if you like."

He rose from the table. "I'll arrange to have the phaeton readied for us... assuming Father hasn't bartered it off."

"He did, but he replaced it. The current incarnation is... well, your stepmother chose it. It's a bit..." Jane stopped, uncertain how to describe the vehicle without appearing unkind or ungracious.

"Garish?"

She nodded gravely. "Some might describe it so. Naturally, I never would, but some might."

His lips firmed into a thin, hard line. "And yet all he talks about are the dire financial straits we are in. Eight years' absence have not afforded him ample to time to realign his priorities, it would seem... I bid you good morning, Miss Barrett, until our appointment."

Jane watched him leave. She would have cursed if she had any inkling how. The few words she'd managed to learn over the years were far too mild to express her current dismay and frustration. Instead, she stamped her foot against the floor beneath the table. It felt shockingly good, so she did it again.

She needed to keep him at arm's length. As charming, handsome and reasonable as he appeared to be, that was a dangerous combination for a woman who had sworn off love and men altogether.

Chapter Five

CHARLES APPROACHED HIS uncle's home with a large bouquet of flowers and a box of sweets. In order to disguise his knowledge of Marcus' return, Cassandra had insisted it was best to proceed as if he'd planned to pursue a courtship with Miss Barrett. And so there he was, playing the role of a calf-eyed suitor. How he despised all of it! He wanted no part of her. But he did want her fortune and he wanted the title. He deserved it, after all. Marcus had never valued it and certainly never understood how their family worked. Their coat of arms should well have been the depiction an animal eating its young. It was their way, after all.

Climbing the steps, he knocked at the door and thought how odd it seemed that the simple wreath with its black ribbon was gone. He'd grown so used to the trappings of mourning that had initially been a constant reminder of his cousin's fate. They were certainly quick to remove all traces of it, he thought bitterly, shaking off the black ribbons and widow's weeds like a wet dog drying itself. The prodigal son had returned, after all. The fatted calf would be slaughtered by sundown.

Riggs, with his typically dour expression, answered the knock and ushered him inside. Charles noted the absence of his black armband and those on the footmen as well. "Riggs, has the house decided to throw off mourning?" Charles queried with false concern.

"We have no reason to mourn, sir," the butler intoned, "and every reason to rejoice. Lord Althorn is returned to us."

Even though he'd expected it, had known it would be uttered, the words still made his heart stutter in his chest. Those simple words represented a threat to every hope for his future. They could well mean that there would be no title, no fortune. Depending on how much Althorn knew, it was quite possible he would go to the gallows. Even if Althorn didn't know the full extent of his war time activities, there was no doubt he'd be banished from the family if his plot failed to rid of him of Marcus once and for all. Cassandra thought it possible to brazen one's way through even the most difficult of obstacles. For himself, he was not so sure.

His cousin had seen him, after all, had called out to him for help as he was being carted away by the French. At worst, he might suss out the truth and determine that it was Charles who'd set the French soldiers on him and that might lead to other questions about his dealings with the French. At best, Charles would be branded a coward and a liar for not helping him and for keeping his fate a carefully guarded secret for five years. Cassandra didn't know that. She didn't know that Marcus had recognized him there. He'd never told her because he'd thought it wouldn't possibly come back to him. A folly he would, no doubt, come to regret.

"When did this happen?" he demanded. He allowed his voice to tremble. After all, no one would have expected he would be happy about the return.

"It was just after you departed last night, sir," Riggs answered. "Why you must have passed Lord Althorn on the street as you were leaving."

There had been a well-dressed gentleman on the opposite side of the street. He'd crossed the street just as Charles had climbed into a hackney. Had that been Marcus lying in wait even then? "You're certain it is him? There's no mistake?"

Riggs didn't answer. His gaze drifted past Charles.

"As certain as anyone can be. It is good to see you, Cousin. Isn't it?" The words were uttered in a deep baritone that he had not thought ever to hear again. They were also heavily laced with suspicion.

That voice was instantly recognizable. They had grown up together, after all. Charles turned. It was him, of course. Against all hope, he had to admit that it was true. There was no chance it was an imposter. A harder, leaner and more weathered version of his cousin, but his cousin just the same.

"We thought you were dead," Charles said simply. His tone lacked any real degree of warmth, but then they had long since given up any pretense of familial affection. It was difficult to feign joy when the man's very presence signaled so much disaster for him.

"Thought or hoped?" Marcus asked. The undercurrent of anger and veiled accusation was evident in his tone. "Remind me, Charles… when was it that our paths crossed last? You were at Corunna, were you not?"

"Thought, of course. Who could ever wish you ill? Yes, I was at that horrible place. The chaos and bloodshed has never left me. I took a blow to the head near the end of the battle… I laid senseless for days afterward," Charles lied easily, his tone light and devoid of the fear-fueled rage he felt. That piece of fiction was a last ditch effort to cover his perfidy. "But now we are both here and in the bosom of our loving family. Welcome home."

He despised Marcus. The moment in time when his general disregard had altered into true hatred was unknown to him. It had grown over time, he supposed, watching as every advantage was heaped upon his cousin's head while he faced a life of struggling penury as a clerk or vicar. When Marcus had tossed all of that away, running off to fight in a war he, as a member of the aristocracy, could easily have avoided, Charles had both marveled at and reveled in his stupidity.

For the first three years of that long and arduous war, he'd waited with bated breath to see if his cousin would succumb to the fate of so many other soldiers. But opportunity had presented itself and he'd taken advantage. A well-placed word in the right ears, and Marcus had been taken on the field. His assumption then was that he would be killed, but he could never attest to his certainty of that without offering up a reason and incriminating himself in the process. Instead,

Charles had bided his time and toadied to that vile tradesman, William Barrett, to assess his willingness to transfer the contract to any Duke of Elsingham present or future. Well, they were through waiting for that. Marcus would marry the cow and then they'd get rid of them both.

If it wouldn't have utterly destroyed everything he was working for and everything he hoped to gain, Charles would gladly have run him through right there on the spot.

"Thank you," Marcus said, his tone as equally devoid of emotion. "Is there some reason you stopped by, Charles? Perhaps you heard of my miraculous return?"

The animosity was palpable. Even the servants appeared to be uncomfortable, some of the footmen glancing nervously at one another until Riggs cleared his throat in warning. It appeared, Charles thought, that his recently returned cousin was willing to be much more forthcoming about their mutual antipathy than they ever had in the past.

"No. I was caught quite unawares," Charles lied with complete calm.

Marcus smiled, his lips curving but in an expression that offered no warmth at all. "I understand that you made an offer to my betrothed the evening past. While I thank you for your concern for her future and wellbeing, as I have returned, it will be unnecessary for you to honor those obligations on my behalf. You understand, of course, that we will be using this time to become reacquainted with one another and will naturally want a certain amount of privacy in the family home."

Charles stiffened, his spine going utterly rigid and his chin notching upward. Had she told him that? Had the two of them laughed together at his proposal as if he were some sort of buffoon? "I see you and Miss Barrett have developed a much more intimate acquaintance than you've had in years past... home only hours and already sharing tête-à-têtes."

Marcus' reply did not acknowledge the accusation buried within Charles' own statement. Instead, he said simply, "We are both very appreciative of your wish to look after her but, under the circumstances, feel it is best if such advances were forgotten entirely."

Charles placed the chocolates and posy on the hall table. "Naturally, we will proceed as you direct. Give my regards to Miss Barrett. I have recalled that I am late for another appointment and must be off. No doubt as a member of the extended family, I will be the first to know when you are once again receiving callers."

MARCUS WATCHED HIS cousin leave with a feeling of unease. He didn't trust Charles to simply fade quietly into the distance. Then again, he'd never trusted him at all. Charles' acts of cowardice and self-serving during the war were not the first indications of his true character. The man was grasping, greedy, and begrudging of everything that anyone else possessed and yet careless with anything in his own possession. It was as if he only valued things that he perceived as being out of his grasp. Did Miss Barrett fall into that category?

As if he'd summoned her with the thought, she appeared at the top of the stairs. She wore a promenade dress, but one that lacked much in the way of embellishment. Even the black fabric was completely matte and lacked any sheen whatsoever. There were no pretty trims or bows. While he was not completely cognizant of all the rules of etiquette that governed women's mourning attire, he'd never seen one dressed with such unrelieved austerity.

She cast a curious glance at the abandoned bouquet and box of sweets on the table as she descended the last of the stairs. "Did someone come to call?"

He considered lying to her, but only for a moment. Charles was no competition for her affection. Of that he was certain. "Charles came by," he admitted. He did not believe for a moment that his cousin had genuine feelings for Miss Barrett. He also did not believe that as pragmatic as she appeared to be that she would be fooled by his thin veneer of charm. "I imagine he felt that today was to be the first day of your courtship... instead, it will be the first day of ours."

A thoughtful frown caused her lower lip to turn out slightly and the faintest of furrows to appear between her brows. With her pale blonde hair and rosy cheeks, she was far lovelier than he would have ever imagined her to be. The years since they'd last seen one another had been kind to her, indeed. The awkwardness of her youth had vanished and left in its wake a confident, curvaceous woman who knew her own mind and was not compelled to seek the counsel of others. While he admired those qualities in her, he also recognized that those same qualities would only make it more difficult to win her hand.

Her hands were clenched at her sides and her chin notched upward as she asked finally, "Is this simply some sort of competition between the two of you? I'm well aware of the long-standing animosity—"

"I assure you, Miss Barrett," he replied easily, "that whatever occurs between the two of us is just that... between the two of us. It has nothing to do with Charles, our meddling fathers or an ages old contract that neither of us should be bound by. I want to see if we can make this thing work between us."

Her gaze was level, earnest and unwavering. "Why? Why this change of heart?"

"I'm not sure I understand."

She stepped closer to him and whispered in a lower tone, "Lord Althorn, I have had a great deal of time to reflect upon it and I came to the conclusion that while you opposed marriage to me for a very valid reason that I have since been made aware of, you also opposed marriage in general at that time. One would think that after an eight year absence and five of those years in captivity the taste of freedom would be far too heady to give up so readily." She paused and took a deep breath. "Why have you changed your mind about marriage and more specifically, marriage to me?"

"I will happily answer any questions but in private, Miss Barrett. Join me for our drive this morning and I promise to explain my reasons to your satisfaction," he promised.

She considered the offer for a moment and then gave a curt nod. "Very well, Lord Althorn, we may go for our drive as planned, but do not think to evade the question."

"I wouldn't dream of it," he said as he donned his heavy cloak before they walked outside to the waiting phaeton.

He didn't gasp or recoil, but the urge was there. Calling the vehicle garish was a vast understatement. Painted an impractical powder blue and trimmed with white and gold, it was like a lady's reticule on wheels. The interior was white leather and an ermine lap blanket draped the seat.

"For pity's sake," he muttered. "What in the name of all that is holy is this monstrosity?"

"I believe it's called poor taste," she replied easily. "But if one wishes to make a statement, and I assume you do, a better conveyance could not be found for it."

He handed her up and then took the reins from the groom that held them as he climbed up himself. It was an embarrassment to be seen in such a vehicle. Why on earth his father would ever have permitted such license by his bride—well, it was best not to think on why his father had permitted it. In fact, he would rather think of anything else.

Taking Berkley Street to Curzon, he turned toward Hyde Park. There was a distinct chill in the air but, despite that, the streets were busy and crowded with pedestrians and other traffic. More than one person whipped their head around for a second glance at them as they drove past. He wasn't foolish enough to think that it was merely the carriage that had caught their eyes. The stunned expressions of many passersby were all the confirmation he needed that his return had been well remarked upon.

"Well, my lord, if you wished to formally announce your return and have it surprise anyone, you've taken the wind out of your own sails I'm afraid," Miss Barrett offered caustically.

He said nothing, but his lips firmed and his jaw clenched. That was precisely the sort of thing that had made him reluctant to return. He had no wish to be an object of curiosity. Reclaiming his place in society was necessary to his future and thus those sorts of gestures were the most expedient methods of doing so. Conversely, if he wished to ferret out the truth about Charles and what had taken place at Corunna, he needed to be circumspect. He was at cross purposes with himself and would have to simply make do.

"Has no one anything better to do with their time than gossip?" he asked.

"No. They don't. Why should they? Gossip, at least in society, is a kind of currency. If you can provide information or juicy *on dits* at parties, then you are a sought after guest. If you are the subject of these *on dits*, you may also be a sought after guest... because it makes you an object of curiosity and insures that the event will be a total crush so people can get a good look at you." The explanation was offered dispassionately enough but there was a hint of disgust in her voice, as if she were completely disillusioned with society as a whole.

"You speak as if from experience." Had she been a victim of such vicious gossip during his absence?

She glanced at him then. "You fled the country to risk life and limb simultaneously with the banns being posted for our marriage. Suffice it to say there were quite a few whispers. I was young enough then not to be bothered or even aware of them. But as I grew older and was invited to events, naturally before your disappearance and my five year period of mourning, I realized that the low hum of conversation was usually about me. It was occasionally offered up with a helping of false sympathy. After all, what better way to get the juiciest details than under the guise of friendship?"

"It was hardly worthy of gossip!"

"The truth... certainly it wasn't worthy. But gossip and truth bear little enough resemblance to one another, my lord. You detested me. You opposed the match. You were in love with someone else. There was madness in my family and you didn't wish to tarnish the bloodline of your esteemed dynasty—I could go on. A dozen reasons were offered up as to why you chose facing French muskets to marrying me, my lord, and not one of them had to do with the fact that I was simply too young to be a bride," she explained.

"For what it's worth, I am sorry. I handled things very poorly then," he admitted. "If I had known that my actions would have such detrimental consequences for you I would have done things very differently."

She ducked her head as she uttered a grudging concession. "You did handle things rather impulsively, but I don't know that if you'd handled them any other way we wouldn't have both wound up at the altar when we were far too young to be there. They would not have let you simply refuse, as well you know. I'd be locked away at your country estate and you'd be... well, I can't say what, precisely, you'd be doing. But I daresay, it wouldn't involve being a doting husband. Resentment would have set in and we'd have hated one another by now, I imagine."

"Parts of your assessment are true enough. We'd have been badgered and hounded to the ends of the earth," he admitted. He noted how perfect her profile was with her slightly upturned nose and full lips. Her stepmother might have insisted she was too plump, but the softness of her cheeks and the gentle curves of her face were a welcome sight for him. He'd seen too many women haunted and starved during his time on the Peninsula. He never wanted to see that sort of desperation in another person ever again.

It wasn't simply her health and vigor that he was noting, if he were to be honest. Even last night, when he'd first returned to his family's home, there'd been a spark of attraction there. Whether it was that she had blossomed into the fullness of womanhood while he was away or whether it was his own proprietary nature in looking at her and recognizing that she was promised to him, he'd felt the stirrings of lust, of the desire to claim her. Or perhaps, it was because he hadn't touched the softness of a woman's body in more than five years. Regardless, he hadn't anticipated that he would actually desire Miss Barrett. He also didn't anticipate that she would be amenable to any overtures on his part that would reflect that.

"But that still does not answer my question from earlier... why have you suddenly embraced the notion of our marriage so whole-heartedly?" she demanded, her tone sharp and her question quite pointed.

She would not let the matter go and he did not have an adequately prepared answer that would not reveal too much about his own newly discovered feelings for her or about the circumstances of his capture. So he relied on the stoicism that his father had drilled into him during his childhood. "I have several reasons. The first of which is that I ran from my duties, my obligations, and even from myself," he admitted gravely. "In doing so, I paid a very steep price. With that came a great deal of reflection on what my life ought to be and what I wanted from it."

"And what is that precisely? I'm not foolish enough to believe some Banbury tale from you about having realized I'm your destiny," she warned.

He chuckled in spite of the rather intense nature of their conversation. "No, Miss Barrett. But you are very cynical. Has anyone else remarked upon it or do you save your acerbic wit for my sole enjoyment?"

She pursed her lips in a familiar expression of disapproval. "This is very serious, Lord Althorn. You've professed a desire to court me that is supposed to have nothing to do with our fathers' agreement, the wedding contracts or your desire to access my father's vast fortune. There must be a reason."

"Very well... I am weary of being alone. I spent far more time isolated in a tiny, rough-hewn hovel of rock and dirt than I care to even comment on. While there, I realized that no one would miss me... they might miss the role I was to fulfill or the obligations that it was my responsibility to meet, but no one would miss me. As a man, I'd had little to no impact on anyone's life. That was a lowering realization, Miss Barrett, and I vowed that if I managed to once more set foot on English soil, I would wed. I would have a wife and a family and I would treat them infinitely better than my own father treated me or my late mother."

JANE STARED AT him in complete and utter astonishment. It was as if he'd mirrored her very own thoughts. For years, she'd been painfully aware of that same horrible truth. She was nothing to her father but a means to an end, a convenient way to attach himself to an esteemed title and an aristocratic connection. Had he truly felt the same way?

Refusing to acknowledge the significance of that or the softening of her heart that had occurred at his admission, she asked, "That's all? You're lonely and you think I can ease that loneliness for you?" She didn't want to be moved by him, to feel any sort of kinship with him on such a painful subject. Sympathy might sway her and that could not be.

"Or that we might ease the loneliness for one another... by virtue of the agreement that was made for us by our parents, we have neither one had the opportunity to develop romantic connections elsewhere." He paused then. "That is the case, isn't it, Miss Barrett? Your reluctance to wed is a reflection of your disinterest in being married altogether and not simply that you'd prefer to be married to someone else?"

Lying would be expedient, but only in the short term. In the end, it would create far more questions and controversy than she wished to contend with. So, Jane opted for the truth. "You are correct in your assertion that my objection is to the state of marriage and not the groom in question."

He continued to stare at her, studying her face as if she were some strange specimen. When at last he nodded and looked away, Jane felt oddly bereft at the loss of his attention.

Althorn spoke again, using the same reasonable tone that had prompted her presence in the phaeton to start with. "We have been isolated from the world in many instances by the same set of circumstances. In that regard, Miss Barrett, we understand one another."

Suspicion reared its ugly head and she said, somewhat snidely, "There's more, isn't there? Some other reason why you want to wed me and not just any other girl who strikes your fancy, isn't there?"

He stared ahead, his expression clearly denoting his inner turmoil as he weighed and measured what to say to her. Then he uttered the sad and soul shattering truth. "I won't lie to you and say that the existing contract and the accompanying financial settlement is not a factor. Money, Miss Barrett, speaks volumes even in affairs of the heart. There are things I wish to do, changes that I wish to enact in how the men returning from the Peninsula are treated and the opportunities that are available to them. I cannot undertake the tasks I have set for myself without appropriate financing and our present arrangement would allow that and more."

It shouldn't have hurt. She didn't want to marry him, after all, she reminded herself. But it did. It stung her pride, her heart, and the remnants of that little girl she'd once been who had quietly worshipped him from afar. "No one can fault you for your honesty, Lord Althorn. I've never known such a forthcoming fortune hunter."

"A lie is no foundation to build a life together upon," he answered evenly. "I am not only after your fortune, I merely acknowledge that it is not a dissuading factor. I cannot ignore the value it could have in our lives together or all the good it could do—that we could do. And I would have you with me, as more than simply a walking bank note. I want a partner in this life, Miss Barrett, and in all of my endeavors. I will not continue my existence as an idle aristocrat. I want it to have meaning. I mean for my life to have a purpose. Can you understand that?"

She blinked rapidly, attempting to fathom how stupid one man could possibly be. "What I understand is that the men of your family have absolutely no qualms in insulting me to my face. Whether you're a fortune hunter to your own benefit or to others is of no consequence. Ultimately, I am not wanted or desired for myself at all but only for the funds I can bring. Between you telling me that I'll do, especially since I have money, and your cousin telling me that he's known me long enough and is fond enough of me to overlook how singularly unattractive I am," she paused and drew in a calming breath. "I detest the lot of you. You're all just as greedy and self-serving as your father is."

"But I don't wish to be self-serving. I'm talking about making sweeping changes in the way wounded soldiers are cared for—"

"To soothe your own conscience," she snapped back at him. "Are you really so obtuse? This isn't about them at all! It's about you. Everything, from the moment you left me here to face the censure of our families and society all by myself, to the moment you returned and once again upended my life and everyone else's... it's all been about you."

"I'm sorry you feel that way," he said.

"Take me back. I've no wish to continue our drive," she insisted.

"Whether you wish to continue it or not, we are committed to this. The line of traffic will not permit me to turn around and I daresay this conveyance with its dainty wheels would not survive being turned in the grass," he replied. "I had hoped being honest with you would be the right decision to make... and I still feel that it is. You asked for my motives and I've given them. I stand by what I told you last night. We will continue our courtship for the next six months and if at that time you wish to bow out, I will not protest."

Her eyes rolled of their own volition and her tone, when she replied, was caustic. "The degree of your magnanimity is boundless, my lord! Boundless!"

"It is the way of society," he replied quietly.

"It should not be," Jane retorted hotly. "I should not have to give my life over to a man who only values the money I bring and not the person I am. If you can't understand that then there's no hope for you at all!"

"And am I not valued for the title I bring?" he asked, somewhat indignantly. "Is the fact that you will one day be addressed as her grace, the Duchess of Elsingham, not a point in my favor?"

"No," she said. "To my father, yes, of course, it is. But it has never been something I valued."

"Then what do you value, Miss Barrett? For I find that I cannot fathom what goes on inside your head... at all."

"Your kindness at breakfast was a point in your favor, but you have effectively wiped that clean."

"That's all?" he asked. "In all our years of acquaintance, I've only ever managed to do one thing right in your estimation?"

"We have no years of acquaintance! We barely knew one another. Beyond a simple greeting at family gatherings, you could never even be bothered to speak to me!" Jane literally wanted to scratch his eyes out. The man absolutely infuriated her and the fact that he was so patently oblivious to his own failings only goaded her ire more.

"And what should I have said? That's a nice doll you have. By the way, I'm to be your husband!"

"Well, you might have said something! This is obviously not going to work and I don't understand why we can't simply end it right here," she said. "You have no real desire to be with me... only with my money. And frankly, the more time I spend in your presence the less inclined I am to like you at all."

They grew silent after that heated exchange. Sitting in the gaudiest and most ridiculously luxurious phaeton in Hyde Park, they were both stiff, tense and clearly unhappy with one another as some of society's most vicious gossips looked on.

Chapter Six

AFTER FOLLOWING THE bickering couple through the park, Charles had returned to his rooms and consumed a goodly amount of the brandy that Cassandra had obtained for him—no doubt pilfered from her ailing husband's cache. Regardless, there was enough of it in his belly that he no longer felt the burning anger that had overtaken him when looking at Marcus' smug face.

A glance at the clock and he knew she'd arrive shortly. Her nighttime visits were more sporadic, but every afternoon she came to him. Even at the thought, the door opened.

Heavily veiled and draped in black, she'd have come by hack rather than her gaudy phaeton. It had been a brilliant maneuver on her part. Purchasing such a distinctive vehicle, all she had to do was send her maid out in a veil for a drive and Cassandra herself was free to move about as she wished while the whole of society could attest to "her" whereabouts.

"We might as well hang it up. It's over, my darling. The prodigal son has returned. I'm just a poor relation, once more, with no prospects and no chance of taking you from this place," he confessed. "Assuming I don't hang that is."

She shushed him. "Stop it. Stop feeling sorry for yourself! Our ultimate goal remains unchanged. Why on earth would you hang? Really, Charles, all this maudlin obsession with your cousin is very tiresome!"

"It's impossible. Althorn has returned. Their engagement is doomed. She may revile him even more so than she does me," he complained.

"Charles, we will find a way! I've not suffered years with that disgusting old letch only to be left an impoverished widow when he finally dies! Stop this at once!"

Charles looked at her and smiled. She wasn't as young as when they'd first begun their affair, but she was even more beautiful, if such a thing were possible. The icy blonde perfection of her had always suited him perfectly. It concealed her fiery nature and the very passionate woman beneath.

"I recall when I returned home from the Peninsula and first set eyes on you," he mused. "I'd never seen a more perfect example of fine English beauty."

"Only English?" she asked.

He sipped his brandy before answering. "You will always be the most beautiful woman in the world."

"It was a scandalous and foolish thing to do," she said. "Embarking on an affair with my nephew-by-marriage. But you were so charming and so utterly wicked. And I think no one else on earth could understand how much I despised Elsingham but you."

He reached for her hand, tugging her down beside him. "I do hate him. Both he and Marcus can go to the devil!"

"But not before we both get what we desire the most," she reminded him gently. "We deserve it, Charles, for all that we've had to endure."

He sighed heavily. "He saw me at Corunna," Charles admitted. "Marcus knows I was there and likely suspects that I was the one who outed him to the French. If he wonders at that, he might begin to wonder what other intelligence I shared with the French. It could be disastrous."

"It will be fine, my love!" Cassandra insisted. "Have we not managed to carry on a clandestine affair under the nose of your uncle and all of London for nearly five years? From the moment you returned from the war, I knew we were destined for one another. I will not allow this minor setback to change anything!"

The room was spinning for him, so he closed his eyes for just a moment. She was his destiny. Maddening, demanding, by turns cruel and kind, she was a vexing creature but one who incited a passion in him like nothing else. It was she who had taken his idle hatred for his family and sculpted it into their current plan. It was she who had encouraged him to make himself invaluable to his uncle in the hopes of increasing the man's willingness to have his only son and heir declared legally dead, paving the way for Charles himself to take the title. Her mind was always spinning and whirling, one insidious plan after another to get them what they both craved—freedom to be together and wealth to support them in the lifestyle of their choosing.

"And if he ever discloses that I set those soldiers upon him... that I orchestrated his capture, I'll be hanged. Do you not see that?" Charles protested.

"Stop being melodramatic. You're worse than a woman at times, I swear! He will not see you hanged. He wouldn't allow for such a scandal to taint the family. Now sit up, for goodness' sake!" She snapped the words off sharply, her tone brooking no argument.

Reluctantly, Charles sat up and attempted to feign composure even if he truly lacked it. "It is all lost," he repeated for emphasis. Could she truly not see that?

"He may have returned, but that is not as problematic as you make it seem," she insisted. "We no longer have to go through the turmoil of having him declared dead. They will marry. There is no other option!" She turned to face him more fully, cupping his face in her hands as she looked deeply into his eyes and whispered, "And before they manage to produce an heir, we'll eliminate them both."

"She's refusing him. Quite adamantly. You know that... she's difficult," Charles pointed out.

"Then we'll be certain she's so hopelessly compromised she'll have no choice but to wed. This is a gift, my darling, and we will not squander it," she said reassuringly. "We get all that we wanted without you having to marry the wretch. Can you not see?"

He smiled drunkenly up at her. At times, she was a vicious bitch who made him want to strangle her with his bare hands. At others, she appeared an angel there to save him. "You always know what to do. What ever would I do without you?"

She kissed his brow. "Go upstairs, my darling, and rest. You've gotten far too foxed this morning for our afternoon play."

He lunged for her, dragging her to him and kissing her rather clumsily. "I'm never too foxed for that."

"You certainly are," she protested. "I'll not struggle out of this gown for you to rut on me for two seconds and then pass out! Let go of me."

He did as she instructed. Charles knew only too well the cost of crossing her. She'd scarred him once already. "Not even a peck and a cuddle, my darling?"

She shook her head firmly. "No. You need to sober up. You'll be joining the family for dinner tonight. Once I've formulated a plan, I'll be sure it is passed along to you."

He frowned once more. "I was dismissed this morning… informed that the family was not receiving anyone by no less than Marcus himself."

"It is my home," she stated firmly. "And we shall receive whomever I choose. Not to worry, my love. Not to worry at all."

***

JANE STORMED UP the stairs as soon as they were home, not even bothering to excuse herself or offer a by your leave. Retreating into the sanctuary of her chambers, any of her guilt or remorse at having painted him a potential imposter for the gossip rags had long since fled. He deserved that and more.

Sarah entered and, upon seeing her mistress' thunderous expression, offered, "I'll come back later, miss, when you're not—that is, when you have had time—I'll just come back later."

"He is a complete and utter cad!" Jane said. "I cannot believe the gall of that man!"

Sarah gasped, "Did he take liberties, then?" Oddly enough, the maid sounded more titillated than scandalized.

Jane rolled her eyes. "The very fact that he still breathes is a liberty I would not grant him! Do you have any notion of what he has said to me?"

"Well, no, miss. I don't," Sarah said as she began undoing the laces of Jane's gown. "Was it something very wicked?"

"He said," Jane began, the words strident and with far more volume than was appropriate, "that he was marrying me for my money. Just admitted it, as if it were the most normal and natural thing in the world! And then had the audacity to be shocked that I was offended!"

"Begging your pardon, miss, but haven't you always known he was to marry you for the money?" Sarah asked.

Jane whirled on her and snapped, "That is hardly the point. He could have said anything else!"

"Should he have told you that he loved you then?" the maid queried. There was clearly a point to her questions.

Jane scoffed, "Well, of course not! We hardly know one another!"

"That he was overtaken by your beauty and couldn't help himself and that he had to have you for his own, then?" Sarah continued, her tone both patronizing and maddening.

Jane stamped her foot. "Sarah, you are being utterly ridiculous! Even if he'd offered such drivel, I would not be fool enough to believe him!"

"So he doesn't know you well enough to love you, you don't think yourself beautiful enough to have captivated him through such means, and he's not allowed to want to marry you for money. You'll forgive me, miss, but you've just eliminated the three reasons that all men marry... well, unless they've no choice in the matter," the maid finished smartly.

Furious at the maid's logic, Jane demanded, "Precisely what are you implying, Sarah?"

"Only that you were ready to refuse him whatever his reasons were. He could have said everything right and done everything right, and it might still be wrong in your eyes because you want it to be."

There was no denying the truth in that. "Yes! I was. I still am adamant in my refusal. I've no wish to be married! It's not as if I'm being unfair... he doesn't want to marry me either, not really."

"You're awfully set against it when you barely know him." Sarah helped Jane remove the heavy promenade gown and exchange it for a simpler and lighter weight day dress that was more appropriate for indoor wear.

"Whose side are you on, Sarah?"

The maid pursed her lips. "I'm always on your side, miss. I'll never work for anyone else as kind to me or as willing to treat me more like a friend than a servant. And it's because I'm on your side that I'll say something to you that you won't like much but is true nonetheless... you're letting pride rob you of a chance at happiness. Maybe he won't be a grand husband or the love of your life... but you could have a child that would be. Don't you want that? To hold your own children in your arms?"

The longing that it incited in her was more than she could bear. Of course, she wanted to have children someday. She wanted to know what it was like to love unselfishly and to be loved as fiercely as she had loved her own mother. "Is that reason enough to marry him?"

The maid's reply was thoughtful and persuasive. "He's a handsome man and, by all rights, a kind one... if not kind then far from cruel by what the servants say. Maybe you don't like what he said, but he didn't lie to you, and there is something to be said for a man who will at least be honest."

Jane sank down onto the edge of the bed. "I don't want to be my mother, Sarah. I don't want to love a man who is incapable of loving me."

"With all due respect, miss, it wasn't your mother he was incapable of loving. It's everyone. Your father is a cold man... cold and cruel to the bone. That's not the marquess. And we both know it. Give him a chance, miss. Give yourself one."

As Sarah left, Jane forced herself to consider what the maid had said rather than simply allowing her knee-jerk reaction to take precedence. It was all temper and pride for her when it came to him. She was constantly reduced to that not quite fourteen-year-old girl who'd had her heart broken by words taken out of context. It was that and, if she were completely honest, the horrible memories of how her father constantly belittled her mother. He'd despised her and made little effort to conceal his disdain. That her father was, if not kind, at least cordial to his new bride was a testament to the woman's rather shocking beauty but also her vicious nature. Her father actually feared her stepmother or, at the very least, would do whatever was necessary to avoid the unpleasantness of her wrath.

As if her thoughts had summoned the demon herself, there was a knock at the door. The sound and pattern of it were distinctive—three short, sharp raps that sounded impatient and angry.

Rising to her feet, Jane reluctantly opened the door and faced the woman who lived to make her life a misery. "Yes, Mrs. Barrett?"

Her stepmother marched into the room, her stride stiff and angry. "You are purposely trying to sabotage his courtship of you to be an embarrassment to your father and me," she accused. "You ungrateful, spiteful wretch of a child!"

Jane offered no defense of herself. She had learned that to do so would only lengthen the torment. Instead, she stood there with her hands clasped in front of her and bravely faced the tirade that was to come.

"We have done everything for you. There are few women, Jane, who would tolerate having their husband's grown daughter remain in their house as a constant reminder of the woman that came before her! That I was so warm and welcoming to you in spite of your rebellious and contentious nature is a testament to my moral fortitude," the woman continued, oblivious to her own hypocrisy. "The reward for tolerating you was that one day I might have a familial connection to a duke. I don't need to tell you exactly what sort of elevation that brings socially! Would you really deny us that? Your father, who has sacrificed so much for you? Have I not been kind?

Have I not treated you as I would my very own daughter had I been blessed to have one? I have offered you countless hours of advice, applied discipline to correct your weaknesses of character! I have monitored your food consumption to keep you as trim and attractive as you can possibly manage to be given your unfortunate figure! Why, Jane, you should be ashamed of yourself!"

Jane fumed silently, but said nothing. It was far from over and they both well knew it. The next bit would be even more unpleasant.

Mrs. Barrett's gaze traveled over her from head to toe. "I suppose it's a good thing we'll be throwing off our mourning clothes now that he has returned. Naturally, you'll need a trousseau. Given your love of cakes, the amount of fabric we'll have to purchase could very well send us into the poorhouse! Do try to control yourself, Jane. You don't have to eat every morsel put in front of you!"

"I will try to do better," Jane offered.

"Try! What a useless word that is! You either will or you will not… that you cannot even commit to losing the extra stone you're carrying is evidence to me that my best efforts to mold your character have failed. Well, the fault does not lie with me, Jane Barrett, for I have done all that I could! Marry this man, Jane. With your dull appearance, sharp tongue, unfortunate penchant for reading and, let us not forget, your too-ample figure, it's undoubtedly the best offer you'll ever receive!"

With that parting insult, the woman whirled on her heel and exited Jane's chamber as if she'd been exiting a grand ballroom. When she was gone, Jane sank onto the bed again, exhausted by the litany of complaints about her once again.

"I ought to marry him, just so I can be a duchess and give that vile creature the cut direct in front of everyone!"

UNABLE TO TOLERATE being in the house and listening to anyone else tell him what he should do to win the hand of a very unwilling woman, Marcus had sought relief in the one place that would always be a bastion for men. His club. As he approached the door, it was opened and he was greeted by the majordomo. "Good afternoon, my lord."

"Thank you, Alberts. I assume I'm still a member here?"

The man smiled, but the expression was restrained. Effusiveness would never do for such an exclusive club. "For life, sir, and I must say we are very glad to have you back with us."

It was the warmest welcome he'd gotten since he'd been home, he thought. "Is Highcliff in?"

"Yes, my lord. At his usual table. Shall I send over a bottle of brandy?"

"Two bottles," Marcus corrected. "It shall be a long day."

"Very well, my lord. I will see to it."

Marcus stepped into the luxuriously and masculinely-appointed interior of the club. Dark wood, rich leather and not a dainty, gilded chair in sight—it was a welcome reprieve. Highcliff was at a table in the back. The man was dressed in a garish fashion, but far less so than was typical of him. Of course, he knew why.

"Well look what the cats have dragged in," Highcliff said at his approach. "You're dressed better today, but I daresay far more glum than at our last meeting. Are you here to discuss any new developments regarding your cousin and his peccadilloes?"

Marcus seated himself. As the footman approached with a tray laden with snifters and bottles of brandy, he answered, "In part, yes. Charles claimed that he was injured at Corunna, suffered a head wound and lay senseless for days afterward. Is that something that could be verified?"

"Easily enough. I can track down the physicians and surgeons who were stationed there and see if they recall him... it's very likely they may not. I daresay, they saw so many wounded it would be hard to keep track."

"What about members of his regiment? They would likely recall better, I think," Marcus said. "If they had to pick up the extra slack of keeping watch and the various other unpleasant duties of an enlisted man while he recovered, they'd recall it well enough, I think. Before I decide whether or not to see him punished for his actions toward me, I need to be certain that others didn't suffer from his misdeeds, as well."

Highcliff nodded sagely. Their club, a haven for men such as themselves who had committed to doing whatever was necessary for king and country, was one of the few places where Highcliff could drop his dandified facade. "I'll set about finding them then. What exactly is it that you fear he may be guilty of?"

Marcus sighed heavily. "Charles was hardly the sort to seek out a military career, was he? That sort of work has never appealed to him. The only thing that would induce Charles to risk life and limb that way would be a significant amount of money, and we both know that he didn't earn that as a soldier."

Highcliff nodded in agreement. "There have been rumors that someone betrayed us at Corunna... that information was leaked into enemy hands that forever altered the outcome of that particular battle. You think it was Charles?"

"I think it could have been, but I have no proof," Marcus answered evenly.

"I will look into that, as well. But that isn't why you're here, is it? What else brings you to the club in the middle of the afternoon?"

Marcus sighed wearily, "Please share with me any wisdom or insight you have!"

Highcliff arched one eyebrow, "That certainly sounds dire."

It was. His life, his future depended upon it. "Do you understand anything at all of the workings of the female mind?"

Highcliff laughed, the deep sound booming throughout the room. "My friend, no man understands the workings of the female mind," he finally answered, still chuckling under his breath. "We are not meant to understand them anymore than we are meant to understand any of the great mysteries of life. Women are meant to be enjoyed, to be worshipped, to be seduced... they are never meant to be understood."

"I am not speaking of affairs of the heart, Highcliff... it is a business arrangement perpetrated between my father and the father of my betrothed. We are supposed to be wed and she is not just reluctant but altogether unwilling. I cannot say if it is marriage altogether she is opposed to or simply marriage to me."

Highcliff shook his head as he opened one of the decanters of brandy and poured liberal amounts into each snifter. "Althorn, I've known you since we were boys. I daresay, I am the closest thing to a friend you have. You have always been too proper, too stiff, and too antiquated in your thinking. The business is between her father and yours. The romance of the thing should be between you and your bride. All women long for seduction, for romance, for desire. If you are not offering those things to her then, of course, she is reluctant to wed you."

"I have been honest and forthcoming—"

"About your very rational and practical reasons for marrying her at someone else's behest?" Highcliff interrupted. "It's no bloody wonder she turned you down flat. She ought to have slapped your face in the process."

Marcus took a healthy swallow from his own snifter of brandy before demanding, "Are you my friend or hers?"

"If she is to be your bride, they are one and the same. Tell me, Althorn, do you find your bride attractive?"

"Of course, I do. She's quite lovely." Marcus didn't add that she had a delightfully curvaceous figure and golden blonde hair that made him itch to wrap those strands about his fingers. To do so would be counterproductive. They couldn't even speak to one another without snapping like vicious dogs. To attempt anything further would likely result in significant maiming.

"And does she have any indication that you find her so… or have you simply allowed her to believe that you're not unwilling to marry her? Because eager to do so and simply willing to are very different things," Highcliff pointed out.

"I informed her that I wished for us to have a partnership and that the funds made available to us through marriage would be put to good use in our life and in my endeavors to aid returning soldiers," Marcus explained. His reasons were sound, he thought. Not romantic, but certainly sound.

Highcliff shook his head. "You are an absolute fool... a fool, my good man. Apologize. Profusely. I'd tell you to write a sonnet to her beauty but no doubt you'd muck that up as well. Just tell her that you find her attractive, that you desire her... or do one better and show her. I have to imagine that you'd do a damned sight better with action than words."

"She is a gently-bred young woman."

"What the devil has that got to do with anything? Women are women regardless of the quality of sheets they were born in or lie upon. They crave pleasure as surely as men do. They simply have to hide it more," Highcliff explained. "If you want her to be your wife, you must first show her that you want her—not as a bride or a prize to be won, but as a woman. That is all."

Marcus sat back in his chair and sipped his brandy thoughtfully. He'd never entertained the notion of treating Miss Barrett as he might have treated a woman he truly had to woo. It had seemed to him that, with the decision effectively taken from their hands, there'd been no need. Even his suggestion of courtship had not been intended that he should win her hand but that they should publicly display their relationship to prevent any gossip that their wedding might not occur as planned.

"Dammit," he said and placed his snifter back on the table. "I have to go."

Highcliff smirked. "Of course you do. Go forth and seduce with great success, my friend. I'll just stay here and finish off this fine brandy so it doesn't go to waste."

Chapter Seven

J ANE WAS STILL hiding in her room. It was tea time and all the others had gathered in the drawing room. She'd have rather starved, contrary to her stepmother's opinion of her appetite, than walk into that nest of vipers.

As Sarah entered, carrying a tray laden with a pot of tea and cucumber sandwiches, Jane eyed them dubiously. "I take it my stepmother has put cook on alert again about what I am and am not permitted to eat?"

The maid ducked her head. "If I can, I'll try to sneak something else up later."

Quietly furious and emboldened by Lord Althorn's words to her just that morning, Jane decided to take action. "Don't bother. I can fend for myself. I'm going to the kitchen to get what I want and *she*—that hateful, vile, witch of a woman—can go to the devil as far as I'm concerned."

With that, Jane left her chambers, left her maid gaping in her wake, and made for the stairs. She intended to go and fetch herself a decent meal and have a word with the cook. It was, at least as far as anyone else knew, to be her house someday, was it not?

As she strode down the corridor, she was formulating in her mind precisely what she intended to say to the cook. Because she was so intent upon that, she was not paying proper attention to her surroundings. As she rounded the corner, she propelled into a solid form clad in a satin brocade waistcoat and a coat of blue superfine. The light scent of sandalwood teased her senses.

"You appear to be in quite a hurry, Miss Barrett."

The slightly amused tone made her want to kick him. But as he wore boots and she had only her slippers, she resisted the urge. Besides, it wasn't him that she was angry at. Not any more, at least. It was herself. The things Sarah had said to her that morning had penetrated the haze of her anger and she'd accepted that there was some truth to what the maid had said. She was looking for reasons to find fault with him and, as was the way of things, would always find it.

"I was just on my way to the kitchen," she said. "Excuse me, my lord."

"Miss Barrett—Jane," he said.

It was the first time he'd ever called her by her given name. She looked up at him then, noting not for the first time how tall he was and how impossibly handsome. "Yes, my lord."

"Marcus," he corrected. "My name is Marcus and I would have you use it. Can we speak privately?"

"Is there something wrong?" she asked. He was behaving very strangely. Even as she questioned it, she caught just a hint of brandy from him. "Are you foxed?"

"No. I'd made all the necessary arrangements to get myself well and truly foxed but then thought better of it. I really must speak with you privately," he insisted.

"Very well," she agreed, wondering what on earth he was about. Perhaps, he had decided to call off the entire business as well and save them both the inconvenience.

He took her hand, a far more intimate gesture than she was accustomed to from anyone and certainly from him. As he walked her toward the door that led to the narrow portrait gallery, she couldn't help but wonder at his sense of urgency.

Once they were alone, concealed by the heavy curtains that sectioned off that area of the house from all others, she stopped. "What on earth is this all about?"

"I made a mistake," he admitted. "I've made nothing but mistakes since I've returned here."

Slightly disappointed in his answer, and even more disappointed in herself for feeling anything at all, Jane said, "Then you agree that it's best we not proceed with this ridiculous betrothal?"

His expression shifted into something altogether unfamiliar to her. "No. That's not it at all. A very good friend has informed that I am being an absolute fool and I have to admit he's quite right. I've told you all the reasons why it's wise for us to wed, but I've yet to tell you any of the real reasons why I want to marry you."

"So you can have my father's fortune," she snapped. "You don't have to tell me that, Lord Althorn. I'm well aware."

Marcus frowned as of weighing his options. Then with a slight shrug, he stated, "That isn't what I meant at all. But telling you things is not working to my advantage. So perhaps, it's time I show you."

Before Jane could react to that at all, he had pulled her close to him, until her breasts were crushed against his chest and she was so near him she could see the faint shadow of his beard beneath his skin. "What on earth are you doing?"

"What I should have done earlier," he said. And without further warning, his lips descended upon hers.

She didn't struggle or try to break free of his hold. In truth, she was so completely stunned she didn't know what to do other than stand there and let him kiss her.

Jane had never been kissed before, but she'd spent an awful lot of time imagining what it might be like when it finally occurred. None of her imaginings had come even remotely close to the real thing. She'd had no notion of just how firm his body would feel pressed against hers, or that the mingled aroma of sandalwood, soap and brandy would be so infinitely appealing and so capable of clouding her judgement. There would have been no way to predict that her own response to his nearness, to the taste of his lips and the rasp of his whiskers over her skin would be so intense.

Tentatively, Jane kissed him back, moving her lips against his in the same manner with which he'd kissed her. She felt him tense, muscles bunching and rippling beneath the fabric of his clothing as his arms encircled her more fully. She didn't think she'd done anything wrong. Rather than push her away, he pulled her even closer. The pressure of his lips on hers altered slightly. Uncertain of what she was supposed to do, Jane gasped softly as he clasped her more fully to him.

With her lips parted, his tongue swept inside, tangling against hers in a slow and sensual movement. It wasn't entirely unknown to her, that manner of kissing. She'd heard maids giggling about it and she'd even questioned Sarah about it once. Her answer had been subpar at best, a trite *"you'll like it well enough with the right man"*. It appeared that against all reason and better judgement, Marcus Edward Balfour, Marquess of Althorn and heir to the Duke of Elsingham, was, in fact, the right man. Because she liked it very much. A shocking amount, in fact. With every stroke of his tongue against hers, every nip of his teeth and the soft sweep of his lips over hers, she found herself wondering what else she would like and what else he could do to evoke such a strange maelstrom of sensations inside her. Blood rushed, her heart quickened, and heat blossomed inside her along with a strange anticipation that she could not name. Whatever he was doing, she wanted more of it.

⁂

PERHAPS HE'D OVERESTIMATED his own self-control. Or perhaps he'd underestimated how responsive Jane Barrett would be to his kisses. Regardless, Marcus found himself struggling to rein in his growing desire for her. He'd intended only to kiss her, to introduce some physical intimacy into their acquaintance to begin building a romantic connection with her. He hadn't foreseen that it would escalate so quickly or that her body would fit so perfectly against his own.

The softness of her breasts crushed against his chest and the flare of her hips that fit his hands so perfectly were not conducive to having a chaste kiss as it should have been. She was completely innocent, sheltered, isolated even. And yet, her untutored response to his kiss enflamed him more than the tricks of even the most notorious courtesan could. Forcing himself to break the contact and to draw back from her, he met her heavy-lidded gaze.

"It isn't simply about your fortune. And if you ever think it is again, you should remember this moment," he said.

"Is that why you kissed me?" she asked. "Just to prove your point?"

"I kissed you because I wanted to. If it proves a point, then we shall just consider that a lucky happenstance," he answered. "I've wanted to do that since you fainted in my arms last night."

"I didn't faint in your arms!"

"You did," he insisted. And in spite of the agony of his leg, he hadn't been able to forget the feeling of her lush curves pressed against him just as they were in that moment.

"It was hunger from being starved by my odious stepmother!"

He didn't laugh, though the desire to do so was there. Forcing himself to be completely forthright, or as forthright as he could be with her about his unexpected feelings for her, he explained, "I had intended to come home and to marry you as per the agreement. I had not anticipated that I would be eager to do so. Rest assured on that front, I am quite eager for our wedding to take place."

"Just because you can kiss me senseless doesn't mean I'm willing to marry you. I haven't made up my mind," she insisted.

"If I had the wherewithal to kiss you again... and only kiss you... I would do so until you relented," he said. "But alas, I cannot trust myself. Make no mistake, Miss Jane Barrett, there are many things in life far more valuable than something as dirty and coarse as money... and this is one of them."

She said nothing for the longest time. When she turned to walk away, he saw her falter. She paused just before the curtained partition that separated the gallery from the hall and glanced back at him. It was an unconsciously seductive pose, looking over her shoulder, biting her lip, her hair slightly mussed from his hands that had roved of their own accord. He drank in the sight and savored it long after she fled.

He wanted her. Not because she was intended to be his bride. Not because she had a fortune. He wanted her solely for her, for her lush figure and the sweet curve of her face, the softness of her lips and even the barbed wit that sometimes cut him into ribbons. He wanted her because she was her and no other. That was a complication he had not foreseen, but a welcome one and one he meant to explore fully.

JANE DIDN'T GO to the kitchens after all. She fled back to her room and tried desperately to make sense of what had just occurred.

Sarah was still there, tidying up her meager wardrobe and undoubtedly hiding from other tasks that might be assigned to her. She took one look at Jane, in her current state, and asked, "Good heavens, what on earth has happened to you?"

Jane shook her head. "I don't know. But it can't be good. I need to stop the publisher from putting out that pamphlet, Sarah. What if I'm too late?"

Sarah frowned. "But isn't that what you want? For the pamphlet to go out and him to be forced to prove that he is, in fact, the marquess? It was all part of your plan."

Jane stepped deeper into the room and sank heavily onto the small bench before her dressing table. "My plan has to change. He kissed me, Sarah."

Sarah guffawed. "A kiss? And that was enough to make you want to marry him?"

"No... but it was enough to make me question my adamant refusal. I may still renege, but I need to be certain I haven't done something so awful that option is taken from me altogether."

Turning to her dressing table and the writing box she kept hidden beneath it, Jane pulled out some foolscap and her quill. "I hope I'm not too late."

Scribbling furiously, she dashed off a letter to the publisher stating that her sources had been wrong, that he was the marquess and publication of the pamphlet would make them both laughing stocks. When it was done, she sealed it and then sent Sarah below stairs to bribe one of the kitchen lads to deliver it. If it wasn't enough, if the publisher chose to go ahead with the printing, she'd be ruined. Althorn would not rest until he discovered who had defamed him so thoroughly, and if he were to discover it was her—

"I just need time to decide," Jane uttered to the now empty room. "I don't know what to do."

Cursing herself, cursing him and that blasted kiss for making her question her own mind, Jane ate her miserable cucumber sandwiches and tried to regain some modicum of resolve. It was as useless an endeavor as trying to fill her belly with the loathsome little sandwiches.

Chapter Eight

DINNER THAT NIGHT was an uncomfortable affair. Neither her father nor stepmother spoke, nor did the Duke of Elsingham. Conversation consisted primarily of whatever the Duchess of Elsingham was spewing about fashion, purchasing new gowns in bright colors, attending balls and all other manner of nonsense. At the far end of the table, Charles Balfour sat in stony silence.

Jane noted the undercurrent of animosity between Charles and Althorn. They did little enough to disguise it, she mused. Of course, it might have been that she was so painfully aware of him after their earlier encounter. She couldn't stop thinking of it and remembering just how it had felt. While she did not possess the words to describe it, she did know one thing with utter certainty—she wanted it to happen again.

As if he'd read her thoughts, Althorn looked at her over the rim of his glass. His gaze was heated, direct and spoke volumes about his feelings on the matter, as well.

Her face flushed with embarrassment at having been caught staring, but also with something else altogether. Averting her gaze, she willed her pulse to return to its normal rate and tried not to let herself be distracted by him. It might all be for naught, anyway. She had yet to hear back from her publisher and if the pamphlet was printed as per the usual schedule, it would come out two days hence. Her entire world could come crashing down then.

"Perhaps we could manage an outing tomorrow night?"

The suggestion had come from Charles. Jane blinked in surprise as she glanced up at him and then back to Althorn who appeared singularly nonplussed by the suggestion.

"That would be a lovely idea," the duchess said, clapping her hands in delight like a child. "The theater perhaps? Oh, we haven't attended the theater in an age! Wouldn't it be delightful, Miss Barrett?"

Very much on the spot, Jane fumbled for a response. "While the theater would be lovely, I am not quite certain we should be making such public appearances just yet—Lord Althorn has only just returned and it might be... the etiquette of this situation is very much uncharted waters."

"Pshaw!" the duchess countered with a dismissive wave of her hand. "We ought to be hosting a ball given the joyous occasion of his return! But alas, that might be too much for my dear husband's health."

"And for my dear pocketbook!" the duke shouted. "There will be no ball!"

The duchess smiled even brighter, though it prompted a slightly maniacal gleam in her eyes. "Then the theater it is! We'll go tomorrow night. Do we know what play is being performed? Not that it matters! Not a whit. I'm just so excited to go!"

Jane dared a glance back at Althorn. His expression was grim but he gave a curt nod before turning to Charles. "We shall attend tomorrow evening then. I'm sure no one can fault us for it. After all, my return was a joyous occasion. Wasn't it, Charles?" His tone was goading.

Charles smiled coldly. "My dear cousin, I must admit to being quite overcome at the sight of you. I'll make the arrangements," he offered.

"There's no need." Marcus dismissed his offer summarily. "I have the use of a box. I had planned to take Miss Barrett for an evening, but there is no reason that we cannot all enjoy Lord Highcliff's bounty."

Charles' expression was etched with resentment. "Of course. Always the best of everything for you, isn't it, Marcus? Heaven forbid you have to rub elbows with the rabble... Highcliff's box will do nicely."

The undercurrent between them was positively vicious, Jane thought. She half-expected them to come to blows at any minute.

As dessert was served, her place was obviously devoid of any of the delicious fruit trifle that had been prepared.

"Are you not a fan of trifle, Miss Barrett?" Althorn asked.

Jane glanced at Mrs. Barrett who was eyeing her with diabolical glee. "I quite like trifle, in fact," she replied. "Mrs. Barrett and I disagree on what my proper diet should be."

Mrs. Barrett laughed uncomfortable, clearly stunned that Jane would make such an admission. "My dear girl! It's only so that you will look your best on your wedding day!"

Althorn nodded sagely. "I daresay that Miss Barrett could not look any more perfect on that day than she does right now." He gestured to one of the footman, "You will serve, Miss Barrett. And from this moment forward, no one, aside from Miss Barrett herself, will have any say in what she does and does not eat."

The footman nodded, clearly aware that a war had been waged and won in that dining room. He fled back to the kitchens immediately after serving up another helping of the trifle.

With the decadent concoction placed before her, Jane took a small bite and enjoyed not only the flavor but the victory. She would pay for it later. But for the moment, she was thoroughly elated by the discomfiture of her vicious stepmother.

"Well, I daresay, we'll only have to purchase a bit of extra fabric for your wedding gown. It's hardly the end of the world," Mrs. Barrett finally said.

"If we had a ball and Miss Barrett could dance, she could eat all of the sweets she wanted and it wouldn't make a bit of difference," the duchess suggested with a slight pout.

The ridiculousness of it all struck Jane then. The entire house was filled with Bedlamites it seemed. Looking up, she met Althorn's gaze and for that small moment, there was an understanding between them. Everyone in the house was positively mad but the two of them, and that was less an endorsement for them than an indictment for the others. Still, it helped the remainder of the meal to pass in relative peace.

IN THE LIBRARY after dinner with his father, Mr. Barrett and his scheming cousin, Marcus wished himself anywhere else. He'd faced less animosity on the battlefield than he faced in that one room. Given what he'd seen at dinner, he doubted very seriously that Miss Barrett was faring any better in the company of his vapid stepmother and her beastly one. Mrs. Barrett was attractive enough but he'd encountered warmer corpses.

"When are you going to finally make good on this betrothal, Alt-horn?" Mr. Barrett finally said, skirting anything that resembled small talk and even civility. The man took a deep draw from his cheroot and then immediately followed it with a healthy swallow of brandy.

"When Miss Barrett feels comfortable enough to proceed, we shall. I daresay, sometime in the summer," Marcus offered. There was a finality to his tone, a warning to those who might try to push either of them. More than ever, he was determined to make it work, but only on their own terms.

"The summer?" the duke scoffed. "That girl is practically in her dotage!"

"Hardly that," Marcus replied dismissively. She was just shy of two and twenty. Did everyone really think that a girl of her age was too old to not have already been shackled to a husband? "It has been some time and many things have changed since last Miss Barrett and I met. It is only natural that we should take our time and get to know one another again."

"You didn't know one another to start," Charles pointed out less than helpfully. "I think you are making a mistake, Cousin. You are creating an opportunity for her to develop cold feet and renege on the contract. You should pursue her more forcefully."

The duke laughed as Mr. Barrett nodded. "Yes, indeed!" His father wheezed as he continued to chortle. "I'd never thought to hear such sensible speech from you, Charles! He's quite right, Marcus. Marry the girl now before it's too late!"

Mr. Barrett sighed heavily. "She's willful and headstrong. Quite like her mother was in that regard... it took years to make that woman see reason. I fear you'll have your work cut out for you with Jane."

Charles continued, "If you took her off to Scotland in an elopement, it wouldn't much matter if she consented or not."

Marcus rose to his feet. "I've heard about enough of this. Miss Barrett and I will wed when she is willing and ready. Not before. If you'll excuse me, your grace, Mr. Barrett, Charles... I've some correspondence to attend to."

"You've only just returned," Charles uttered in mock protest.

Marcus turned toward his cousin, noting the gleam in his eyes and the cocky grin that curved his lips. He'd never wanted so badly to plant his fist in anyone's face. "And that is precisely why I must attend to things. Too much has been neglected in my absence."

"Surely you needn't rush off so soon," Charles cajoled in the same grating tone. "Why don't you share with us something of your experiences while we all languished here in London... bereft in your absence."

Marcus met Charles' challenging gaze levelly. "While my memories of Corunna and what happened afterward would be of particular interest to you, Charles, I doubt very much you'd wish for me to air such putrid recollections to everyone gathered."

"Quite right," Mr. Barrett interrupted. "Never understood the fondness some men have for sharing old war stories. Deucedly boring!"

"Then we are in agreement," Marcus said. "If you will excuse me."

"Before you go, Althorn," Barrett said, "Summer won't do. Two months hence you'll be married to my daughter or I'll be contacting my solicitors. I don't like to be difficult... but we've all waited long enough."

"I won't be threatened or bullied, Barrett," Marcus snapped. "You might have been able to get away with that before, but not now. I'll marry her or I won't, but it isn't up to you or to my father. It's between Miss Barrett and myself. And that will be the end of it."

⚜

CHARLES WATCHED HIS cousin leave. It couldn't have gone any better than if he'd planned it to the last detail. As Barrett and the duke argued amongst themselves, Charles refilled his brandy snifter and then offered the prize he'd been instructed to dangle.

"What if it wasn't up to them at all?" Charles murmured.

That softly uttered question halted the conversation between the patriarchs. They turned and looked at him suspiciously.

"What do you have in mind?" the duke asked.

Charles nodded his head. "Marcus has always been a firm believer in what is right and proper... what if the proper thing to do was to force the marriage? What if the threat of scandal was so great he had no other option but to press the match more forcefully than he has to this point?"

Barrett scowled. "Are you suggesting that he should compromise my daughter?"

"No. Because he wouldn't," Charles answered. "Marcus is far too much of a stick in the mud to ever give in to passion in such a manner. The girl doesn't have to actually be ruined. There only has to be the illusion of compromise. Tomorrow night's outing would be perfect."

Barrett took another hefty swallow of his brandy. "What are you planning?"

"Nothing yet," Charles lied. "I'd never think to act without your approval... but if Miss Barrett and Althorn were to be caught in a compromising situation—say alone in a darkened room at the theater as if they'd snuck away for a tryst—the only honorable thing he could do would be to proceed with the wedding posthaste."

The duke chortled. "I don't know what you're about, Charles, not when you were angling for a go at her yourself only days ago! But if it'll get the job done, you may do whatever is required!"

Charles glanced at Barrett. The other man nodded his agreement. "Very well, your grace, Mr. Barrett. I have arrangements to make. I bid you adieu until tomorrow night."

"I HAVE NEVER been so mortified! Naturally, he is her betrothed, but until such time as he can call himself her husband it is her father and I who should be in charge of her behavior!" Mrs. Barrett was speaking far more forcefully than was wise in the presence of a duchess. Overset by Marcus' interference at dinner, she paced the room, alternately bemoaning her ill treatment and maligning the character of her stepdaughter's betrothed.

Jane didn't roll her eyes, sigh heavily or do any of the other things that fully expressed her misery at having to listen to her stepmother going on and on about Althorn's high-handed tactics at dinner. It would only draw attention to her and, for the first time, it appeared her stepmother's ire was directed elsewhere. Doing anything to jeopardize that was not in her best interest.

"I really can't say what on earth has gotten into him," the duchess chimed in. "Although to be fair, I hardly know him. I only met him a handful of times before he departed for the army. How strange it is to be his stepmother when he's actually the same age as I am. I don't even know what his favorite foods are. My goodness, what a terrible hostess I've been. I should find out straightaway what his favorites are and have cook prepare a special meal for him!"

"No doubt, it'll be horribly fattening and he'll grin like a fool while my worthless stepdaughter inhales half of it!" Mrs. Barrett snapped, her ire once more aimed in Jane's direction.

The duchess tittered, casting a sidelong glance at Jane before falling into peals of giggles. "Oh, dear! It is ungenerous of me to say so, but you are growing quite plump, my dear Miss Barrett! Perhaps, you'd best accept Marcus' offer while it still stands?"

"Is there anything else about my person you wish to discuss?" Jane demanded. "Perhaps we should look at all the ways my hair is displeasing. The color is not blonde enough to be fashionable. It refuses to heed pins and resists all attempts at taming and proper curls. Or mayhap, my eyes are the wrong shade of blue. By all means, Mrs. Barrett, your grace… please, feel free to pick me apart and identify every flaw. But then, I've never had to invite you to do either, have I? You've both willingly done so for years!"

The duchess' smirk turned icy cold and her eyes gleamed. "My goodness. It appears that having a present and very much alive betrothed does not suit you at all, Miss Barrett. Why, I daresay it has made you an utter termagant."

Mrs. Barrett was gaping at her like a fish for a long moment before gathering herself enough to scold. "How dare you speak so ill to our hostess! Have you no notion of how poorly your behavior reflects upon your father and me? What on earth must her grace think of us to see you so poorly behaved?"

"I am poorly behaved?" Jane queried with a bitter laugh. "I am insulted at every turn by the both of you. Snide, nasty comments about my age, my weight, my figure, my general state of attractive-ness—or unattractiveness if the two of you are to be believed! I am told over and over again how very grateful I should be for any male attention but specifically from one so exalted as the marquess! I refuse to be the butt of your jokes or the whipped dog at your feet anymore! I'm done with it, I tell you!"

Both women gaped at her, but it was the duchess who recovered first. Her eyes were overly bright and though she smiled, the expres-sion showed an inordinate amount of her teeth, giving even such a beautiful woman a somewhat feral appearance. "If our company is so disagreeable, then perhaps you should not suffer it any longer."

At that point, Jane rose to her feet and summoned all the wounded dignity she possessed. "I'm quite tired. It's probably the aftereffects of having a full stomach for the first time in ages. I believe I shall retire.

Good night, your grace. Good night, Mrs. Barrett!"

Without waiting for either of them to grant her leave, Jane fled the room in full retreat. All she wanted was an escape from the constant badgering and the general unpleasantness of her stepmother's company. The Duchess of Elsingham was tolerable, most of the time, if vapid. A thoroughly self-centered person, she at least wasn't full of spite and vitriol. Or hadn't been until Charles Balfour had proposed to her. At that point, the woman's demeanor had become much more vicious. Jane had often thought over the last few years of how strange their bond seemed to be, but now uglier suspicions were supplanting those vague notions she might have had about the nature of their relationship.

Leaving the drawing room, she made quickly for the stairs. She didn't want to give her stepmother a chance to recover her composure and call her back. As she rounded the corner and reached for the banister, she found it already occupied. Lord Althorn was there, a few steps ahead of her.

"Are you fleeing the baying hounds, as well?" he asked with an amused curve of his lips.

His lips were a dangerous place for her gaze to fall, she thought. She didn't need any further reminders of the kiss they'd shared earlier. "Something to that effect. Is everyone in this house simply impossible?"

"In a word, yes."

The drawing room door opened. Panic took over in that instant, spurring her instinct to flee further from danger. "Hurry," she whispered. "Before she sees either of us!"

Together, they fled up the stairs and disappeared once more into the shadows of the curtained gallery. From below, as they huddled together behind the curtain, Jane could hear her stepmother's voice. "How on earth did she vanish so quickly?"

The duchess' musical laughter tinkled like bells. "I have no idea. It's best to let her go, however. She's in a snit and will likely stay that way for some time. Imagine being so overset by simple words of advice on how best to please her husband-to-be! Let's have some sherry, shall we? Sherry always makes things better!"

When their voices trailed off, Jane breathed a sigh of relief. It faded into something far different. She hadn't realized how close they were standing or that they were, once more, in the very same spot where he'd kissed her just that afternoon.

"Pray tell, Miss Barrett, what words of wisdom did they impart on how to please your husband-to-be?" The words were whispered against her ear, softly and with enough heat to make her shiver.

"It doesn't bear repeating," she said. "It's the same sort of nonsense they always spout off."

"I take it your stepmother is displeased with you?" he queried.

"In spite of my rather improper retort to their well-meaning advice, I believe she is more put out with you at the moment," she answered, striving for a light tone and failing miserably at it. "Mrs. Barrett does not like to have her authority questioned... not by anyone."

He moved closer, so close that even in the dim light she could see the dark shadow of his beard just beginning to form. She could smell the faint scent of her father's cheroot clinging to his clothes and the scent of brandy. "I take it you are fleeing my father?"

"And mine," he admitted. "I dislike being bullied... but more than that I dislike sitting there while Charles plots and schemes against me."

She frowned at that. "Do you really think he would do that?"

His expression shifted, becoming darker and infinitely more grim. "I know it beyond question. It would not be the first time he has betrayed me. But I do not wish to discuss my cousin with you, Jane."

She felt her breath shudder from her as he uttered her name. It was like a caress—titillating and forbidden. "Then what is it you wish to discuss, my lord?"

He lifted one hand and grasped the single untamed curl that had escaped from her chignon. As he rubbed the strands between his fingers, he said, "The most pressing topic on my mind at the moment is whether or not you mean to let me kiss you again."

"I shouldn't," she whispered. Her voice wasn't pitched so low and breathlessly on purpose. It was simply all that she could muster at the moment. As a protest went, it was quite possibly the weakest one ever offered.

He leaned in even closer, until he could whisper in her ear as his breath ruffled over her skin and made her shiver.

"That wasn't a no, Jane."

"I don't think I can say no. I know that I ought to... for so many reasons. For propriety, for my own peace of mind, for my previous certainty that there could never be anything between us but a contract. And yet, I cannot make myself utter the word," she admitted grudgingly.

He smiled then, and his hand that had been caressing that single curl suddenly delved into the mass of her hair. Pins scattered as her hair spilled over her shoulders and into his waiting hand. "An unwillingness to say no isn't precisely a yes but, at this point, I'll take what I can get."

She wasn't caught off guard or taken unawares. This time, there was anticipation, there was foreknowledge of what was to come. Even then, she wasn't fully prepared for it. As one arm snared about her waist and pulled her even closer, his other hand tangled in her hair, tilting her head back. The only thing that shocked her was her own eagerness. And when his lips pressed against hers, the frisson of excitement carried with it something else—longing.

Jane realized, in that moment, that she'd been waiting for him to kiss her again almost from the second their first kiss had ended. It was as if every moment of the day had just been a delay until they could get to this. She would never have considered herself a passionate person. She certainly wouldn't have ever entertained the possibility that she might be a wanton. And yet, she found herself accepting that fact with far more ease than she should have. Given that she was still uncertain of the desired outcome of their courtship, her capitulation could not have been more unwise.

As his lips moved over hers, his tongue sliding between them to tangle with hers in a sensual dance, thought fled. Jane gave herself up to the kiss, sinking against him. Her hands locked behind his neck, holding him close. It was an unconscious gesture, but a telling one. It might have been minutes or it might have been hours that they stood there, locked together, sharing what, for her, was the most intimate encounter ever.

When at last he dragged his lips from hers, she whimpered a slight protest. It was soon lost in a soft sigh of pleasure as his lips trailed over the sensitive skin of her neck. The scrape of his teeth elicited a shiver from her as the sensation of it aroused a yearning inside her she had never known. What would it feel like to have his lips on her elsewhere? To feel the gentle sting of such a bite on even more tender flesh?

"Jane," he whispered, "We should stop... while I still have the strength to do so."

"How is it that we've gone from snapping at one another to this? How?"

He shook his head. "I can't answer that. I can only say that this is far preferable to me than us forever being at odds with one another."

"It doesn't change anything... I still don't know if I want to be married."

He took a step back but didn't let go of her entirely. "I didn't expect that you would have such a complete about-face. You have reservations and I won't press you for more than you are willing to give me."

And that was the crux of it. Because when he was kissing her, she would willingly give him everything. It didn't escape her notice that both of their more intimate exchanges had only halted because he had done so. Had it been left up to her, they would have gone on indefinitely, and likely culminated in an act that there was no returning from.

"Be truthful with me, Althorn."

"Marcus," he corrected.

"Marcus, then... do you really want me or is this just a convenient way to manipulate my feelings so that I do what you want."

At first, she thought she'd angered him. He was silent for the longest time. When he did answer her, he did so in a manner she could not have anticipated. He clasped her hand in his and brought it between them, pressing her palm against the front of his breeches. The hardened flesh beneath her hand pulsed at her touch.

"Rest assured, Jane, that my response to you is very real. I want you. My body does not lie," he said.

"But your lips do?"

"I have not told you everything, but I have not told you anything that is untrue," he said. "I mean to marry you. I mean to fulfill my contractual obligations. But this... this thing between us is something else, something I could not have anticipated. Regardless, I am grateful for it. What better omen could one have for a betrothal than to have such a keen desire for one's betrothed?"

"Desire is not love," she protested.

"No... but I daresay that desire is the seed from which it can grow. Love isn't simply one thing, Jane. It's a combination of them. Desire is part of that. Trust is another."

He kissed her again, a surprisingly chaste brush of his lips against her cheek. With that, he turned and vanished into the shadows of the darkened hall beyond, leaving her to ponder the weight of what he'd said. Could she love him? Could he love her? And would she ever be able to trust in the sincerity of his love when the marriage itself had been bought and paid for?

Chapter Nine

THE NIGHT HAD been long and restless for him. As Marcus descended the stairs, he was feeling the strain of that. He hadn't anticipated wanting her to the degree that he did even after acknowledging his initial attraction to her. And it went far beyond just the need for feminine companionship. He could easily have found a willing woman to slake his lust. But therein lay the crux of it. They were only substitutes. Because he didn't want just any woman. He wanted *the* woman. Miss Jane Elizabeth Barrett.

"A missive has arrived for you, my lord," Riggs said, approaching with a sealed letter on a salver.

Marcus took the document, scanned the contents and sighed heavily. "I must go out, Riggs. If anyone should inquire, I will be home before tea time."

The butler frowned. "I see, my lord. Is there a problem?"

"Nothing to worry about. Riggs, be certain that no one bullies Miss Barrett today or interferes with her breakfast, if you please."

The butler didn't smile, but he had a wicked gleam in his eye at being trusted with the role of white knight. "Certainly, my lord. I shall gladly see to it that Miss Barrett is not disturbed or importuned in any way while she enjoys her morning meal."

With that, Marcus left the house and headed toward Highcliff's residence near Bruton Place. The man wouldn't have sent for him if he did not have news to impart. The short walk in the crisp air would clear his head and mitigate the effects of his lack of sufficient sleep, or so he hoped.

When he arrived, the butler opened the door before he had even knocked and ushered him inside. Highcliff was ensconced in his study, still wearing a banyan with his hair mussed from sleep. He was also drinking copious amounts of strong, black coffee.

Marcus grimaced. "How you can tolerate that abominable concoction, I've no idea!"

"It clears the mind," Highcliff answered. "From the bags beneath your eyes, I daresay you could use a cup or two."

"I'll have tea, thank you. Like a proper Englishman."

Highcliff laughed. "I'm neither proper nor entirely English, am I?"

It was an old joke between them, going back to their school days. "I assume you have news or I wouldn't have been summoned here at this ungodly hour."

Highcliff nodded, took another sip, and then answered, "I tracked down a member of Charles' regiment. He was not injured. Not at Corunna nor in any other battle. He was always curiously devoid of even the most minor of scrapes. According to this man, it was almost as if the French tried to avoid shooting the bastard."

Marcus sank down into one the chairs facing the desk. "Perhaps I should have brandy instead of tea. It's worse than I thought, isn't it?"

Highcliff sighed wearily, a sound that belied his normally carefree attitude and sometimes dandified experience. No one knew better than Marcus just how much of his true nature Highcliff concealed. The man was deadly and had done things for king and country most could not imagine. Even now, his life as a scandalous bachelor concerned only with fashion and the seduction of merry widows and unhappy wives was largely a ruse.

"Charles' movements during the war perfectly coincide with significant losses that potentially resulted from the leaking of invaluable information about munitions and troops," Highcliff replied. "You suspected him of it years ago. You brought those suspicions to me in Portugal months before Corunna, did you not?"

Marcus heaved a weary sigh of his own. "I did. But I desperately hoped to be wrong. A traitor in the family... a man guilty of treason and in line for a dukedom? And then, of course, there are the lengths he would go to in order to have the title. I've no proof but there isn't a doubt in my mind that he was fully responsible for my capture. The soldiers ignored him and took me instead. Yet, I was dressed as an enlisted man. In my borrowed uniform at that time, Charles gave every appearance of outranking me."

"Not to mention that he knew you'd been captured and informed no one. Some whispered that you were dead, others a deserter... and he possessed knowledge that not only would have quelled any gossip or conjecture, but could well have led to your rescue and return," Highcliff pointed out. "This patently false tale of a head injury at Corunna is simply a way of covering his tracks and hiding, if not his involvement, then at least his inaction on your behalf."

"And in my absence, he waited a full five years before making a play for Miss Barrett's hand. Why now? He didn't know I was returning. No one could feign the shock that I saw on his face when we met," Marcus mused. "There must be some reason for his sudden ambition on that front."

"Debt, my friend. Your cousin likes to gamble, but he does it poorly. He spends a great deal of time at a gaming hell and brothel by the name of The Prickly Thorn. It's hardly a respectable establishment... I strongly suspect that it's the lovely Helena who lured him there."

"Helena?"

"She's a soiled dove who styles herself as a demirep. There are wild stories about her being the illegitimate daughter of a Prussian count. I don't believe it for a minute. She's beautiful enough but a more grasping woman I've never met. Oddly enough, she bares a shocking resemblance to your stepmother. And as Lady Cassandra's father was both notoriously faithless and fertile—it could be worth looking into. I will say this for the lovely Helena, even in her silks and satins, there is something of the gutter about her... and I ought to know. Takes one to know one and all that. And she's got her claws into Charles all the way to the hilt. She's been seen coming and going from his apartments at all hours of the day and night... always heavily veiled and dressed as a widow. Probably in castoffs from her illegiti-mate half-sister."

Marcus considered it. "Did Cassandra introduce them? Perhaps she thought to establish Charles as her sister's protector when she believed he'd inherit the dukedom. Regardless, you think she's the impetus for his sudden pursuit of Miss Barrett and his play for the title?"

Highcliff picked up a letter opener from the desk and twirled the blade between his fingers with a skill and agility that was mind boggling to those who hadn't seen him do so before. "I think he can't hold her if he doesn't have the funds to pay her. She's the kind of woman who can drive even the best of men to their knees," Highcliff answered. "Charles has never been the best of men."

"He's hardly the sort to fall arse over head in love," Marcus retort-ed. "Charles has never given a fig for anyone else... not in the entirety of his life."

"It's not love, my friend. It's obsession. And unless your cousin is a eunuch, trust me when I say that she could sway him to her cause." Highcliff paused and took another hefty swallow from his coffee before continuing, "That woman is the devil's own. Mark me on that."

"We're supposed to attend the theater with him tonight. It's a family outing. My stepmother is coming as well, though my father has begged off." Marcus said. "At the Royal... you'll be there?"

Highcliff grimaced. "I hate that bloody place. I'll have to play the ham-headed fop since it's such a public appearance, but I'll be in attendance, as well. This was Charles' idea?"

"Yes. I can only assume that he is planning something. What, I cannot guess. Rather than allow Charles to make the arrangements, I said you had obtained a box for us. Can you?"

Highcliff sighed heavily. "Yes, I'll get you a box. You're very de-manding for a man who's been dead for five years, Althorn."

"I have a great deal of time to make up for... I didn't trust Charles. I think it's best he doesn't know where we'll be in the theater until we arrive there. I can't say for certain that he would plant an assassin but, given his past behavior, I can't be certain that he wouldn't," Marcus explained.

"Keep a close watch on your Miss Barrett. I wouldn't trust him as far as she could throw him," Highcliff stated firmly. "I'll have a few friends at the theater, as well, just in case something goes wrong."

Marcus gave a curt nod. "Agreed. There's something sinister afoot. There's an investigator you've used before?"

"Harrison," Highcliff replied. "He's good, especially in places that are not entirely respectable. The man blends well with the worst of society. It's a damnable skill to have in a man that, far as I know, is completely honorable."

"Set him on this Helena. I know enough about Charles, even if his strategy isn't completely obvious to me yet. But she's an unknown and that makes her dangerous."

Highcliff nodded his agreement. "I'll see to it. You're off to squire Miss Barrett around the city, then?"

"No. I'm off to obtain a ring for her. Most of mother's jewels have been showered on the current duchess, more's the pity. Vapid as she may be, I think if someone were to attempt to take her jewels, they'd have nothing left of their hand but a bloody stump."

Highcliff scribbled an address on a piece of parchment. "Tell him I sent you. He'll do right by you and by Miss Barrett."

Marcus nodded his thanks and left. The waters were growing murkier by the minute, but all of the ripples seemed to center on Charles and his greed. If he'd been selling secrets, it was no doubt for money. But if his gambling was as bad as Highcliff suggested, it was a certainty that the money was already spent. So he'd be looking for a new revenue stream and a woman with Miss Barrett's fortune, not to mention her father's desperation to see her wed to a title, would have suited him perfectly.

Hailing a hackney, he climbed in and muttered under his breath, "If anyone has a more worthless family than I do, I pity the poor bastard."

"What was that, guv'nah?" The driver's accent was harsh, mimicking the sounds of Seven Dials.

"Nothing. Take me to Bond Street."

"Aye, guv'nah!"

JANE HADN'T EATEN her breakfast. She had waited with bated breath for the morning papers to arrive, including her little scandal sheet, as her stepmother referred to it. The woman had no idea just how accurate her description was as the scandals originated at the very tip of Jane's own quill. It was a strange reversal of circumstances that she was finally permitted to eat whatever she wished and her nerves were such that she couldn't tolerate a single bite.

Eventually, the footmen had cleared away the breakfast dishes along with her untouched plate and she'd retreated to the morning room. She'd mangled her already pitiful attempt at embroidery under her stepmother's reproachful eye. Even the Duchess of Elsingham, possibly the least skilled lady in embroidery Jane had ever seen, had given her an arched look upon noting the tangled mass of threads that was supposed to have been a chair cover.

Unable to sit still a moment longer, Jane set her embroidery aside and rose to look out the window at the street beyond. When she saw the shabbily-dressed lad run down the stairs to the servants' entrance carrying a bundle of papers, she nearly danced with excitement.

"Excuse me. Our news sheets have arrived and I need to see if there is a new edition of the London Ladies' Gazette," she said.

Mrs. Barrett harrumphed loudly. "That rag! I cannot understand how a girl who styles herself as a bluestocking, and with your love of books you could be nothing less, could bear to read such utter nonsense!"

"We all have our small indulgences," Jane answered, the words hurried as she was even then making her way to the door. "Excuse me, Mrs. Barrett, your grace."

Leaving the room and the two women gaping after her, she ran down the stairs to the kitchen, but she was too late.

"Where are the papers that were just delivered?" Jane asked. If the servants thought it odd that she'd entered their domain, their expressions were carefully schooled to conceal it.

"Well, Miss Barrett, they were already taken up to the library... straightaway as soon as the lad brought them and the day's mail. I'm sure his grace wouldn't mind you popping in if there was something important you were expecting," the housekeeper, Mrs. Oliver, said. Her tone clearly indicated that she felt there was nothing important enough to warrant interrupting his grace.

Panic. Terror. Painful regret. There were a dozen or so ways to describe just how Jane felt at the prospect of that article finding its way into Marcus' hands. It would be well worth braving the duke's wrath to avoid it. Turning on her heel, she all but ran up the stairs and toward the library. By the time she reached the double doors, she was breathless and her face was flushed. The footman opened the door for her, his expression implacable even if she did appear ready for Bedlam.

"What is it?" the duke bellowed from within.

"Really, Father. Could you possibly be more unpleasant?" Marcus replied from behind the doors.

Jane froze. Her feet were rooted to the floor as she was assailed by a dozen visions of how horribly wrong everything could go.

"Girl, come in or go on about your day, but do not stand there gaping at us a moment longer!"

The barked order from the duke roused her to activity. Forcing one foot in front of the other, Jane entered the room and curtsied. "Good morning, your grace, Lord Althorn. I believe one of my publications was delivered with your mail by mistake."

The duke picked it up from the stack and waved it about. "This piece of drivel? 'Marquess A Returns From Captivity... Or Does He?' This is preposterous! I will not have such rubbish in my home!"

Jane watched Marcus for his reaction. He frowned, then arched one eyebrow before crossing to his father's desk and picking up the small pamphlet that Jane had been secretly writing for since his disappearance. As he thumbed through the pages, his eyebrow rose further. Then he looked up and she could see that he was furious.

"This has Charles written all over it," he said. "That greedy, grasping, worthless nephew of yours has once more tried to sabotage everything I hold dear for his own gain!"

"I'm certain it isn't so very bad," Jane offered in what she hoped was both a reassuring and placating tone.

"Not so very bad? He's branded me an imposter, a confidence man and that's just with the headline! Heaven only knows what sort of depravity I'll be accused of in the article itself," Althorn snapped.

"Well, don't take the girl's head off! It isn't as if she wrote the blasted thing!"

At the duke's reprimand, which was, of course, patently false, Jane's heart began to palpitate. Her nerves were strung tighter than a bow and she very much feared she would either faint again or cast up her accounts. Neither of which would endear her to the duke.

"Father is right, Jane. I'm sorry for behaving so boorishly but this kind of subterfuge is precisely the sort of thing Charles has always engaged in to get his way in things. I'll not have it. With all that the other prisoners and I endured in captivity and the danger we faced in our attempts to return home... I'll not allow an insult such as this to pass!"

"I'm sure he meant no insult. And you know how gossip is... a person might have simply remarked that you had changed in the interim and suddenly it's a headline!" she fibbed. "I wouldn't think a thing of it. Truly."

The duke waved his hand dismissively. "Get out. The both of you. Take that worthless piece of nonsense with you. There is too much emotion in this room by far! I'm done with the lot of it!"

Marcus strode forward, grasped her hand and pulled her from the room with him. "Where the devil can we go in this house that won't involve seeing my relatives or yours?"

"The garden," Jane suggested. "Cold as it is, no one else goes there."

"Get your pelisse," he instructed. "We need to speak privately about this, with no prying ears or eyes. And there are other matters to address."

Did he know? Had he somehow, in that short span of time, pieced together the truth? That she was responsible for the rumors that would now be circulating that his claim of being the Marquess of Althorn was fraudulent? She'd given it away, Jane thought. Somehow her cursed inability to ever conceal her feelings had somehow exposed her guilt to him.

"I'm very warm actually... I don't need my pelisse. Let's just get on with it."

He looked at her oddly then, taken aback by her abrupt reply. "Very well. We won't be long."

As if she were facing her very own execution, Jane walked with him into the garden and wondered what on earth she would say to her father when he rightly withdrew his offer.

Chapter Ten

MARCUS TOOK IN her hang-dog expression curiously. Jane appeared utterly morose and he had no idea as to why. Unless it was the article, he thought bitterly. What woman would wish to attach herself to a duke who might not actually be a duke? To go through with their marriage and navigate society with their rank questioned at every turn would be difficult to say the least.

"About this article, Jane, rest assured that I will find the person who wrote it and see that every word is retracted and a full rebuttal printed. I've no doubt whatsoever that these are more of Charles' machinations," he said, striving for a tone that was both confident and reassuring.

It infuriated him beyond end as the article not only indicated that he was not who he claimed to be, but painted him as a fortune hunter, a confidence man and little better than a criminal completely lacking in honor. It was heavy handed even for Charles.

She looked up at him, her lips parted in surprise. "You mean you don't know who wrote it?"

He glanced back at the paper. "There are only initials—J.E.... I will find him though. That is a promise. And when I get my hands on Charles—"

Taking a deep breath, Marcus attempted to reel in his temper. "I apologize, Miss Barrett. But this is piece of drivel is more than I can tolerate. I suppose I shall have to challenge him to a duel. It is the most expedient way to satisfy my honor and also to end whatever plot he has afoot!"

She blinked up at him in surprise, her expression blank as the enormity of what he said slowly sank in on her. "You can't do that! You must not challenge him!" She protested after a long and very silent pause.

"He's left me with little choice. This is an insult that cannot be easily forgiven... certainly not when considering the other crimes he has committed against me. If you are concerned, I assure you that I am an excellent marksman and am quite skilled with a sword, regardless of which weapon he might choose."

"I'm not worried about the type of weapon or even how skilled you might be with it! Do you honestly presume that if Charles were to accept such a challenge that he would fight fairly?" she demanded. "And while I harbor no great affection for him, you are grasping at straws. There is no proof at all that Charles is responsible for this!"

"I do not need proof," he stated firmly. "This is precisely the type of underhanded thing he'd do. Do you not see that he wants my title along with your fortune and will stop at nothing to get it?"

"I do see that! That is precisely why I refused his proposal! Think of the scandal, Marcus!"

Marcus had been thinking of the scandal. He'd also been thinking of the peace of mind that would be had when he no longer had to wonder from one moment to the next what sort of scheme Charles might be hatching to gain control of everything that was his. "Scandal be damned," he said and turned from her to re-enter the house. He'd ask Highcliff to be his second.

"Charles had nothing to do with it," she blurted out quickly.

Marcus halted then, his steps faltering. He turned to her. Her expression was a strange mix of panic and guilt. Seeing that written so plainly upon her face, he began to see exactly what had unfolded. "You sound terribly certain of that, Jane."

She clasped her hands in front of her and looked unwaveringly at the ground at her feet. "I am certain. I have never been more certain of anything in my life."

Having the blame taken from Charles and placed on her lovely shoulders did a great deal to soften his anger. But there were still matters that had to be dealt with. "Did you seek out this person and start this rumor, Jane?"

"I didn't have to seek anyone out," she admitted tearfully. "I am J.E.—Jane Elizabeth Barrett. You asked what sort of endeavors I had taken to support myself and now you know. I've been writing snide, nasty, gossipy columns for the *London Ladies' Gazette* for four years. I've saved every guinea I've been paid for them in order to escape my father and stepmother. I wrote that column the first night you returned. It was just panic, blind panic! If I had it to do over, I wouldn't have! I swear it."

Marcus couldn't quite believe what he was hearing. He blinked at her for several moments as he tried to formulate an appropriate response. He'd expected after her initial statement to hear that she'd had some involvement. He had not expected to learn that she was the author of such a piece.

She continued, truly distraught, "I tried to stop it. I sent a letter to the publisher and pleaded with him not to go ahead with it, but he never replied and I've been watching for the delivery ever since, hoping to intercept it so that you wouldn't see it. It was a horrible, sneaky, dishonest thing that I did. I wrote that knowing full well that you were precisely who you claimed to be. I was only trying to delay our nuptials by forcing you to provide some proof of your identity... that's all."

"I see," he finally managed. Taking several steps, he settled himself on one of the small, garden benches. To say that he was stunned was an understatement. Shocked, but strangely defused of his anger, Marcus allowed the reality of the situation to sink in. It was by no means laughable, and yet he found no small amount of humor in it. "It will be all right."

"No, it won't! You'll never forgive me for it! And even if you could... your father... and your stepmother... and my father... and heaven knows Mrs. Barrett hates me enough already! I've ruined everything by being reckless and stupid!" She was practically shouting by the time she reached the end of her long list of potential and actual detractors.

"Nothing is ruined, Jane," he said. "And frankly, the fact that this was you and not Charles changes everything. I daresay, I find the entire thing rather amusing."

She whirled then, facing him for the first time. Her lashes were dark with tears and her eyes absolutely luminous. Her lower lip trembled slightly as she said, "Amusing? You find all of this and the potentially catastrophic consequences of it amusing?"

"I do... I'm sorry," he said, trying to curb his laughter. "I realize you're very upset, but the entire situation is like a farce fit for Drury Lane."

"And when your father demands that the contracts be dissolved and my father demands recompense for it? Will you find it amusing then?"

"That will not happen," Marcus assured her, though the thought was somewhat sobering. "Because there is no need for them to ever know that you are the J.E. responsible for this. I will keep your secret and in exchange, for the time being at least, you will keep mine."

"What secrets are you referring to?" Jane demanded.

"My suspicions of Charles are well founded. I cannot tell you everything, but what I can tell you is that he is not to be trusted and not to be trifled with. You, I, and our impending marriage mark three very real obstacles to everything that he wants."

"Charles is unpleasant, to be sure! But I cannot imagine that he is truly a danger to either one of us."

Marcus shook his head. "There are any number of serious matters that we must address and Charles is but one of them. You must be very careful of him, Jane. He is not to be trusted... not at any cost."

"Why would you say such a thing? I know Charles is somewhat unpleasant, but he's hardly a criminal!"

She was too intelligent and too stubborn for her own good. If he wanted her cooperation then it was time to confess everything. "He is a criminal, Jane. In fact, I'm fairly certain he's guilty of treason."

Her tears stopped. Shock had taken precedence over everything else at that point. "You can't be serious! Charles is—he's certainly not someone that I would trust implicitly, but to be a traitor to one's own country, especially during a time of war, is something I can't imagine he would be guilty of."

"I know it's difficult because, frankly, it goes against everything that I hold dear. But for some men, money holds more sway than honor. I fear Charles is amongst their number. I need proof. And I have a friend who is helping me to obtain it. Regardless of the scandal and regardless of how Charles wronged me personally, treason cannot go unpunished. So while you were creating a scandal in the hopes of halting our marriage, sadly, one already existed that could have done so."

"I don't understand," she said.

"Jane, your father is after a connection to a dukedom... he wants a title in his family and an esteemed one at that," Marcus explained. At her continued look of confusion, he said, "If our reputation is tainted by what Charles has done, if it should become public, it is very likely that your father will void the contract and, perhaps, even forbid a marriage between us."

"He can't," she said after a moment's pause. "That contract is binding and, scandal or not, our inability to move about in society during your absence has destroyed any potential connections he has in the aristocracy. He wouldn't accept anything less than a marquess and, frankly, lofty, titled men who are poor enough to marry the plump, bookish daughter of a man not even one generation removed from trade—well, they're hardly thick on the ground."

"You can't be certain of that... and this could be precisely what you wanted. Your freedom."

JANE LET THAT sink in, absorbing the knowledge that he'd willingly handed her what he believed to be the key to ending their betrothal.

But he didn't know her father or his motives. "Questioning your claim to the title was the only thing I believe would have swayed him, farfetched as it may be. This is about his ego, you see. He wants to know that someone of his bloodline will muddy the pristine waters of the aristocracy. It's pettiness really, I suppose. He has always resented those born not to wealth, but to rank, because, try as he might, putting on whatever airs he could mimic, he would never be accepted there. But by marrying his daughter into it, one day his descendants will be. Possibly even in his lifetime."

An awful thought occurred to Jane then, one she was terrified to voice. But proceeding without knowing the truth would be infinitely worse. "Would you rather use this information to end our agreement?" she asked softly. "I understand if you have had second thoughts—"

"I have no second thoughts. I know precisely what I want, Jane. I want to put this mess with my cousin behind me, I want us to be married, and I want us to settle into a life together at Thornwood Hall. I think we could be happy together, Jane, if you're willing," he offered earnestly.

"Two days ago, I would have refused quite adamantly… because I was still holding on to old resentments and old hurts. I didn't think that you and I would suit one another at all. But I'm no longer entirely certain of that," she admitted hesitantly.

"You don't have to be certain," he offered. "Not yet, at any rate. We have a bit of time before they begin braying at us again. But if you're willing to proceed with the betrothal, if not necessarily the wedding itself just yet, I have something for you."

When he produced the small box that she could only presume held a ring, Jane felt her heart skip a beat. Theirs was not a love match, and yet they were carrying out the very scenes that she'd fantasized about as a child. His chivalry in battling her brutish stepmother, his forgiveness and even amusement at what most men would have found to be an unforgivable offense, and now a romantic gesture that typically happened between people who were very much in love—all of it rekindled the infatuation she'd held for him as a young girl. But she wasn't a girl, she was a grown woman with a woman's doubts and fears. It took more than a pretty ring and a proposal to ensure a happy marriage.

She'd never thought to have love in her life. But having sampled desire, one of its many components if her betrothed was to be believed, she wasn't certain she could willingly settle for less. Of course, that did not mean she could not love him and he her. Regardless of where they currently stood on that front, he had done everything that was right and proper for a perspective bridegroom.

"I'm still not sure."

"You are not wearing the ring because we are to be married. You will wear the ring because you are considering it… that is all, Jane. Our personal agreement from that first night still stands," he vowed. "When you are legally able to take control of the annuity your grandfather left you, then you may tell me to go straight to the devil."

"I don't think I will do that." Her reply was accompanied with a rueful chuckle. "I've been rather impossible to you since your return."

"I've had moments of being rather impossible myself," he admitted. "Let us try. That is all. And tonight, when we are at the theater, be mindful of Charles. He would not have suggested this outing if he didn't have something planned."

His tone was sharp and his expression guarded. It was becoming a familiar expression from him for he wore it whenever he spoke of his cousin. Suspicion reared and Jane elected to be blunt. "You said he might be guilty of treason… but there is something more, I think. Something that he has done to you personally. Tell me."

His answering sigh was all the verification she needed that she had been correct in her assumption.

"At Corunna, I saw Charles. And he saw me… hours before I was captured. But our paths crossed again. He was standing only yards away from me when the French soldiers took me captive. I was dressed in a lower ranking uniform than Charles was at that moment—and I cannot tell you the reasons for that. I did many things in the war that still cannot be discussed openly."

"So they didn't take him... only you, when by all rights he should have been the more valuable captive?" Jane allowed the enormity of that accusation to sink in. "And then he lied. From the moment he returned home, he denied any knowledge of having witnessed what happened to you there. Why would he do such a thing?"

"Because he wants the title for himself... and he pursued you because he wants a fortune to go with it. Charles, regardless of my return, would not simply forgo his ambitions. I've no doubt he still has his gaze fixed firmly on both of his aims."

The warning elicited a shiver of fear from her. She'd never truly feared Charles, only been mildly repulsed by his toadying. But if Marcus was correct, the man was far beyond simply greedy. He was also utterly without conscience.

"I will be wary of him," Jane agreed. As she turned to walk back into the house, a horrible thought occurred to her. "You should be wary, as well. There are other heiresses he could hang his hopes upon, but there is only one title he can ever hope to lay claim to. You are far more of an obstacle to his aims than I could ever be."

"We are agreed then to both be on guard," Althorn offered. "Don't run away so soon, Jane. We have this garden to ourselves."

"We do not, Lord Althorn," Jane replied, her tone heavy with reprimand. "The servants are well aware that we are out here together. I've no doubt that several of them are watching us at this very moment."

"Would it be so terrible for them to see a betrothed couple kissing?" he chided softly.

"When one member of the betrothed couple is still having second thoughts about marriage, it could be very bad, indeed. Any hint of impropriety between us, my lord, and any illusion of choice that I have may well be forfeit," she stated firmly. "Pleasant as those interludes have been, I think it unwise to continue them until we are both more certain of our course."

"My course is certain, Jane. But you are the current and I am at your mercy. For now, I will agree to your demands. Should the opportunity arise for us to indulge in such activities without being viewed by others, that agreement becomes null and void," he warned.

Jane wanted to protest, but her own traitorous desires wouldn't permit it. Instead, she offered a curt nod and did the only sensible thing she'd done in days. She fled.

Chapter Eleven

THE THEATER WAS quite crowded. While it had been some time since Jane had been able to attend any performances, the number of people clamoring together to get a good look at the "Missing Marquess" seemed disproportionate to her memories. It also seemed to greatly exceed the number of patrons that the theater could, in fact, safely accommodate.

"Whatever else has occurred, thank heavens your friend, Highcliff, arranged a box for us. It would be positively nightmarish otherwise," Jane uttered under her breath.

She didn't see Marcus smile, but she could sense that he did. The houselights had just been shuttered and the orchestra was warming up.

"Highcliff is full of surprises," Marcus replied, his voice barely above a whisper. "For example, I had no idea that we'd be utilizing the Royal Box and in full view of the entire gathering."

Jane frowned. "Oh my goodness. It is. Such elevated circumstance and I didn't even notice. My father may well disown me."

"Are you certain?" Marcus asked. "If that is the case, Miss Barrett, I assure you that you have never been more appealing than in this very moment."

Jane didn't allow the giggle to escape, muffling it behind her hand. In truth, if they could both be disowned by their families, their lives would be infinitely improved. It would all be infinitely less complicated if they didn't have such a convoluted history together and if there weren't so many other people involved in what should have been a private matter between the two of them. Jane could admit freely, to herself at any rate, that had she encountered Lord Althorn as the man who sat beside her that evening, without any past knowledge of him, she'd have been utterly charmed by him and would likely have had no hesitation in agreeing to his courtship.

Was it spite against her father that prompted her repeated inclination to turn him down? It was an uncomfortable thought but one that had to be entertained. She didn't think that was the entire reason for her hesitation, but she wasn't foolish enough to discount it entirely. There was also a healthy dose of fear that kept her from giving him anything other than a very guarded "maybe" as an answer. She lacked the ability to keep her heart secure against him. The more time spent in his company the more certain she became of that. While his intentions were clear, his feelings for her were not. Being trapped in a marriage, loving her husband and having no hope of ever having her love returned seemed to Jane the worst sort of pain a woman could endure.

Preoccupied with her own thoughts, she found herself paying little attention to the actors on stage. She did, however, frequently steal glances at the perfectly-chiseled profile of the man beside her as she struggled with her own indecision and her own motives.

In fact, Jane was so lost in thought that when the curtain dropped for intermission and the applause began, she was quite startled by it.

"Are you quite all right?" Althorn asked her.

"I'm fine. Just a bit warm in here I think," she said.

"I'll go and fetch you something to drink if you've no wish to brave the crowd," he offered.

"Nonsense, Cousin!" Charles protested. "One does not come to the theater to hide in one's box. Miss Barrett, and you of course, are quite the talk of the *ton*. If you aren't seen talking and flirting amongst everyone else during intermission then the opportunity to see and be seen has been wasted."

"I really don't care to see and be seen, Mr. Balfour," Jane protested. The Duchess of Elsingham had clearly not been so hesitant. The very second the curtain had begun to drop, she'd been out of her chair and diving into the fray.

"You may not, my dear," he continued in his same wheedling tone, "But others do. It would not do as the future Duchess of Elsingham to be seen as standoffish or cold. You must set an example."

"She doesn't feel well, Charles. Leave off. In fact, Miss Barrett, if you prefer, we can leave the performance early and return home," Marcus offered.

"No," Jane replied instantly. It would be utterly disastrous to be alone with him. She didn't trust herself or him. Perhaps being in a crowd of people was the best possible option regardless of how distasteful she found it. "As much as I might dislike admitting it, your cousin is correct. We should socialize and behave as any other affianced couple might... regardless of the rather strange circumstances we have found ourselves in."

"If you're certain then?" Althorn asked.

"I'm not, but it won't hurt anything to be sociable," Jane replied easily.

He only arched one eyebrow imperiously. "Very well then. Let us go and entertain the masses. It's a bit like being a gladiator in Rome, is it not?"

Jane rose and took his proffered arm. "They likely fared better and were less likely to be eaten alive," she replied, her voice dripping with sarcasm.

He was still chuckling under his breath as they made their way out into the lobby where the other patrons were gathered, drinking their lemonade and gossiping at a volume that was positively deafening. As they walked down, the crowd parted. Voices dropped to the merest whisper, but the sheer quantity of whispers still created an undeniable hum.

"Will it ever stop?" Jane asked softly. "Will we be objects of curiosity forever or will your disappearance and reappearance fall out of fashion as a topic of conversation?"

"There will always be new gossip, Miss Barrett," he answered levelly. "Besides, isn't this your stock in trade?"

"It's very ungentlemanly of you to bring that up," she pointed out. Then she teased in return, "One might think you weren't brought up as a gentleman, in fact. You might not even be a real marquess!"

MARCUS BIT BACK the retort that instantly sprang to his lips. She wouldn't appreciate offers to behave ungentlemanly enough to make her forget that she was a lady. Not to mention that they were hardly in a place to make such ribald comments. "Miss Barrett, you wound me. I've been devoid of the comforts of my English home for so long. Is it any wonder that I have forgotten such things?"

She didn't laugh, but he could see the amusement in her eyes as she lifted her glass of watered down lemonade to her lips and sipped daintily. The round of well wishes began immediately. A nameless and faceless throng of people descended upon them, congratulating them on their betrothal, on his delayed return home, on the end to their enforced period of mourning and how lovely it was to be seen out in society again.

"Were you out in society all that much?" Marcus whispered to her.

"I was never out in society. There was no need for it. My father's fortune had already caught a husband for me," she answered rather acerbically.

"Oh, my dear heavens! We thought you were dead, my boy! Dead as a doornail!"

Marcus groaned. A simple outing with his betrothed and a small flirtation had now turned into a farce, except it wasn't even remotely amusing. Lady Olmsworth was the last person in the world he wished to get stuck conversing with. She always had rather unfortunate breath and a propensity to be long-winded. The two did not go well together. Not to mention that she'd been half in love with Marcus' father for the entirety of his young life and would, no doubt, wax poetic about just how much Marcus looked like him, just as she had on every other occasion.

"I am quite hale and hearty, as you can see," he assured her. "Please excuse us... Miss Barrett has grown overly warm with the crowd. We must get her some air. Pardon me, Lady Olmsworth, Lady Devers."

Taking Jane by the elbow, he led her toward the door. "If you could faint, much like you did at your first sight of me, it would be greatly appreciated."

"I cannot faint on command!" she hissed back at him. "Where on earth are we going?"

"Anywhere that Lady Olmsworth is not," he answered. "And unless you want to be regaled with tales of how handsome my father was, what a wild buck he was back in the day, and just how many times she cuckolded her late husband with him, you'll try to look a bit peaked and wan right now."

Jane blanched at is description. "Oh, dear heavens."

"That'll do nicely," he said, taking in her horrified expression.

"Lord Althorn!"

They both glanced back at the bellowed greeting. It was Lord Ainstruther, a family connection to the duchess, who'd often been in attendance at the family's home. The man was long-winded, loud, rather smelly and had an unfortunate habit of staring at Jane's breasts as if they might actually pop out of her gown at any moment.

"If I feign a swoon, you must promise to catch me," she said.

"I swear it on my life."

Dutifully, Jane sank against him. It was overdone, possibly the worst display of acting in the history of the theater and would likely fool no one. It did give them a convenient excuse.

"It's the heat," he said. "Charles, we must go... I'm terribly sorry."

Charles smiled. "Not to worry, Cousin. I've seen this piece performed several times already. Let's get Miss Barrett home, shall we? I'll collect her grace if you want to get her bundled into the carriage."

"Straightaway," Marcus agreed as he ushered the unnaturally limp form of his betrothed out the door. Next to her ear, he whispered,

"You'd make a terrible spy."

"Were you a terrible spy?" she asked.

"I was a very good spy. Maybe I'll tell you someday," he offered suggestively. "I've heard such tales of daring are very seductive."

Her eye roll was all the answer he required. "Just get me into that coach before I trip and do injury to us both."

Marcus glanced up and their carriage was in the line that flanked the street. It was already being pulled forward. By the time they reached the bottom of the stairs, it was just in front of them.

Helping Jane into the conveyance, he climbed in after her. His intent had been to leave the door open for propriety's sake as they awaited Charles and his stepmother. But the carriage door closed with a remarkable amount of force and the horses lurched forward almost instantly.

Marcus reached for the handle of the door only to discover that it was curiously absent. His banging on the ceiling of the carriage was ignored by the driver.

"What is happening?" Jane asked.

"I believe we're being kidnapped," he replied easily.

"Surely you jest!"

"I do not jest... not now. We are being abducted and for what reason I cannot begin to say, but I've little doubt that Charles is behind it."

CHARLES WAITED FOR a full five minutes, giving the carriage ample time to get away. The driver had clear instructions to take them to a small cottage near one of Marcus' lesser estates. He would recognize the dwelling and also recognize just how far removed it was from any other residence, including his own. In the dark and the cold, they would have no option but to spend the night there together without a chaperone. Unless, of course, he elected to jump from the carriage, but Charles wasn't worried on that front. Marcus would never dream of abandoning Miss Barrett to the less than tender mercies of whomever might be responsible for their abduction.

Just as he'd imagined, the duchess cried out in dismay. "Where on earth is our carriage? Surely they would not have gone off without us!"

"I confess, my dear aunt, that I overheard them speaking of an elopement," Charles said, just loud enough to be overheard by anyone else who'd stepped outside for some air.

"What a silly thing to do when they are already betrothed!" she pouted.

"They have waited far too long already... or so I heard Marcus profess to dear Miss Barrett," Charles continued. "No doubt they will be wed by the time they return."

The duchess cried out in dismay. "How could they do this to us? How could they deprive of us of the joy of planning a wedding... and a ball? And all of those lovely gowns we were going to shop for together! Oh, that hateful, vile wretch! I know it was all her idea!"

By the time the Duchess of Elsingham had finished her litany, two dozen eager ears were trained on them. Charles patted her arm congenially. "There, there! My poor, dear aunt! I'm certain that when they return from their elopement we can plan a proper ball to celebrate their marriage. Who could refuse to pay homage to such a joyous occasion, after all?"

The duchess sniffed and wiped away her feigned tears. "You're quite right, Charles. I'm certain they didn't mean to be selfish."

It was all going just as they'd planned. "I'll get us a hack for the journey home... I do apologize for the terrible inconvenience and for you having to ride in such a low conveyance."

One of the many men listening intently stepped forward. "Nonsense, Balfour! I'd never dream of letting her grace ride in a lowly hack. Let me see you both home in my fine barouche!"

"Thank you, Lord Ramsleigh," the duchess gushed. "How very chivalrous you are!"

He patted her arm and then brought her hand to his lips. "Think nothing of it, my dear. I couldn't help but overhear what a trying evening you've had. How very thoughtless of your stepson and his betrothed to take off in such a manner and leave you stranded!"

She tittered and smiled as if on cue. "You are too kind, Lord Ramsleigh."

Charles watched the other man lead her off and then fell in step behind them. The entirety of London society would be talking about the elopement. If they refused to marry when they returned, they would both be ruined. Smiling, Charles thanked his lucky stars for his love and the twisted machinations of her mind. Watching her with Lord Ramsleigh, even he was half-convinced she had been taken completely unawares by the absconding couple, much less had a hand in it herself.

Chapter Twelve

THE CARRIAGE HAD rumbled along for what seemed to be hours. They were well out of the city and the carriage lamps only provided so much visibility in the yawning darkness. But as the vehicle slowed, Marcus sat up straighter. He could hear other voices and the sounds of other horses. It was obviously a prearranged rendezvous.

"If they ask you to get out of the carriage, do not," he warned. "You'll be safer in here."

"They? How many of them do you think there are?" Jane asked, a hint of panic creeping into her voice.

"No more than one or two, I imagine. If they mean to ransom us back, they will likely not harm either one of us, but we should take no chances," he countered, trying very hard not to alarm her. In truth, he suspected many more than that, but there was little point in increasing her fear which was surely considerable to begin with.

But Jane, even in their current predicament, was thinking everything through. "And if they don't mean to ransom us back? If they mean to eliminate us so that Charles can have the title?"

"It's a title with no fortune at present and I don't believe that Charles has the kind of time necessary to court and woo an heiress. He's been gambling, you see, and losing very heavily," Marcus reminded her. He prayed fervently that those responsible for abducting them were not after repayment of one of Charles' debts.

But as they sat there, the coach grew quieter. The creaking of the box as the driver disembarked faded into silence and no one came to the side of the carriage. Even the horses had stopped their whinnying and snorting. The stillness was almost unnatural. They had gone, Marcus realized, and left them there.

"They're not coming to let us out, are they? We're locked in this carriage!" The panicked tone of her voice was not one he was accustomed to, but then being locked in such a small space was not something she was accustomed to. He was altogether too familiar with it.

"No," he said. "I can get the carriage door open. As long as it isn't moving, we can get out safely. Get back as far as you can."

When Jane had eased to the far corner of the carriage, Marcus gripped the frame near the door and brought his foot up, kicking it until the latch finally broke loose and the door swung open. By the end of it, his leg was aching, his recently healed wounds protesting such strenuous activity.

Easing out into the darkness, he cursed softly. It was nearly pitch black, but it didn't matter. He recognized the countryside and the surrounding landmarks well enough. He felt Jane moving behind him, leaning out the carriage door.

"Where are we?"

"South of London... near Whitehaven, one of our smaller estates," he said.

Jane breathed a heavy sigh of relief. "Then we can get help from the staff!"

"When the sun comes up, yes... but not before. This is the countryside, Jane. They've brought us out into the middle of nowhere, really... it's all farmland and woods. There are wolves, Jane, and in the long winter months they grow very hungry. We cannot risk it until daylight."

He saw her pause. Then he saw that the reality of their situation and the knowledge that they faced just as great a danger from nature as from men settle in upon her. "So we wait in the carriage then?" The question revealed her reluctance to stay cooped up in the small enclosure any longer. He didn't relish it either.

"There is a house just there," he said and pointed beyond the carriage on the other side. "It's a small cottage. No one lives in it, but it's kept stocked with blankets and firewood for the gamekeeper when he's out this far from the house. We aren't just near one of my estates, Jane. We're on it. But we're still at least a mile from the house in the dark, and that's if we go cross country. If we follow the road, we're at least three miles and heaven knows what we might encounter along the way."

"So we'll spend the night there... alone? Just the two of us? You can't be serious."

Marcus sighed. "They took the damned horses. We can't even drive the carriage ourselves. We've no other option."

"Did you plan this? Is this your way of forcing my hand, of forcing me to agree to marry you? I'll be ruined!" she protested.

"I have more honor than that. I asked you to be my wife and I agreed to give you the time to make a decision on your own, Miss Barrett," he said, biting the words off sharply. "I'll not be impugned in such a manner by you or anyone else! Have I done anything that would make you think so ill of me, Jane? Do you honestly believe I am that lacking in honor?"

"Who else has anything to gain from seeing us wed?"

Charles. "I can't say for certain... I would imagine that my cousin, and his outing to the theater, were all part of a much bigger plan. No doubt, he has been offered ample financial compensation for his role in this and, no doubt, my father and your father were quite thrilled with the plan."

She looked away then. It wasn't an argument that could be easily refuted. "Do we really have so little say in our own lives? You've been home for less than a sennight and they've already managed and schemed us into an impossible situation. There is no coming back from this, Marcus... now neither one of us has a choice!"

"Let's get inside before we freeze, Jane. I'll build a fire. When we're both warm and reasonably more calm, we'll discuss it further." Marcus offered her his hand. He watched her hesitate. Dark as it was, there was just enough moonlight in the small clearing for him to see it.

"This isn't how things should happen." Her voice was tremulous and she was clearly overset by all of it. He couldn't blame her.

"For what it's worth, I'm sorry... but it cannot be undone."

She took his hand then and allowed him to lead her toward the house. It was a small gesture, but it proved that despite her earlier suspicions, likely borne out of nothing more than panic and the trauma of the evening, she trusted him. That, in and of itself, was more than enough to appease him.

⚜

CHARLES ENTERED THE house with the duchess. They hadn't returned straightaway but had enjoyed a long drive that allowed them to indulge their own passions. Ramsleigh was an old friend, after all, and had been more than willing to be dropped off at his club and allow them use of his conveyance. If anyone asked, they would simply state that they were keeping up the appearance of searching for Marcus and his stolen bride.

As they stepped into the foyer and divested themselves of their cloaks, they could hear shouting from the library.

"Riggs, what on earth are they going on about now?" Cassandra asked, her tone clearly revealing her impatience with both her husband and Mr. Barrett.

"Your grace, I believe that Mr. Barrett is somewhat upset about rumors that were circulated in a publication by the name of the *London Ladies' Gazette*. They have been arguing quite bitterly for the past hour," the butler informed her gravely. "I am fearful for his grace's health, under the circumstances. Such tempers are not good for him."

Cassandra nodded. "We'll attend to it, Riggs. Thank you."

When the butler had vanished, presumably to do whatever it was that butlers did, she whirled on Charles. "Do you know anything about this? Have you done something utterly stupid that will wreck our plans?"

Charles glared at her in indignation. "I've done only what we agreed to. What the devil would I know about the Ladies of London Gazette?"

"*London Ladies' Gazette*," she corrected. "The only person in this house who even reads that nonsense is Miss Barrett! One would think with her obsession with puerile gossip, she'd be a more interesting companion!"

"Whatever rumor this is, it appears dire," he said. "They sound like they're ready to do murder in there."

Cassandra cocked her head to the side. "I'm tempted to let them, but we can't risk it until Marcus and that little mouse of his are finally married. Let us go and see what sort of disaster awaits us."

As they neared the library door, the shouting grew worse. Barrett was screeching so as to be nearly insensible. Throwing open the door, Cassandra marched in with all the regality of queen. Charles took a moment to admire her and then quickly followed behind her.

"What is the meaning of this? I will remind you, Mr. Barrett, that my husband is in poor health! I would also remind you that, contrary to your current behavior, you are supposed to be a gentleman! How dare you shout and carry on in here as if you were little better than a dock worker!"

Barrett turned on her then. "How dare I? I will tell you how I dare, madam! Your stepson is a fraud! An imposter... little better than a confidence man courting my daughter to get access to my fortune!"

"You're being utterly ridiculous, Barrett!" the duke snapped. "He's my son, isn't he? I'd know my own son!"

"Hardly," Barrett retorted. "You had little enough to do with the boy before he left! And as your wife said, you are in poor health. We all know that fit of apoplexy has affected your mind, your grace! What's to stop someone from challenging his claim to the title? I'll not see her wed to someone and then disgraced!"

"With all due respect, Mr. Barrett," Charles interrupted. "I am the only person who would be entitled to challenge his claim to the title, and I have no desire to do so." There was no point in adding that it was easier to let him ascend to the title and eliminate him than to go through legal channels.

Barrett's eyes were flashing daggers at him. "You and your plans and schemes! Where is my daughter now?"

Charles shrugged. "I can't say precisely other than that she is with Marcus. You wished her to be compromised to force the marriage and so she has."

Cassandra placed a staying hand on his arm. "They 'eloped' albeit with some assistance from us during the intermission at the theater... in full view of most of those in attendance. Whether he is the heir or not, she'd be more disgraced now by not marrying him. You cannot stop it now, Mr. Barrett, not without doing irreparable harm to her reputation."

Barrett glared at them both as he growled. "I'm going after them and you, Balfour, are going with me. We'll see about this elopement. It can still be salvaged."

"To what end?"

Barrett shrugged. "It might not be a duke, but there are enough desperate nobles out there with crumbling estates that I can still get her wed to a title... virtuous or not."

When Barrett stormed out, the duke collapsed back in his wheeled chair. His face was still purple with rage but it was clear that the exchange had overly taxed him. His hands trembled and the palsy that affected him was significantly worsened.

"My dear," Cassandra said, "I'm having the footmen take you straight up to bed. You need to rest."

"That man! For nearly a decade, he's hounded me to get them married off and now suddenly he wants to call a halt! I've never dealt with a more infernal and fickle creature in my life than William Barrett!" the duke groused.

As Charles looked on, Cassandra crossed the distance between them and petted him much the same way one would soothe a child. "It'll be fine, darling. Charles will take care of everything. I promise."

The old man nodded and was quickly whisked away by the footmen that she'd rang for. When they were alone, Charles asked pointedly, "What are we to do about Barrett?"

"Delay him, mislead him, lay false trails… whatever is necessary, but do not allow him to interfere. If they do not marry, all is lost. When all is said and done, he will not seek a divorce or annulment because that would render her utterly useless to him."

"And if he will not be put off?" Charles demanded.

Cassandra shrugged. "The contracts are signed. It would be more complicated for the conditions of it to be fulfilled with Barrett dead… but not impossible. Do what must be done, Charles, whatever it is."

And that was why he loved her, he thought. She had the ability to see through to the heart of every situation and boil it down to the most necessary course of action. "Whatever it takes, then. I'll get our horses readied."

⚔

THE INTERIOR OF the cottage was quite dark. The windows were shuttered so tightly that the pale moonlight had no hope of penetrating. Jane paused inside the door.

"I can't even see my hand in front of my face," she muttered.

"Wait here. There's a tinderbox at the hearth with candles or a lamp… always. I'll get that going and then work on the fire. You're half-frozen," Marcus replied.

She was. The muslin gown she wore had once been a pale pink but had been dyed the most alarming shade of drab gray. It had been the only gown in her meager wardrobe fit for an outing to the theater in spite of that. It was not, however, fit for traveling through a cold night in a carriage with only a thin wrap for warmth. The cold had penetrated so deeply that she no longer even felt it.

When the lamp on the mantel flared to life, she could finally see the interior of the cottage. It wasn't so bad, though it was hardly luxurious. There were several wooden chairs around a somewhat rickety table. Pots and kettles hung from timbers above on hooks along with bunches of dried herbs. In the far corner was a bed draped with patched coverlets and a trunk. It was not grand by any means, but had its own kind of charm.

"You said the gamekeeper uses this cottage?" she asked, somewhat puzzled.

"It used to belong to an old woman whom my father was just superstitious enough to fear. They'd called her a witch when he was a boy and he wasn't taking chances. When she died," Marcus explained, "he made it over into a camp for the gamekeeper so that he might have a better chance at catching any poachers who dared set foot on the estate."

"And did he catch the poachers?"

Marcus shrugged as he retrieved several logs from a stack beside the hearth. "I couldn't say. He had not prior to my leaving for the army but it's anyone's guess what has happened here in my absence."

"It is rather fine for a gamekeeper, isn't it? Velvet coverlets, even if they are worn and patched, are hardly what one would expect to find here," she pointed out. In truth, the cottage's description tended more toward cozy than utilitarian, hinting at being used for far more than simply a gamekeeper's stopover.

Marcus shrugged. "I have little doubt that either my father or perhaps my stepmother has been making use of this place for some time. They often spend months at Whitehaven in the autumn, I believe. My father, prior to his recent illness, has never been faithful in any of his three marriages and I doubt very seriously that my step-mother is under the illusion that she owes fidelity to a broken down old man."

Fidelity amongst the nobility was never a question of absolutes. She had learned during her time as a gossip columnist that many couples had their own definition of fidelity, such as not taking on the friends of one's husband as a lover, or avoiding siring children outside of the marriage. Her own parents had been no exception. She had no illusions about the relationship between her own father and mother. He'd never been faithful. Jane also wasn't foolish enough to think that, even as beautiful as her vicious stepmother undeniably was, that he had changed his philandering ways. Mrs. Barrett's fidelity wasn't an issue. The woman was colder than ice and likely encouraged him to seek such comforts elsewhere. Shuddering at the thought, she moved toward the fireplace and the low blaze that had finally ignited there.

"I'll get you a chair," Marcus offered and crossed the room to the small kitchen. He returned with two of the wooden chairs.

When Jane was seated before the fire, soaking up the warmth from it like a sponge, he moved toward the bed and retrieved one of the blankets piled there and brought it back for her. With it draped about her shoulders, she wasn't exactly warm yet, but she was certainly more comfortable than she had been since leaving the theater.

"What happens now?" The uncomfortable question hung between them for a moment. So long, in fact, that Jane almost regretted asking it.

Finally, Marcus answered after a heavy sigh. "We marry. If either one of us refused at this point—well, I don't have to tell you how unkind gossip can be or how unforgiving our society is."

"So we go back to London and proceed as planned, then?"

Marcus shook his head. "No. We've been playing by their rules. We've been doing what they wanted and living under their roofs for far too long. My father has used this estate for years, but it isn't his. Whitehaven belongs to me. While it may be small, it is profitable—something many of his estates are not. My father has largely been living off the money earned by the few small estates that I have inherited. His own estates are a shambles."

"How have your estates remained in such good standing when his have not?"

Marcus smiled. "My father may make use of the estates as he pleases, but the running of the estates is entirely off limits to him. I have a man of business who sees to everything for me... someone I trust implicitly and whom my father has no wish to deal with at all."

"Oh," Jane said. "I didn't realize. Even in your absence they were well cared for?"

"Better than I could have done myself," he admitted. "The ledgers were delivered by courier to me just yesterday. I am not wealthy by any means… but I am not impoverished at least."

"Well, that's something to celebrate I suppose."

"I only mention this to say that we can live here at Whitehaven instead of Thornwood Hall. As far as I'm concerned he, Charles and your father are not welcome here. Here, I would have the authority to enforce that more so than at the family seat."

Could she really do that? Could she honestly cut ties with her family entirely? The thought of it should have been terrifying but, instead, it gave her the first glimpse of true freedom she'd ever had in her life. "Will we marry here?"

"We'll stop at Whitehaven so that I can get the necessary funds and we'll travel to Scotland. They wanted an elopement and so we'll give them one. Straight to Gretna Green and if they dislike the scandal then they can bloody well hang," he answered angrily. "This isn't how I would have done things, but if it gets both of us out of their clutches, so be it."

"We do this thing that they've forced us into and then that's it… we're free of them? What about the money? Your father has always insisted that the marriage contracts had to be upheld because of the financial aspects of it," Jane mused. "How will we live?"

"The money is ours, Jane. My father has labored under the false pretense that I will allow him to continue living in the manner to which he has allowed himself to become accustomed… and I will not. He and my stepmother can retire to a country estate and live off what that estate earns. I'll happily supply him with a skilled steward who can make the estate more profitable, but I'm done with him. This, what he and your father have done to us here, taking the very last vestiges of choice from either one of us—that is unforgivable to me."

So many things were unforgivable in her eyes. The way her father had destroyed her mother, little by little and day by day, the way he'd stood by as her stepmother attempted to do the same to her, the fact that he'd told her throughout her life that the only use he ever had for her was to help him attach himself to a more well connected family via the husband he'd purchased for her—those things were unforgivable. In truth, what they'd done that night wasn't so different from any other. But if it meant she could live her life free of her father and stepmother, free of social obligation to the current Duke and Duchess of Elsingham, did it matter?

"It will create a scandal. If we break from them entirely, especially after an elopement such as this—are you prepared for that?" Jane asked.

"I've been presumed dead for five years, Jane. Everything I do is a scandal," he replied.

Jane's lips quirked of their own volition. "And I probably haven't helped on that front... insinuating so boldly that you are, in fact, not the Marquess of Althorn but some imposter. You don't think that will be problematic do you? If you deny your father's requests for money, he could disavow you... claim that you are not his son."

"He could, but he will not. I will develop a plan to pay his debts, but only those he already has. I will not allow him to accrue more... and with the creditors hounding him, that is the best he can hope for. Are you willing to see this through, Jane? To marry me, live here in the country, rarely go to London and rarely, if ever, see my family or yours?"

"It seems wrong somehow to run headlong into marriage just to escape my father and stepmother... yet I find myself tempted to do just that," Jane mused.

"It wouldn't be the only reason," he said.

There was something in his tone that alerted her, some undercurrent that flowed between them as they sat there in the darkness broken only by the dancing light of the fire. Jane met his gaze then, noting the tension between them and the way that he looked at her as if she were beautiful. It wasn't self-pity to acknowledge that she wasn't a beautiful woman. Attractive enough, yes, passably pretty, without a doubt—but not beautiful. But she felt it in that moment. Beautiful, desirable, all the things that she'd read about in novels that had seemed so incredibly far-fetched for a girl like her now seemed to be perfectly within her grasp.

"Why are you looking at me that way?" The question wasn't censorious but simply curious. It would be too humiliating by far to misread the situation.

"Because I enjoy looking at you, Jane. Surely you must know that by now?"

She could feel herself blushing. "I never imagined—that is, when I was younger, I never imagined that you would see me as anything more than an inconvenience... an unattractive heiress with no rank or circumstance to lend cache to your already esteemed line."

His lips firmed into a hard line. "If I ever made you feel that way, I assure you it was not my intent. I was young, stubborn and, frankly, rebellious... I did resent being betrothed to you, but never because it was you. I simply resented the intrusion of my family into a choice that I thought I ought to be able to make for myself."

"And now?"

He sighed but it wasn't a long-suffering sound as much as a rueful one. "Now, I have to concede that my father may finally have, if inadvertently, acted in my best interests."

"I didn't think that I would ever want to marry you... I honestly didn't think I'd ever like you overmuch, to be completely forthcoming on the matter," she admitted.

"And now?" he challenged her with her own question.

"Now, I'm willing to admit that I may have been hasty in my judgement. Of course, it no longer signifies. Whether we wished to marry or not, now we must," she admitted.

"It doesn't have to be a chore, Jane... not unless we choose to make it one. I, for one, am eager to be married to you."

"Eager?" Her tone was incredulous. "Willing, I understand. Eager seems a bit overdone!"

"I concede that we haven't had time to form the kind of attachment you would wish before going into a marriage... but I cannot and will not deny that I have feelings for you, that I am beyond simply attracted to you, Jane. I have wanted you from the moment I walked back into my father's house."

There was no mistaking his earnestness in the admission. There was also no denying her immediate response to it. Her pulse raced and blood rushed in her veins as she considered the implications of what he'd said. She had always found him attractive. As a young girl, she'd woven hundreds of fantasies, albeit innocent ones, about him. As a woman grown, when he'd walked back into her life, those fantasies had taken a far different turn. Even more so after he'd kissed her.

Emboldened by his admission, by the stark realization that her reputation was in ruins even if her virtue was intact, Jane made a choice that only days ago would have shocked her to her core. "We are already the most scandalous couple in London... you a dead man, me a bluestocking, both of us eloping to Gretna Green from the steps of the theater in full view of all of society."

He nodded rather sagely. "So we are. Quite wicked, in fact."

"We could be more wicked still," she uttered softly. With far more courage than she'd ever realized she possessed, Jane made the most improper of offers. "As I am ruined in name, why should I not be ruined in deed, as well?"

Chapter Thirteen

MARCUS FELT HIS blood heating at the mere thought of it. Temptation was an ugly thing clawing at him, testing his morals and his honor.

"You've no idea what you are suggesting," he replied, half-hoping that he was wrong.

"Really? I thought I was suggesting that you should make love to me. But if you interpreted it in some other manner, please allow me to clarify. I may never have experienced that activity myself but I am quite well aware of what occurs." Even in the dim glow of the fire, the blush that stained her cheeks was plainly visible.

She'd effectively eliminated every single halfhearted argument he possessed. Left with only one, he said, "I would not have you regret this. Some things about our union could at least happen in the proper way and order."

She laughed at that. "Why on earth should they? Nothing else about the way this has occurred has even been remotely proper or normal. Arranged marriages are out of fashion, so we have one. Child brides are out of fashion, so your father tried to procure one for you. You returned from the dead, Marcus… impatience in consummating our union would be the most normal thing about it."

That was a point he had to concede. In that assessment, she was entirely accurate. But he was beyond discussing it any further. Instead, he rose and returned to the narrow bed in the corner. Gathering the remaining blankets, he brought them back and spread them before the fire to form a makeshift pallet for them. Once the task was done, he remained crouched on his haunches on the floor, and held his hand out to her. She was barely an arm's length away, but for his own peace of mind, he needed some show of willingness on her part.

When she lifted her hand and placed it in his as she rose from the chair, he had all the confirmation that he needed. As she settled onto the floor with him, the firelight danced on her skin and the pale strands of her blonde hair picked up the red and gold of the flames.

"I may have overestimated my degree of knowledge," she admitted hesitantly. "I do understand what is to take place... but in a very vague manner and without the faintest notion of how to begin."

Marcus felt his lips twitching at her chagrined admission. "I rather thought that might be the case. If you're amenable, perhaps it might be best to treat this as you would a dance... in other words, allow me to lead."

Jane made a slight moue that did not fully conceal her reluctant amusement. "Very well. I concede to your greater knowledge and expertise. You are an expert, aren't you?"

That was not a question he meant to answer. Ever. "I'm familiar enough with the particulars that it will be a more than satisfactory experience for us both."

She inclined her head much like a queen would to her subjects. Marcus reached for her simple wrap and slid it from her shoulders, letting the garment fall to the floor. Then he brought his hands up to her hair and tugged each of the pins free until the mass of it tumbled down, the golden curls spilling over her shoulders and the swells of her breasts.

"I have wanted to see you like this from the start," he confessed.

"You did see me this way at the start... running about Oakhaven with a doll under one arm and grass stains on my dress which the governess scolded me for quite bitterly, if I recall."

He chuckled then. "That wasn't the start I was referring to... you really were a child when I left. And while I understood that you would certainly mature and become a woman while I was away, I never quite imagined how satisfying a vision that would be."

"You don't wish that I was less plump or more plump, or shorter or taller, or any of the other things that I've been told I was too little or too much of over the years?"

With complete gravitas, he said, "I do not wish you to be anything other than exactly as you are. If others cannot see the value of that, they do not deserve to be in your presence."

"Kiss me," she urged him fervently. "I don't wish to talk anymore."

He could do nothing but comply. Leaning in, he captured her lips gently, his touch coaxing and tender. But that wasn't what she wanted. She pressed herself against him, seeking and yearning, her lips parting beneath his in blatant invitation.

Marcus had intended the seduction to be slow and careful, to afford her ample time to change her mind should she begin to have second thoughts. But as she clutched at his shoulders and pressed her chest to his, all thoughts of tenderness and taking his time fled.

They were two people who had never been quite enough for anyone in their lives. But for one another, they were quite perfect. She fit to him like a glove, but even that wasn't enough. As the kiss deepened and a soft moan escaped her, he wanted to consume her. The need to feel the softness of her body beneath his, to feel the satiny warmth of her skin against him, overwhelmed any good intentions he might have possessed.

Marcus never broke the kiss as he pressed her back onto the mound of blankets. As she returned the kiss with equal fervor, he needn't have worried that she was having second thoughts. Taking a deep, shuddering breath, he forced himself to slow down, to introduce her to passion slowly rather than simply making a mad dash for the finish line.

Easing back from her, he noted the flush in her cheeks and her kiss-swollen lips. He'd thought her lovely before, but with the bloom of passion, she was exquisite.

"Why did you stop?" she asked.

"I haven't stopped... only slowed the journey. There is too much to learn about one another, too much to enjoy with one another, to rush through it all," he answered. "And we're both far too overdressed for the events planned for this evening."

"Oh," she said and cast her gaze aside. "I hadn't considered that... we would... that you would..." She trailed off then, unable to complete the sentence.

"That I would what?" Marcus queried.

"Well, that you would see me," Jane admitted softly. "I hadn't really thought much about it."

"I have... I've thought of nothing else. I've imagined it dozens of times in dozens of different ways every night as I close my eyes," he offered.

"I don't want you to be disappointed."

"That is impossible." Marcus realized that giving her an excessive amount of time to think was not helping the matter at all. Jane didn't have any doubt about their course of action, but she did have a wealth of doubt about herself and her own attractiveness. All of that could be laid squarely at her stepmother's feet, no doubt. The best way, in his mind, to combat that was to simply face the fear head on and conquer it. With that thought in mind, Marcus reached for the bib front of her gown, carefully undoing the buttons that held it in place. As the fabric fell away, revealing the delicate embroidery of her chemise, his eyes were drawn to the swells of her breasts above the fabric and the darker shadows of her nipples just visible above her stays. Brushing the back of his hand over that tender flesh, he felt her shiver.

"Perfect," he whispered. "Perfect in every way."

As if his words had given her courage, she sat up and shrugged the gown from her shoulders, letting it fall to her waist. "If we're to remove my clothing, Marcus, I feel it is only fair that some of yours be shed as well."

Shrugging out of his coat, Marcus let it drop to the floor. "Never let it be said that I was anything but fair." His cravat and waistcoat followed. Clad in his shirtsleeves and breeches, he raised one eyebrow at her. "I've called your bluff, Jane. It's time to show me your cards."

JANE DREW IN a deep and bracing breath as she faced her fear and removed her gown entirely. Rising on her knees, she reached for the laces of her stays and loosened the garment until it to fell away. Clad only in her chemise and petticoat, she met his challenging gaze. "I think we're at a stalemate."

"Hardly that," he offered in a teasing manner. "I would call it a detente."

Before she could think of an appropriate reply, he was kissing her again. His lips moved over hers voraciously, as if he wished to devour her. And heaven help her, she wished to be devoured by him. So long as he was kissing her, she couldn't think. And if she couldn't think, she couldn't list all the numerous flaws and negative attributes that she so desperately wanted to hide from him.

When his hand cupped her breast, his touch gentle but not in the least hesitant or unsure, she was incapable of describing the sensation. It swept her away entirely. From that single point of contact, she felt it throughout her body. It was as if every sense and every nerve had been awakened in that one precise moment.

And yet that single touch led to more. His hands roamed over her, touching her, coaxing her body to blazing life. With his hands roving her flesh and his mouth burning a trail from her lips to the tender column of her neck where he nipped and scraped only to soothe with the sweep of his tongue over her rapidly heating skin, she had become a mindless thing. Animal, primal, hedonistic... wanton. He gave and she craved more.

At some point during his more than simply adequate seduction, the remainder of her garments had simply vanished. Where and when he removed them she could not say, but when he parted her thighs and touched her intimately, she was very aware that no barriers remained between them.

"It isn't too late," he said. "If you have any doubts, now is the time to utter them."

"I haven't the will to ask you to stop," she confessed breathlessly. "Nor the desire to."

He kissed her again, muffling the sound of her cries as he moved his fingers inside her, stoking her desire to a fever pitch. With every touch, her body burned hotter for him. Muscles tensed and quivered as she strained toward some unknown destination.

Jane gasped as he pulled his lips from hers and dropped them to her breast. His mouth closed over the taut peak as her hips arched toward him. Her eyes closed tightly and she let out a strangled cry as the tension he'd built so skillfully suddenly broke inside her. It wasn't simply pleasure. That was far too tame a word to describe it, but it was the only one she possessed. The breath rushed from her and her belly quivered as it washed through her.

SHE WAS STILL breathless and languid when Marcus parted her thighs wider and slipped between them. Nestled there, the welcoming heat of her body pressed against him, he didn't take the time to marvel at his good fortune as he wished. Other needs were more pressing. Watching her discover her passion had fired his blood to the point of madness.

Opening the fall front of his breeches, he moved carefully as he nudged the blunt head of his cock inside her. "It will hurt, but only for a moment."

She wrapped her arms about him, pressing her palms to his back. "I've been warned... repeatedly. By every female member of our combined households."

It was little wonder then that she'd had no wish to marry, he thought. But then she moved beneath him, hitching her knees higher on his hips and granting him entry. With one small movement, she'd robbed him of thought entirely. Flexing his hips, he plunged into her welcoming heat. She was so tight, her flesh closing about him like a fist, and then he felt the delicate barrier of her innocence. Withdrawing slightly, he thrust once more, breeching her maidenhead and seating himself fully inside her.

Jane didn't cry out. She didn't utter a sound, in fact. But she did go completely still beneath him, every muscle tensed and not even a breath escaping her. Marcus held himself in check, wrestling with his baser self for control. When at last she began to relax again, her body going, if not lax, then at least mobile, he let out a deep shuddering breath. "Are you all right?"

She blinked several times and then, in typical pragmatic fashion, stated, "They lied. That was significantly more than just a little."

"And now? Does it hurt still?" he asked. It would kill him if she asked him to stop, but he would regardless.

A slight frown pursed her lips and created a furrow between her brows. After a pause, she answered, "It doesn't hurt anymore. But I'm not quite sure I like it."

"It gets better. I swear it," he replied. To prove his point, he shifted his hips slightly, a short and shallow thrust that had her eyes widening and her lips parting on a soft "o" of surprise.

"I can certainly see that it does," Jane agreed.

Marcus managed to keep his smile hidden, but only just. It was not an appropriate time to crow in victory. That, he would save for later, assuming he didn't embarrass himself like an untried schoolboy.

Setting a slow and easy rhythm, watching her reaction to each and every thrust, learning precisely what she liked, Marcus could feel the sweat beading on his brow. His breath was ragged and harsh as he struggled to keep that pace and not just lose himself inside her. When she arched her back, her head falling back and hair spilling around her, it took every shred of self-control he possessed. But as her legs locked around his hips and he felt the first quivering of her release, he was lost.

Any thoughts of gentleness or taking care fled. Instinct drove him as he buried himself inside her. His body tensed and his own release claimed him, sending him hurtling over the edge with pleasure so intense it was blinding.

Marcus collapsed against her, his forehead resting against hers as they both slowly returned to earth.

Chapter Fourteen

THE GRAY LIGHT of dawn was still and a heavy shroud of mist clung to the small clearing as Charles and William Barrett neared the abandoned carriage and the small cottage where Marcus and Miss Barrett would have spent the remainder of the night.

In the yard, Barrett dismounted. "If she's been ruined, I'll see him dead," he said fiercely.

"For someone who's never seemed to have a particular care for his daughter, you've made a sudden change of heart, Barrett," Charles pointed out.

"She can toss her skirt up for anyone she likes once she's wed to a legitimate title," the man snapped. "But she's only of value to me as a virgin who can be married off to the highest ranked bidder!"

Charles smirked behind the man. "He's not an imposter. I promise you that he is the real Marquess of Althorn. You're doing all this for naught!"

"It doesn't matter whether he is or not," Barrett responded. "Only that other people believe it without question. I've spent a fortune to connect my line to that of a duke, and forever more that union will now be tainted with doubt!"

"You really are a grasping, social climbing weasel," Charles said softly. Luckily, Barrett was too far ahead of him on the path to the carriage to have heard the whispered insult. Whether it was necessary or not, Charles decided that the man would have to meet an unfortunate accident on the road. They would all be far better off without his coarse manners and foul temper about them.

IT HAD BEEN just after dawn when they left the small cottage. The abandoned carriage, horseless and mud splattered, was parked in front of it. Marcus had led them into the woods, to a narrow and slightly overgrown path. He said it would lead them to the main house, but had been far too dangerous to attempt at night.

At the noise of approaching riders, he'd placed a staying hand in front of her and insisted they conceal themselves behind several trees. At the first sight of her father and Charles, she'd thought perhaps it was to be a rescue attempt. After overhearing their conversation, she knew it was anything but.

"What are they about, do you think?" Jane queried in a near silent whisper as she glanced at Marcus. He frowned in response and kept his gaze trained on the cottage door.

"I believe your father is attempting to halt our marriage for the first time in our lives," he answered. He then added with quiet menace, "And he will not succeed."

"And Charles? Why would he be here to help him when it's clear that he orchestrated all of this?" Jane asked.

"I don't know the answer to that. I only know that we cannot trust either of them… and we must get well off this path or risk discovery. Come with me, Jane," he said and held out his hand to her.

Jane glanced back at the cottage. Two days earlier, any hint of her father having second thoughts about the marriage between herself and Marcus would have been viewed as a miracle. But the tides had turned irrevocably. Placing her hand in Marcus' she allowed him to lead her deeper into the forest.

It was dark, the heavy woods not yet penetrated by the weak sunlight. She could barely see and had to allow him to guide her. It was an apt metaphor for everything in their lives at that moment.

Jane followed him along what might have been a path at one time but was now overgrown and difficult to traverse. She stumbled occasionally, but he was always there, steadying her and helping her when the way was rough. Evening slippers were hardly meant for such terrain, she thought grimly. Still, it was only a mile or so to the house. She could endure that. But then another thought entered her mind, one that induced panic.

"What if they go on to the house and are waiting there for us? Surely on horseback or by carriage they will beat us on foot," she asked.

"We won't go directly to the house. There's a man nearby, someone we can trust implicitly, who will allow us to remain there until Charles and the others have gone. It's very likely they will go on to Gretna Green in pursuit... so we may have to change our plans. How do you feel about being married by special license in London?"

"So long as it's done, I don't care where or how," she answered. It wasn't entirely true. Every young girl dreamed of a beautiful wedding in a church with flowers and a lovely gown. Of course, she'd also once dreamed of having her father's affection and transforming into a rare beauty overnight. It seemed none of those things was to occur. Despite those things that might be lacking, her future and her present were far better than she'd thought possible. To ask for more would only have been greedy on her part.

"You do care," he countered. "Very much. And I'm sorry for that. Deeply sorry that this cannot be what you want it to be."

Jane considered her answer carefully. "Many young women have beautiful weddings and abominable marriages. I would much rather thwart convention and go the other route."

"Abominable?" Marcus repeated with a chuckle. "Will it be as bad as all that, do you think?"

"Well, no. But we have been browbeaten, abducted, our reputations thoroughly compromised—"

"More than just your reputation," he reminded her pointedly.

Jane blushed. "Yes, I suppose that's true. Now, we're scurrying through the woods like criminals in the same clothes we wore the day before. How else would you characterize it?"

He paused to help her over a particularly large fallen tree. "What was it you asked me about my escape from the prison? 'Was it dashing' I believe you said. Is this dashing, Jane?"

She grimaced at having her own words thrown back at her. "That was a terrible thing to ask. Not if you were hurt or injured or unwell... I just wanted something to put in that awful column!"

He grinned. "When we are back in London, married by special license, and all the particulars of the marriage settlement suitably arranged... you can add the woeful tale of our elopement to your column."

"By then it will be old news," she quipped. "No doubt Charles sang it from the rooftops last night."

"No doubt he did," Marcus agreed. "We're almost there. Can you see that small cottage through the trees?"

"I can," she said. It was similar to the one they'd stayed in the night before albeit somewhat larger and significantly more active. Chickens ran through the yard and several small children were cavorting there, as well.

As they approached, the children squealed and ran toward the house just as a tall, dark-haired man emerged. Jane was struck immediately by his resemblance to Marcus. It was quite marked. "Who was it that you said lived here? A friend?"

"I didn't say. But from your expression, I daresay you have guessed that he is more than simply a friend. His name is Thomas Carter and he is my half-brother... illegitimate, of course, because my father was a faithless scoundrel who couldn't keep his hands off of the house maids," he said bitterly. "Thomas was born nine months to the day after my mother was buried. It was quite obvious how my father consoled himself after her death."

"I'm sorry," she said, uncertain of how else to respond to that.

"There's no bitterness toward Thomas," Marcus added. "Only toward my father. Thomas has always been a blessing to me... I always promised him that when I had control of the estates and my own fortune that his circumstances would be better. He's the one who is largely responsible for making Whitehaven a profitable estate. He's seeing to both our futures it would seem."

With that, he stepped away from her and approached his waiting half-brother. They embraced warmly for a moment and she could hear Thomas speaking.

"I'd heard you returned," Thomas said warmly. "It is good to see you. Better than I can say."

"It's good to see you, as well," Marcus replied easily. "But, alas, we are not here to visit. We need your help."

"You may have whatever you need," Thomas answered immediately. "All that I have is yours."

"We need a coach to get us back to London and, if possible, does Ann have clothing that Jane could borrow?"

Thomas looked at her then, his eyebrows arching upward in a very familiar expression but one that was quickly masked. "I daresay we can come up with something. Do come inside," he urged.

As they approached the door, Marcus added, "And Thomas, if Jane's father and Charles should happen to come by here asking after us, as much as I hate to ask it of you, please lie."

Thomas' expression firmed. "I've never known you to be dishonorable when it comes to ladies and I don't think you would be, whatever the situation. I can assume you plan to do right by the young miss?"

"As soon as possible… and for what it's worth, we wouldn't be out here in this condition at all were it not for Charles' scheming. Miss Jane Barrett is my betrothed and has been for years. Charles has elected to move up the timeline of our nuptials by putting us in a compromising position. But some rumors were inadvertently begun in London that I am not who I claim to be and now her father wishes to renege on the marriage contract."

Thomas' scowl deepened. "Charles will have some way to profit from it or he'd never have put in the work… a lazier man I've never encountered. As for her father, title or no, you've clearly been alone together in a situation that could only be rectified by marriage. He must see that."

Jane stepped forward. "My father is a bit of a social climber. He's more concerned with the validity of Marcus' title than with my virtue or reputation."

"That is true enough," Marcus agreed.

Thomas frowned and shook his head sadly. "I cannot fathom how people can be so greedy and cruel! Let's get you both inside. While you're getting changed, I'll head to the inn at Gravestead and see about obtaining a coach for you."

"Thank you, Thomas. I couldn't ask for a better friend or brother," Marcus said, clearly moved by the other man's easy acceptance and willingness to help.

"Anne will be eager to meet you, miss," he said and clapped Marcus on the back as they all entered the small cottage.

Anne, Thomas' wife, rushed forward and immediately took Jane under her wing. "Come with me, my dear! We'll get you a nice pot of tea and some warmer clothes! Why you must be half-frozen!"

"Thank you," Jane said, taken aback by the warmth and kindness of total strangers. She looked back over her shoulder at Marcus as Anne led her away. He and Thomas were already deep in conversation.

)🌿

"SO WHAT'S HAPPENED?" Thomas asked. "What has driven you to the middle of nowhere with your betrothed... months before you're to be wed, alone—not even a whisper of a chaperone! Never in my life, Marcus, have I known you to be reckless. So give over. What has Charles done?"

Marcus sighed heavily and took a sip of the heady brew that Thomas had poured for him. He coughed. "Good God! Warn a fellow, won't you?"

"Don't change the subject!"

"I wasn't," Marcus insisted, shaking his head to clear the fog created by the drink. "I simply wasn't expecting such potent spirits before breakfast."

Thomas laughed. "We're farmers, Marcus! The day is halfway done by now."

"So it is... Jane and I were attending the theater last night. Charles and my dear stepmother were in attendance as well. Jane begged off because the crowd and the gossip were simply unbearable. But when we entered the carriage, where we were to wait for Charles and Cassandra, the door slammed, the vehicle shot forward and we were carried off into the night."

"The both of you were abducted in plain view of everyone?" Thomas asked. "Why? What would Charles get from that?"

"I've no idea, honestly," Marcus admitted. "Before my return, he was pursuing Jane for himself. Now, he's throwing the two of us together in an attempt to force our hands into marriage much sooner than either of us had agreed upon."

Thomas shook his head sadly. "You don't see it, do you? I know about her fortune. Everyone does. I'm sure that Charles has plans that include you giving him a great deal of money... perhaps settling his debts."

Marcus grimaced. "Charles would never expect generosity from me... not now. Not after Corunna."

Thomas frowned. "What happened at Corunna and why would that change anything between you and Charles?"

Marcus wanted to tell him, but until there was evidence of Charles' crime, the less said the better. "I would tell you if I could. But Charles is not to be trusted... not at any cost."

"Those are wise words, Brother, and words you should heed. If Charles thinks you will not give him the funds he needs, then rest assured he will have a plan to take them from you," Thomas warned. "No one knows his viciousness better than I do."

It was true. In their childhood, Charles had been three years Thomas' senior. Young as they were, three years had given him quite the advantage. He'd beaten Thomas to a pulp at every opportunity. Even the duke had grown disgusted with it and finally intervened, forbidding Charles to ever come to Whitehaven again. It had been the only time in their childhood that the man had ever acknowledged Thomas at all.

"I'll be careful of him. Tell me about the estate," Marcus suggested, changing the subject to one that better suited them both. "I looked over the ledgers and what you've achieved here is remarkable."

"You've no wish to talk about that now. Not when you've a bride waiting for you," Thomas declined with a smile. "I'll head into the village and obtain a vehicle for you. Stay out of sight here."

Marcus nodded. "Of course... Thomas, I meant what I said. When I have the means, you and Anne will be able to live far differently if you choose."

Thomas shook his head. "I don't mind the farming, or the looking after your estates. In truth, Marcus, I'm a simple man with simple needs. What I will ask for is that you help my children. See them situated in life. Beyond that, I could not and will not ask for more."

"Whatever they require... education, dowries... they will not want," Marcus vowed.

Thomas nodded. "Then we shall do our catching up another time. For now, let me do what I can to see you and your bride safely away before the villains come a-knocking."

Marcus watched him exit. Sitting there alone in the small room that served as both dining room and parlor, Marcus considered Thomas' life. He'd once thought his brother very poor. Spoiled and used to luxury as he had been, the idea of living in such a small home with children underfoot and chickens screeching in the yard had been distasteful to him. But his time in prison had changed him. The things he had once reviled as the hallmarks of poverty now appealed to him far more than a grand estate with servants always underfoot and people always gossiping.

He longed for a simple life and he prayed that Jane would be content with such. It would not bode well for their union otherwise.

AN HOUR LATER, Jane was dressed in a borrowed gown of simple blue wool and a heavy cloak. "I can't possibly take these. They are very fine and I've no notion of how I'll be able to return them to you," Jane protested.

Anne Carter smiled. "You needn't worry, Miss Barrett. Our Marcus has always taken care of us... well, until he couldn't. These last five years have been hard for Thomas. He worried something fierce over what might have become of his brother... I know it's frowned upon my most folks for us to acknowledge that they're related, but it's so plain to see when you look upon them, I feel foolish pretending otherwise!"

Jane smiled at that. "The resemblance is rather remarkable. I'm glad that he'll be able to continue helping you all... I'm sure your farm is quite successful, but with four children, help must surely always be welcome."

Anne smiled and walked to the crib in the corner, picking up the youngest of her brood. The baby was less than a year old, but a more beautiful child she'd never seen, Jane thought. Dark-haired and dark-eyed, the baby bore a marked resemblance to his father and uncle. "That is true to be sure, miss. But do not worry yourself over the gown and cloak. They were gifts from Marcus to us and now they will be gifted back to you so that you may travel home to London in comfort. I swear you must have been half-frozen in that gown! And lovely as those slippers were at one time, it's good I had those boots for you!"

It was a relief to be dressed in warmer and sturdier shoes. The walk through the woods had not been kind to her feet nor to her stockings. One would recover but the other most assuredly would not. It was also quite a relief to be wearing something other than a ruined evening gown. It would at least give her the illusion of respectability even if any shred of it had been eagerly sacrificed the night before.

Jane said nothing further as she heard carriage wheels rumbling just below. Going to the window, she saw that Thomas had returned from Gravestead with the vehicle. It was nondescript, older and clearly worse for wear, but it was also inconspicuous. Given that her father would stop at nothing to stop the marriage he'd once fought so desperately to have occur, discretion was the order of the day.

"Thomas has returned," Anne said. "So you and Marcus will be off now. Before you go, I just want to say that I hope you both have even a tenth of the love and happiness that Thomas and I have been blessed with."

They didn't, Jane thought sadly. They had desire, passion, those things that Marcus had stated were necessary for love to grow, but not love itself. But with a glance at Anne Carter's earnest expression and the warmth in her lovely gaze, Jane didn't protest. Instead, she said, "I hope that, too. Thank you, Anne… and since we are to be sisters, you will call me Jane. I hope to come visit you again soon." Jane reached out and stroked the baby's dark curls. "And this one."

Anne smiled. "Mayhap you'll be working on having one of your own the next time we meet."

Jane was overwhelmed at the thought. Marcus had indicated that he wanted a family, that he wanted to be the kind of father that neither of them had been blessed with. She'd seen him downstairs with Thomas' and Anne's children, playing and roughhousing with the older boys before being thoroughly charmed by their sweet little girl. It had sparked a yearning in her for a family of her own, a longing that she'd felt before but had always tamped down and repressed because her circumstances had seemed to preclude it altogether. But all of that had changed. And as long as they could manage to avoid her father and Charles, it was within her grasp.

"Maybe I will," Jane agreed softly.

There was a sharp rap at the door and Marcus called out to her from beyond it, "Are you ready? We had best be underway in case Charles should happen to remember that Thomas is close by."

Jane hugged Anne. "Thank you for everything."

"Thank you for giving Marcus a chance at happiness. He deserves it so," Anne whispered as she hugged Jane just as fiercely in return. "You both do. I can see it in your eyes."

Jane still wasn't entirely certain that happiness was in store for them. But she was, for the first time in her life, willing to hope for it. Crossing to the bedchamber door, she opened it and stepped outside. Marcus smiled at her.

"I've not seen you in anything but black or gray since returning home. Blue suits you," he said softly. "It matches your eyes."

Jane noted that he'd obtained clothing from Thomas as well. They were dressed well enough, but looked nothing like the heir to a dukedom and his bride. "Do you think we've concealed our identities well enough?"

Marcus ushered her toward the door with a hand at the small of her back. It was a familiar gesture, an intimate one that could only remind her of all the ways he'd touched her the night before. Jane felt her pulse race at the thought and her face heated with a blush.

"I think it should suffice," he said as they exited the cottage. In a lower voice to keep the hired coachman from overhearing, he continued, "Thomas told the coachman that he and his wife were traveling to London. He and Anne will remain inside while you and I take their places in the carriage. With my hat pulled low, Thomas and I look enough alike that the coachman should not notice."

"Then let us go before we bring more danger and difficulty to their door. I worry what Charles might be capable of, but I also worry at my father's temper if he were to catch us here. He's obsessed with having a title, Marcus. It could go very badly for you. If he challenges you to a duel—"

Marcus shushed her softly as they neared the carriage. As the driver made no move to come down from the box and aid them, Jane was forced to have Marcus assist her inside. Again, each touch reminded her of the night before and all that had transpired. Reminders were unnecessary of course. Those moments in the darkness of an abandoned cottage had marked her forever in ways that he might never know. For the first time in her life, Jane had felt truly beautiful. More than that, she'd felt wanted. Beyond simple desire, it was something infinitely more. She had believed when he looked at her that he wished to be there with her and only her, that for him no other woman would do. It was a novel experience and one that she would treasure regardless of what else might transpire.

Once inside the carriage, settled on seats opposite one another, Marcus replied in a serious tone. "You father will not challenge me. If he does, I will refuse... no one could fault me for that. It is an impossible situation. To kill or be killed by the father of my betrothed? It will not happen, Jane. I vow it."

"You say that as if he will give you a choice!" she cried as the carriage lurched forward. "His pride has been wounded. He will not be reasoned with in such a state!"

"We will work this out. In the meantime, we go to Highcliff. He'll help us make the necessary arrangements to be married in secret. I wish it were not this way. I wish that you could have the kind of wedding I know all young women dream of."

"I don't need orange blossoms and a massive wedding breakfast," she said softly. "I just need for this to go smoothly and for my father and your cousin to stay far from London long enough for us to see this through."

Without warning, Marcus reached for her. He tugged her across the expanse of the carriage until she was sprawled rather inelegantly across his lap. "All will be well. I promise."

"You cannot promise that because it is not within your control," she pointed out. In spite of her fears and misgivings, there was a strange comfort in being so close to him. In the circle of his arms, with his strength surrounding her, sheltering her—she felt safe there.

"I can. I have a sense about these things," he teased.

"You do not. If you did, you wouldn't have wound up spending five years in a French prison!"

He laughed at that. "I have no rebuttal to that... so perhaps it's best if we just not talk at all."

"All the way to London?" she asked. "It will make for a very boring journey!"

"There are other things we can do with our lips to while away the hours, Jane. Shall I remind you?"

Her breath caught at the sensual promise in his voice. "I may have forgotten. Perhaps a little reminder wouldn't hurt."

She closed her eyes as his lips pressed to hers and vowed that it would only be a kiss. She would not behave scandalously in a carriage on the open road. But she did.

Chapter Fifteen

I T WAS LATE afternoon by the time they reached London and the relative safety of Lord Highcliff's home. As the ill-sprung conveyance halted in front of the handsome and somewhat intimidating townhome, Jane couldn't help but glance furtively over her shoulder. She was expecting either Charles or her father to pop out from behind every tree or lamp post, much like scary stories her governess had told her as a child to make her behave. It did not escape her notice that it should have been a very unnatural thing to fear one's father, but then he'd never had any compunction about declaring just how little paternal affection he had for her. She was only any good to him so long as she could be of use to him and as she was now thoroughly compromised, she was of no use to him at all.

"Even if they've come back to London, they won't know we've come here," Marcus offered reassuringly.

"My father and Charles are both aware of your long-standing friendship with Lord Highcliff," she pointed out. "It's not unlikely that they would come here seeking information on our whereabouts or on the suspicion that we might have sought refuge here."

"That is true enough, but they would find themselves more than a little taken aback at the reception they would receive. Most think Highcliff is nothing more than a ridiculous dandy… a fop who cares more about fashion than fighting. They'd be quite wrong. He's skilled at misdirection and subterfuge in ways they will not begin to understand. Trust me, Jane, when I tell you that if he does not want them to know we are here, they will not."

Jane blinked in surprise at that. Highcliff, though tall and cutting a powerful figure, had always tended toward the ridiculous in his over the top mannerisms and outlandish dress. "Is he spy the way that you were?"

"He was… in a slightly different capacity. My specialty was foreign intelligence, ferreting out those who might betray us overseas. Highcliff's position was to identify domestic traitors. He is very good at what he does."

Jane was still processing that as he opened the door to their shabby, rented coach.

"Let's get inside and see what can be done about obtaining a special license," he suggested, and offered his arm to help her down.

She nodded her agreement and quickly followed him from the street up the steps. They hadn't even lifted the knocker before the door opened. Marcus let out an exasperated sigh. "Do all butlers do that? I thought it was a skill possessed only by Riggs, but you've an uncanny ability!"

"My lord," the butler inclined his head as they entered the foyer. If he thought it unusual that Marcus was accompanied by a woman when visiting a bachelor residence in the afternoon, he gave no indication of it. "I'm afraid Lord Highcliff is not home at present. He was summoned to your home by the Duke of Elsingham."

"We should go," Jane said in a slight panic.

"Highcliff can handle my father," Marcus said firmly. "It will be fine."

"Lord Highcliff," the butler continued, "instructed me that I should show you to a suite that has been prepared if you were to seek asylum here. I am to assume that you and the lady are seeking asylum then, my lord?"

"We are," Marcus admitted ruefully.

"Follow me and I will show you to your rooms. It is likely best that you not be below stairs if possible," the butler warned. "Lord Highcliff anticipates that a Mr. William Barrett will appear at some point and that if he were to see you—either of you—that it would create unnecessary difficulties."

"Is there anything that Lord Highcliff doesn't know?" Jane asked, somewhat dumbfounded by the man's degree of forethought and preparation.

The butler smirked in a very superior way. "Very little, miss. Very little, indeed."

At the top of the stairs, he turned toward the left and led them to a set of rooms directly across the hall from one another. Jane's was decorated in cream and gold, but the entire room was so luxurious that she couldn't quite fathom that it was in a simple townhouse and not a palace. "I do not believe I have ever seen such a beautiful and ornate room outside of paintings of Versailles," she said.

The butler inclined his head. "Lord Highcliff's mother was French and spent her childhood in the palace as a lady-in-waiting to Marie Antoinette. She remembered those years fondly and decorated the house accordingly, miss. I will have a bath prepared for you."

"Thank you," Jane muttered. "I am looking forward to conveying my gratitude to Lord Highcliff. He's been most kind and generous to us."

The butler nodded again, his expression softening. "I have been with his lordship since he was a boy, miss. He thinks very highly of the marquess. He was quite beside himself when Lord Althorn was missing and infinitely relieved when his friend was returned to him. He devoted a great deal of time during his lordship's absence to tracking down information related to his rumored fate or his whereabouts. Sadly, very little came of it. That, in and of itself, was suspicious."

Jane frowned. "Why would that have been suspicious?"

"Had his lordship died, then there would have been those who had documented it… even if it was under a false name. Some record would have been found or a witness account. Deaths are easy to discover. But disappearances that have been carefully arranged are not."

"You're far more than just a butler, aren't you?" Jane asked.

The butler smiled. "A good butler always matches his skills and abilities to the requirements of the house he serves, miss. To that end, Lord Highcliff and, by extension his staff, will do whatever is necessary to ensure that Lord Althorn is safe and happy."

It was an odd statement. It was impossibly verbose and yet in the end said very little. Jane was still puzzling over it as the butler left her in her impossibly luxurious chamber.

ACROSS THE HALL, Marcus was looking through the packet of information that Highcliff had obtained in his absence. There were sworn affidavits from several of the men in Charles' regiment that Charles had disclosed to them that he'd seen his cousin at Corunna. There were other sworn affidavits that Charles had not been injured during any battle. But it was the last and most damning bit of information that was of the most interest to him. After the Battle of Corunna, Charles had sold a watch to someone in the regiment. That watch had been repurchased by Highcliff and left with the papers.

It was a familiar piece. Marcus had worn it almost daily since he'd been a boy. It had been a gift from his mother before she passed away. Charles could only have gotten it if the French soldiers who had taken him had given it back to the very man who'd turned him over to them. It was still attached to the same fob he'd worn it with. Though the embroidered monogram had been painstakingly removed, the fabric was faded around where those threads had been revealing the tattered outline of an "M".

While the information and the watch were not definitive proof that Charles was a traitor, they were enough to warrant a full-fledged investigation by the war office. It had taken his return, alive and capable of telling the tale, to point Highcliff in the right direction. But now that he had his sights on Charles, not even hell would bar his way.

Scandal was unavoidable at that point. But if Charles was guilty of selling information to the French about munitions and man power, then he'd cost thousands of lives and countless injuries that might have been prevented. There were other consequences—both financial and political in nature—that impacted the country as a whole. The question remained, just how far would Charles go to hide his involvement?

Marcus knew that his return had put a wrinkle into Charles' ultimate plan—to gain control of Jane's fortune and claim the title for himself. But his return also posed a significant threat because he could place him at Corunna and with the French soldiers and their commander. It was the combination of evidence and eyewitness accounts that could see him hanged. It stood to reason that by openly supporting the marriage and even creating compromising situations to ensure it would take place, Charles' ultimate goals had not changed, only the steps he would have to take to reach them. Marcus knew that his cousin meant to see him dead as it would not only clear his name of any accusation, it would also get him all that he wanted.

There was a sharp knock at the door. It wouldn't be Jane, he was sure. It could be Highcliff or it could be Barrett and Charles. Surely if it were the latter, he would have heard some disturbance as they forced their way in.

Crossing to the door, he opened it to find Highcliff standing there. "You've certainly made a mess of it all," the man said sardonically.

"You've no idea. How terrible is the gossip?"

Highcliff shrugged. "So long as you actually marry Miss Barrett the gossip should blow over fairly easily. If you fail to marry her, you'll both be pariahs and cast out of society forever. I'm assuming marriage is in the offing?"

Marcus stepped back to allow the other man entry. "That's why we've returned to town. Due to an unfortunate article in the *London Ladies' Gazette*, insinuating that I may not actually be the Marquess of Althorn, Barrett is now opposing the match very vocally. Jane and I barely escaped him to return to town with the help of Thomas."

"And now you're here for more of my help," Highcliff surmised easily enough. "What is it that you need now, my friend?"

"A special license... preferably issued this evening so that we can be married first thing tomorrow morning," Marcus answered honestly. "I fear delaying any longer than that and Barrett might successfully call a halt to it altogether."

"And Charles... what's his stake in this now?"

Jane appeared then, standing in the doorway. Highcliff turned and greeted her. "Miss Barrett, do come in. I don't believe we've been formally introduced."

"Under the circumstances," she replied easily, "I'm not certain an introduction is necessary. Thank you, Lord Highcliff, for all your assistance and in making us welcome in your home."

Highcliff inclined his head. "I owe Marcus my life... several times over, in fact. He's saved my a—skin more times than I can count. It's fortuitous for me that I may now attempt to balance the scales to some degree. Tell me, Miss Barrett, are you amenable to being married to this stick in the mud tomorrow morning?"

Jane stepped deeper into the room. "Very amenable, Lord Highcliff."

Highcliff nodded sagely. "Then we must see about procuring a gown for you and a posy at the very least. Discreetly, of course. It wouldn't do to have it out that you are here just yet. I'll see to it."

Jane inclined her head. "Thank you again. You are too kind and too thoughtful by far, my lord."

Highcliff turned back to Marcus then and looked pointedly at the watch in his hand. "I am glad to see that returned to you, my friend. I don't have to tell you that the circumstances of its migration are very suspicious, indeed."

Marcus rested his hip on the corner of the dresser as he faced the both of them. An idea was forming, a way to put pressure on Charles and to effectively end their current situation once and for all. "There is something about Jane that you are unaware of, Highcliff... and it's something that might be very useful to us in trapping Charles."

Jane gaped at him and, in a panic, uttered, "You can't tell him that!"

Marcus sighed. It was her secret and divulging it was risky, but Highcliff could be trusted. "It's our best chance of pushing Charles to do something reckless. We can trust Highcliff, Jane, or I'd never risk it."

Highcliff stepped in then. "I swear that I shall keep whatever secrets you need me to keep, Miss Barrett. It's a skill I've honed well."

After a moment's consideration, Jane nodded. "Very well... but if it gets out, married or not, I would still be a pariah."

Highcliff arched one eyebrow at that, but said nothing as he waited for Marcus to reveal the tale.

"Jane is the J.E. who writes for the *London Ladies' Gazette*," Marcus stated dispassionately.

Highcliff's response was a bit more animated. Both eyebrows shot up, but it was not the typically sardonic expression he favored but actual shock which prompted him. "That gossip rag which every society matron I know of devours at its every publication? They read it cover to cover praying they won't be in it! You'd be more than a pariah, my dear. They'd hunt you down and carve you into bits!"

"What if you were to write your column and indicate that the 'spare' to a rather exalted title had been your source for the original article?" Marcus asked.

She shrugged. "That's easy enough. But to what end?"

"Because you would also indicate that the spare lied to cover his own perfidy in the disappearance of the heir apparent... and that he did so because he'd been caught by the heir in a treasonous plot." Marcus finished his explanation and waited. It was all very convoluted, but Charles would get wind of it and likely do something very reckless.

"Is there any truth to that?" Jane asked.

"It is mostly conjecture," Marcus answered honestly. "But I believe with my whole heart that it is true. I told you once that I couldn't share with you many of the things I did while in the army. Jane, I was at Corunna because it was believed that a member of that battalion was selling information to the French. They were providing intelligence to our enemy about our munitions, our ranks, strategy—every way that a military strike could be compromised, it was. And all the evidence of that points to Charles."

She gasped in shock. "I know you said treason, but I never imagined... oh, dear heaven. Well, of course, I'll do what I can, but he doesn't read that publication. Neither does the duchess, and I strongly suspect that the two of them are thick as thieves... perhaps even more than that."

It was an interesting theory and one that he could not easily dismissed. In retrospect, it was apparent that Charles and his stepmother were closer than they ought to have been. Charles had clearly made free use of his father's house and had been quite welcome there in Marcus' absence. His father might have been content enough to see the title go to Charles, but he'd never have tolerated his company willingly. There was no one that the old man truly liked. Which meant that Cassandra must have been the one to issue the invitation.

"You think they have an intimate relationship?" Highcliff clarified.

"Yes," Jane replied, blushing. "It's nothing concrete... just lingering glances and when he asked to speak with me privately to extend his offer of marriage, her grace was quite put out with him and with me. I can only assume she knew what he was about, but didn't much care for the notion."

"That is certainly an additional wrinkle in this scenario to be sure," Highcliff said. "It does add an interesting layer to the interplay last night. Your stepmother, the duchess, was quite vocal in her dismay at having been abandoned at the theater while the two of you made for Gretna Green. Vocal, as in shouting it from the theater steps in a way that more closely resembled theatrics than what took place on stage. Even then, I thought she must have had a far more active role in engineering your need for a hasty marriage."

Marcus uttered an epithet under his breath. "And here I thought I would be returned to the bosom of, if not a caring family, at least not a cutthroat one."

Highcliff crossed to the mantel and leaned against it as if deep in thought. After a moment, he added, "It is interesting enough to note that neither of them assumed any sort of foul play. It was immediately assumed that elopement was the only possible explanation. Charles even went so far as to state he'd overheard you talking about such."

"And then there is the conversation between Charles and my father that we were privy to this morning as we hid in the woods like criminals," Jane interjected.

Highcliff shook his head. "Remind me, Althorn, never to take advice about courtship from you. What was it you heard, Miss Barrett?"

"My father is determined to halt the match because these rumors about Lord Althorn, which I started unfortunately, diminish the value of his title in my father's estimation... but Charles was determined to see it through, pointing out all the reasons that the wedding should proceed regardless of whether Marcus is truly Althorn or not."

"I believe I know why... and Charles' relationship with Cassandra would certainly play into that," Marcus answered. "He wanted to marry you because he wanted access to your fortune and he needed it quickly. With my return, the quickest way to get it would be to have us marry and then eliminate us both. He gains the title and your fortune in one fell swoop."

"Then we should delay the wedding," Jane said. "If our marriage is a pivotal piece in halting Charles' plans, getting married tomorrow morning would be a terrible mistake."

"Except you've spent a night alone with him," Highcliff pointed out. "And I'll not hazard a guess as to what did or did not occur, but others shall. If you do not marry immediately, you could face terrible consequences for that later. Given that the family's social cache is likely to take a considerable hit when the truth about Charles comes out, another one might prove too great to surmount."

"I care little enough for what society thinks of us," Jane replied evenly.

Highcliff sighed. "Take it from someone who knows, Miss Barrett, and can attest personally to this—the sins of the father and the mother are often visited upon the child... this is never truer than in London society. If you do not wish for any children that you and Marcus should be blessed with to suffer for this, you need to proceed with the wedding."

Marcus knew precisely what Highcliff was speaking of. He also knew that it was absolutely true. The scandals and gossip, not to mention the cruel teasing of boys too far from home and parental disapproval, that had plagued Highcliff due to his mother's parentage—half-French and half-Gypsy—had been the foundation of their friendship. To some degree, and in spite of his own exalted title and expectations, Marcus had been just as touched by scandal. Had he not suffered the whispers about his grandparents and then about his own father's philandering? He would not wish such a fate on a child of his own. The fact that they had preemptively consummated their marriage meant that a child was a very real possibility for them. They could not afford to delay marrying until the danger was past.

"We won't delay," Marcus stated firmly. It was too late for that, anyway. "Write the article and send it to your publisher tonight. We will attempt to keep the wedding a secret, however, until such time as we can safely announce it."

Jane nodded in agreement and then excused herself. When she had gone, Highcliff turned back to him. "You do realize that this scandal will forever taint you both do you not?"

"I assume you mean Charles' actions and not our unintended elopement?" Marcus clarified.

"Yes," Highcliff answered. "I think you owe it to Miss Barrett to be certain she understands that. Treason from a commoner is horrible, from the gentry it is even worse. But treason from the potential heir to a dukedom—it is an affront that most will find unforgivable. Guilt by association is an ugly cross to bear."

"Guilt by association! The man had me locked in a prison cell, breaking rocks with a hammer to avoid being shot myself!" Marcus snapped.

"And I accompanied my dusky-skinned mother to England with her jewels sewn into the lining of a dress stained with her family's blood. She'd watched every relative she possessed be carted off to the guillotine, other than myself, and barely survived such a fate of herself. She braved living under the roof of my vicious father to carry me to safety. In spite of his coldness, she loved England, adored it and considered it the home of her heart. Yet when Bonaparte started his ugly, little war, everyone began to stare at her with suspicion," Highcliff pointed out. "For nothing more than being a noble who managed to survive the Terror, she became a pariah. Women are strange creatures, Marcus. They need the society of other women, they need acceptance, especially for their children. Warn your Miss Barrett now, so that you do not have to regret the lack of having done so later."

Highcliff turned and walked away, leaving Marcus to ponder the wisdom of such a course of action.

THEIR HORSES WERE beyond exhausted. The beasts were limping with fatigue and lathered with sweat as they guided them into the mews behind the duke's townhouse. Charles was at the end of his patience with Barrett. Had an opportunity presented itself to be rid of the man forever, he would gladly have taken it. Sadly, the roads had been far too busy that day for him to safely assist the man in shuffling off the mortal coil.

"I think we should have pressed on for Scotland," Barrett insisted.

It was a gamble as to whether Marcus and Jane Barrett would have made for Gretna Green or returned to London. Charles was betting on Gretna Green as it posed the least restrictions on getting the deed done. The last thing he needed was for Barrett to actually manage to halt the nuptials of the ill-fated lovers. Would it be too much of a stretch, Charles wondered, for Barrett to be taken out by whatever random illness Marcus and his bride would succumb to? Poison, he'd decided, would be the easiest method of eliminating them, so long as it was easily camouflaged as a natural illness. For that, he'd have to bow to Cassandra's expertise.

"Marcus would not wish to be married outside the Church of England," Charles lied easily. His cousin likely didn't care one whit, either way. "I had anticipated that they'd make for Gretna Green because it's the likeliest point of elopement. But on greater reflection, I doubt that he'd be willing to see it through. I think the likeliest course of action would be for them to return to the city, assess the damage to their reputations, and then proceed accordingly. They may, even now, be awaiting us inside. This is an aberration for him, Mr. Barrett, I assure you. Prior to his imprisonment and return, Marcus never put a foot wrong."

"They damned well better be back in this city or I'll be meeting him at dawn!" Barrett said.

Charles was never one to sing his cousin's praises but, in this instance, it would serve his purpose to do so. "Mr. Barrett, I'd like to point out to you that Marcus is a seasoned soldier. He was not an officer who shuffled off the enlisted men while he hid behind. No. He was at the front lines, in the thick of the fray, battling an onslaught of Bonaparte's finest with muskets, pistols, swords, knives, and when weapons were lost, his bare hands. I would not casually issue threats when the outcome will not be as you desire."

Barrett blustered then. "I'm no milquetoast to be cowed by him!"

"Perhaps you should be. I once saw him kill seven Frenchman. Had he not been vastly outmanned, I daresay Corunna would have taken a very different turn," Charles mused.

"You never saw him at Corunna... so you said," Barrett snapped.

Cursing himself and blaming his slip on his exhaustion and exasperation with his traveling companion, Charles smiled. "I didn't. But like everyone else, I heard the tales. He was well respected in the army, sir. He did not achieve that by being a coward or an easy mark."

Barrett hushed then, for the most part. He still grumbled under his breath as they entered the house and he retreated to his room. Charles sought out Riggs. "I'll be staying here for the night, Riggs. Until we can make sense of what's happened with Marcus and Miss Barrett, it seems best to stay close by."

If the butler thought it odd or had any reaction to the announcement at all, it was impossible to tell. Stoic as ever, Riggs inclined his head. "Yes, Mr. Balfour, sir. Super will be served in your room this evening. His grace is unwell still and her grace felt it best not to disturb him... if that is to your satisfaction."

It was, because he had no intention of being in his room. He intended to be in Cassandra's. "It is quite fine, Riggs," he said and made for the stairs. "Have a bath sent up, would you? I feel as if I've brought half the road in with me."

When Charles had vanished up the stairs, Sarah stepped from the shadows. "I know it isn't my place to say so, Mr. Riggs, but I don't much care for him. He acts like he already owns the place!"

Riggs frowned. "It is not your place to say so, Sarah, but that does not mean you are wrong. See to your duties and I will be certain that Mr. Balfour's demands are met."

Chapter Sixteen

J ANE HAD LUXURIATED in a warm bath, attended to by a maid assigned at Lord Highcliff's behest. The girl had been curiously skilled as a ladies maid in a house that was ostensibly devoid of ladies. It led her to wonder precisely what sort of guests Lord Highcliff entertained regularly.

She'd eaten her supper in her room, alone, while writing the article that essentially proclaimed Charles a traitor without saying it outright. It was a fine line to walk—providing enough information to identify him without naming him directly, indicating that he was guilty of treason without giving away what their evidence was. The goal, Marcus had explained, was to make Charles nervous, to make him anxious enough to want to know what was up their sleeves.

When at last she thought it was complete, she rose from the small writing table where she'd worked. Peering out into the corridor and seeing no prying eyes, she crossed the hall to Marcus' room and knocked softly. After he'd bade her enter, she opened the door and stepped inside. She was unprepared for the sight that greeted her.

He'd just finished his own bath, it seemed. Dressed in borrowed trousers and nothing else, she was immediately transported to the events of the night before. His gloriously bronzed skin still glistened with beads of water and she wanted nothing more than to touch him and feel the heat of him once more pressed against her.

Hastily turning away, she stammered an apology. "Forgive me, I did not mean to intrude. I wanted to give you an opportunity to examine the article before I sent it off to the publisher. I'll come back later."

"Stay," he urged. "I'll look at it now."

Still unable to meet his gaze, more because of her own wayward thoughts than his current state of undress, Jane stepped forward and handed him the sheaf of papers. She waited in uncomfortable silence as Marcus perused them. Seemingly against her will, her gaze continued to wander in his direction, stealing glances at the heavy muscles of his shoulders and chest. Memories of how it had felt to be held in his arms, to be crushed against the firmness of his body were wreaking havoc on her nerves.

After several minutes he looked up at her. "This will do nicely," he said. "Perhaps it was my own response to your article about my fraudulent identity that prevented me from noticing, but you do have a way with words, Jane. It's beautifully written even if the subject matter is somewhat difficult to bear."

"I am sorry," she offered. "I know it must be difficult for you to have been betrayed so cruelly by someone in your own family... that the betrayal has such far-reaching consequences—well, I just can't imagine." It was a weak and ill-worded statement of sympathy, but she found it difficult to think in his presence under the best of circumstances. When he was barely dressed, it was significantly worse.

"It has been difficult... but I've had time to accustom myself to Charles' perfidy. I imagine it will be infinitely worse for those who have yet to ascertain just to what depths he is willing to sink," he replied, sweeping away her concerns.

"He robbed you of five years of your life!" Jane protested. "Surely it is not so easy to just accustom yourself to that!"

He looked at her sharply. "No, Jane. That was not an easy thing to be accustomed to. Being imprisoned, having every thought and action guarded by others, with no privacy, very little dignity and a complete loss of everything that I am—up to an including my very name—was most assuredly not an easy thing to become accustomed to. But I daresay, you know exactly how that feels."

"What on earth do you mean by that?" she demanded.

"Is that not what you've done every day of your life? Denied your true nature, pretended to be meek and subservient, given yourself over to the whims of someone like Mrs. Barrett... all in an attempt to keep the peace and avoid conflict or punishment?"

She frowned then. "I'm not entirely certain what you're alluding to."

"Not alluding, Jane. Stating. I fear that you have been just as much a prisoner as I was."

Those words halted her protest. They robbed her of her very breath, in fact, because they rang with such truth. She had felt like a prisoner. She had felt as if every part of her was stifled and if not stifled, then indulged in only the most furtive of ways like her column or the countless novels she had been attempting to write for years. "I would hardly compare the two. I was not facing the threat of death," she answered, though her words lacked conviction.

"And is there not more than one way to die?" he asked pointedly. "While I was locked in that tiny cell, Jane, I decided several things about myself. The first was that I would be a man of honor. That I would honor my commitments to the best of my ability and that I would not be the kind of man my father had been. In short, I would marry you and I would be faithful to you. It's a concept the men of my family have little acquaintance with."

"Why are you telling me this now?" she asked, wondering at his motives.

"Because in a few short hours, we will be making our vows before a clergyman. I think it behooves us to have an honest conversation about what we expect from one another."

"I never expected fidelity from you," she admitted. "I had always assumed that ours would be a typical society marriage. We would have a child and then you would have a mistress. That is typically the way of it, is it not?"

"I've no wish for us to be typical," he said. Once again, his tone was sharp. "I offer fidelity, Jane, but I also demand it. I want us to be very clear on that front."

Jane drew in a sharp breath, affronted at the very mention of it. "I realize that my behavior last night was hardly that of a lady, but if I've given any indication to you that I would ever behave in such a licentious—"

"I'm not accusing you, Jane. And as for your behavior last night, can you honestly imagine that I would think ill of you for it? Or is it that you think ill of yourself?" he asked.

"Why else would we be having such a conversation?" Her tone revealed her exasperation. "It was imprudent of me and impossibly forward. And I cannot image what you must think of me—"

"Because I'd rather have this conversation now than when it's too late for you to back out," he answered firmly. "I want to be very clear about what I'm offering and what I'm expecting. And if you have any demands or conditions, now is the time to voice them!"

"What possible conditions or demands could I make?" she asked, still uncertain as to his motives. "I offered myself to you last night... freely. I did so because I had made my decision. And I cannot understand why you would ask me to question it now! Unless you want me to back out... is that it? Do you want me to release you from your obligation?" Her heart felt as if it had sunk to her toes. Everything in her rebelled at the thought.

"That is not it at all, Jane! I would never think to abandon you after what we shared!"

"But that's precisely what you're doing," she protested. "You're offering up broad, sweeping statements about what our marriage should and shouldn't be and telling me that now is my last opportunity to escape it! But why, after what occurred between us, should I want to escape an offer of marriage that includes the one thing most women in my position never receive—the promise of fidelity?"

"Because marrying me could ruin your life!" he shouted, clearly overcome by his own temper. After taking a calming breath, he continued. "I know that the scandal would be impossible, but I'm trying, Jane, against my better judgement and against everything that I desire for my own sake, to offer you a chance not to be permanently linked to a family marked by treason!"

Jane paused for a moment, collecting herself and trying to garner some sort of control over her own highly emotional state. "You truly wish to be married to me? Jane, who writes scandalous trash for a publication most people won't even admit to reading and not simply the recognized daughter of William Barrett in order to fulfill the contract?"

He shrugged. "If it will set your mind at ease, your father will likely void the contract. Are you willing to marry a penniless marquess who will eventually be a penniless duke?"

"Yes," she answered without hesitation. "I am... so long as that penniless marquess is you."

It was true. In spite of their difficult and contentious parting before he left, in spite of the years since that she'd spent convincing herself she didn't care for him at all and didn't want to be married to any man, enough of the hero worship she'd had for him as a child remained. He would always be the most handsome of men in her eyes. And over the last days, she'd begun to see that he was also the most honorable. How that had occurred under the influence of the Duke of Elsingham would likely forever remain a mystery.

It was as if her capitulation had unlocked the very tides. He strode toward her, his long legs eating up the distance between them, until he could capture her once more in his arms. Jane went willingly, eager for his touch, eager to experience the passion he had shown her the night before.

"I cannot get enough of you," he whispered. "I swore that I would not do this... that I would wait until we were married before having you in my bed again, but I cannot. I want you too much."

"I don't want to wait," she insisted. "I want to feel what you made me feel last night."

"And what is that, Jane?" he asked, kissing the side of her neck and biting it gently.

Breathlessly, she uttered, "Enough... you made me feel as if I were simply enough. That I was pretty enough, desirable enough, witty and smart enough... that if you had your preferences, there was nothing about me that you would change."

He paused then, drawing back to look at her. "You are enough, Jane. You are everything that I have ever desired in a woman and more. It's a crime that you've suffered under the care of people who would ever try to make you believe otherwise."

"Can we really do this, Marcus? Can we marry and be happy together... or will we succumb to the same ennui and pettiness that all the couples of my acquaintance have?" she queried softly.

"I cannot promise you that we will not... I can only say that I will work every day to avoid that outcome," he vowed. "We have both had enough unhappiness to last us a lifetime. Even though we've hardly led tragic lives, there is something to be said about the continual drain on one's soul of being surrounded by people who will only ever serve themselves."

"Take me to your bed," she whispered. "I've no wish to spend another night alone."

MARCUS WAS HELPLESS to resist that sweet plea. How any man could hold firm against the soft, seductive curves of her body or the delicate beauty of her upturned face would forever be a mystery to him. Of course, there was also the unfortunate truth that he had no real desire to resist her. Her request perfectly mirrored his own selfish needs.

Without any fanfare, Marcus took her hands and led her toward his bed. It took all of his patience to slowly undress her, to untie the laces of her gown with care and precision rather than simply tearing the garment from her. As each layer was removed, he kissed and caressed every inch of skin that was revealed. By the time Jane was clad only in the thin cotton of her borrowed chemise, she was shivering. But he knew from the rate of her breathing and the rapid pulse beating at her throat, that it wasn't the cold that prompted her response.

"I want to see all of you," he whispered hotly against her ear.

"You have seen all of me," she replied.

"No. The dim light of a small fire and a hurried coupling in a cold room hardly counts," he insisted. "All that remains to shield you from my gaze, Jane, is this chemise. Remove it."

It was a challenge, a test of her confidence, her desire, her willingness to let go of what everyone else had said of her and, instead, see herself anew through his eyes. When her trembling hands lifted to the ties of the garment that rested just above the swells of her breasts, his breath caught. As she tugged the laces free and the garment fell, catching briefly on the curve of her hips before falling to the floor, that breath left him in a rush.

She was utterly perfect. Her soft, rounded shoulders, lush breasts and the gentle flare of her hips all reminded him of the paintings he'd seen by the masters of the Renaissance. Voluptuous, with a sweetness of countenance and a quiet beauty that would be overlooked by those who lacked the ability to see past the shy and subservient mien she'd adopted out of self-defense against her tyrant of a stepmother, she was his. He reveled in that fact, rejoiced in it as he had in nothing else for a very long time. If he'd possessed an ability to capture her beauty, he would have done so, but only to hoard it for his own pleasure.

"I wish you could see yourself as I do," he murmured softly. "We will go to the British Museum one day and I will show you the glorious and scandalous paintings that only married women are allowed to view. And from those paintings, Jane, you will learn how perfect you are, for I haven't the eloquence to tell you."

"Then do not tell me in words," she said. "Simply show me."

Marcus stepped closer to her again, kissing her soundly as he bore her back onto the bed. After shedding his own breeches, he joined her there and did as she asked, worshipping her body with his own.

"WHY DIDN'T YOU get rid of him on the road?"

Cassandra's angry hiss roused Charles from the light doze he'd been enjoying as he luxuriated in the tub of hot water before the fireplace in his guest chamber and imagined the day when he occupied a much grander suite of rooms in the house. "It's rather unwise for you to be in here given just how many prying eyes are in this house right now," he warned.

"It was unwise of you to return with Barrett!" she retorted sharply. "You should have taken care of this problem, Charles. He's insisting that the contract be voided, that Marcus' questionable identity is a valid reason to demand a full account of all the moneys exchanged thus far! We'll be paupers!"

"Then point him toward that ostentatious phaeton of yours... a goodly sum of it could be accounted for there," he snapped. He was too tired for Cassandra's scheming that night.

"Need I remind you that if Barrett succeeds... if he even goes to his solicitor and raises the question, it would make his death immediately suspect! My God, Charles, he's a cit! How hard would it have been to knock him off his horse? A broken neck would have been easy enough to explain away!"

"You would know, my dear," he replied menacingly. "Isn't that how the duke's second wife met her maker?"

Cassandra shrugged. "She was in the way. He had a title that I wanted and a son who was supposed to easily capitulate and marry a plain, little heiress to fill the family coffers! If I'd known what a catastrophe catching a duke would turn into, I'd have set my sights on an earl or marquess!"

"I will handle Barrett," he assured her, more to shut her up than because he wanted to. Frankly, the entire scheme to get his hands on the title and on Jane Barrett's fortune was turning into far more work than he had bargained for. "I have a plan to get rid of him, his mousy daughter and my inconvenient cousin in one fell swoop."

"How will you do that?"

"Some bad meat at the wedding breakfast, I think," he said. "We'll take a little something to make us ill enough to be convincing... and they'll all receive a very lethal dose of something else."

Cassandra stopped short. "That will only work if Barrett agrees to the wedding breakfast."

"I don't plan to give him a choice, love," Charles said. "Now either do something with that mouth of yours that doesn't involve talking or go try to seduce your current husband into an already overdue grave."

Cassandra shuddered with distaste as she began removing her gown. "I can't stand the thought of touching him! He repulses me."

Charles felt his body stir. "Then there's a price to be paid for solace here."

Chapter Seventeen

THEY WERE MARRIED in a brief ceremony with little fanfare at St. Michaels' on Crooked Lane. Small and plain by most standards, the church was never frequented by those they knew and, therefore, suited their needs perfectly. The special license had been procured by Lord Highcliff, who, along with his housekeeper, served as their witnesses. It was hardly the wedding she'd dreamed of as a girl. There was no beautiful gown to transform her, though the concoction of pink silk that had materialized was certainly grand enough. It also lacked a certain amount of coverage at the bust which had prompted the vicar to stare stubbornly at the ceiling.

Still, there were no orange blossoms and there would be no elaborate wedding breakfast to return home to. In spite of that, Jane found herself to be hopeful.

As she recited her vows, she was shockingly free of nerves. It was as if every hesitation, every doubt had fled from her. She stood before the cleric with absolute certainty.

The idea of marrying for love rather than duty or to uphold ages old marriage contracts had always appealed to her. While she strongly suspected that her own feelings for Marcus had crossed the threshold in that direction, she had very little inkling of his feelings for her. He desired her, yes, but that was all she could be certain of. Still, she was marrying Marcus completely against her father's wishes. She supposed there was some truth and comfort in the idea that she'd followed her own heart and not been swayed by anyone else.

She'd found herself questioning through the night whether what she felt for Marcus was love. It was an impossible feeling to define, but her own emotions defied definition as well. She was drawn to him, and she'd grown to trust him. While he often failed to go about it in the proper way, she believed with her whole heart that he ultimately always tried to do the right thing. And what men didn't blunder things?

He'd spoken once of love being a combination of feelings. Desire, trust, respect, genuinely liking the other person and wanting to be in their company—those were certainly part of it, she was sure. But there was something else, some ephemeral component that she could not fully identify that created a small frisson of apprehension in her.

In spite of that, she had managed to develop a strong sense of the kind of man he truly was. A future with him, even if he failed to love her in return, if, in fact, love was what she felt for him, was still preferable to the rather lonely future she had thought to console herself with. More pointedly, together, they possessed a far greater chance of standing firm in the face of her family and his.

They had both been used, bullied, and valued for only what they could provide for others. What a glorious life it would be, she thought, if that were never true again. They had the promise together of something many couples did not—contentment. Could that possibly be enough?

When it was done, they signed the register and the cleric bid them good day. If he thought it unusual that someone of Marcus' standing would be married in such a havy-cavy fashion, he managed to school his response very well to conceal it.

"Congratulations, my lord… and to you as well, your ladyship," the rector offered in the same monotonous tone with which he'd performed their marriage ceremony. Again, his gaze was glued directly to the top of Jane's head and did not dare lower by even an inch. He was certainly a dour fellow.

"Thank you, Reverend, for making yourself and your church available to us this morning. I'm afraid we cannot linger," Marcus explained.

Highcliff had made a rather sizable donation to the church. Of that, Jane was certain. As Marcus took her arm and led her outside to the waiting carriage, Highcliff offered his congratulations. "May your happiness match, if not exceed the misery it has caused for others."

Jane shook her head. "Could you not have simply wished us well without addressing the furor we will no doubt create?"

"To be forewarned is to be forearmed, my dear," Highcliff answered as he reached inside the carriage to retrieve a wooden box. "Speaking of forearmed, I might have persuaded your publisher to put out a special edition of his little gossip rag today. No doubt by nightfall, all of London will be clamoring for Charles' head on a platter. That is when he will be the most dangerous. To that end, this is for you."

Jane opened the box and found a small muff pistol inside. It would easily fit into her reticule or the pocket of an apron. "I've no notion of how to use a pistol, Lord Highcliff."

"You do not need to know, my dear. It's primed and ready. Keep it with you always. If necessary, point it at the person you wish to shoot, pull back this hammer," he offered, pointing to the surprisingly pretty and ornate scroll work on top of the handle, "and then simply squeeze the trigger. It will do the work for you... but they have to be close to you. Just beyond arm's length should do it. At that distance, it isn't even necessary to aim."

"Thank you," she said. "For all that you've done and all the many ways that you have helped us."

He leaned in and kissed her cheek. As he did, he whispered in her ear, "Althorn is my only friend. Make him happy."

With that, Highcliff drew back and bustled his housekeeper into a waiting hack, leaving his much finer carriage for them to return to the fold of their less than welcoming families. Watching him Jane was overcome with sympathy for him. He was handsome, wealthy beyond imagining, titled... and yet, she felt he must be the loneliest person she'd ever known, even given her own less than warm childhood.

"He's very sad, isn't he?"

Marcus met her gaze with a level one of his own. "We have too much to deal with right now for you to go matchmaking for Highcliff. He'll find his own happiness in his own way and in his own time."

"But—"

"One crisis at a time, my dear. One crisis at a time," Marcus insisted as he offered her a hand up.

Once in the carriage, Jane carefully closed the box holding her weapon. It was certainly a first for her. "Do you really feel that Charles poses this much of a threat to us? That we might have to defend ourselves with violence?"

"I do," Marcus answered. "For all of our lives, Charles has been not simply envious, but covetous. Everything that was mine, he felt entitled to. And once he took it, he'd break it—destroy it in ways that it could not even possibly be repaired. It's as much spite with him as anything else. I worry that will now extend to you."

She made a face. "You needn't worry on that point. Charles has as much as confessed that he finds me revolting. Even when he proposed, he essentially stated that he was fond enough of me to overlook my unattractiveness."

"While his statement is utterly preposterous, that doesn't change anything. When we were younger, still grown men, but before we both joined the army, I had a beautiful horse and Charles wanted him. Naturally, I declined. The next day, Charles took that stallion from the stable, rode him into the ground with rain pounding them both. At last, when the horse was too exhausted to even walk, chest billowing and lathered with sweat, Charles made him take an impossible jump over a gate that should only have ever been braved on a fresh horse on a dry day... or so witnesses said."

A sick feeling settled over her. "What happened to the stallion?"

"He broke both his legs stumbling as he landed on the other side of that fence. I had to shoot him, because Charles said he didn't have the heart. He left him to suffer in the field for hours before I could get back to him to put him out of his misery," Marcus answered.

"You think he did it on purpose?"

"I know he did," Marcus said stiffly. "The stable master forbade him from that taking horse, stating that, on my orders, no one else was to ride him. Charles ignored that edict, saddled the beast himself, and took him out against my express wishes." Marcus paused, clearly remembering the exchange with no small amount of anger. "I'd told him no in person, the stable master had told him no, as well, but there you have it. He can be a spiteful creature, Jane. He would hurt you to hurt me. I couldn't bear that."

Jane shivered, her skin cold with fear and a sickening sense of foreboding. "There are many obstacles in his path. You and me, your father and mine! While I've little affection for either of them, if Charles intends to ultimately gain control of my fortune, then it's likely he's a danger to them, as well."

"He is… but they are not my priority. You are. I will keep you safe, no matter what it takes. That is why I want to take you straightaway to Thornhaven. You will be safe there while I deal with this."

"No," she stated adamantly. "If we separate so soon after being married, anyone could challenge the validity of our wedding. I will not give them the ammunition they require to see it annulled."

"Jane, I don't know what I would do if you were hurt, or worse, killed. I cannot have that on my conscience!"

"Is that the only reason? Because you'd feel guilty? Or is there something else, Marcus?"

"And if I tell you it is much more, would you go to Thornhaven then?"

Jane shook her head sadly. "If and when you make a declaration of your affections, Marcus, I'd prefer it not to be part of a bargain."

"I'm sorry for that, Jane. It was wrong of me to suggest it. You will, when all this done, have the declaration you desire… and I hope that I will receive one in return. To that end, do please listen to me and do as I tell you once we reach Father's home. It's imperative to keep you safe."

Those words, dire as they were, gave her hope. "Nothing will happen to me… to either of us. We will look after one another. That's what we're intended to do, isn't it? For richer and for poorer and for better and for worse? Did we not just utter those words?"

Marcus didn't answer. Instead, he reached for her, taking her hand and pulling her to him. She settled across his lap, pressing her head to his shoulder as he held her close. It was a gesture of comfort and not passion, but it was just as welcome.

CHARLES WAS ENJOYING a leisurely breakfast. Alone in the breakfast room, his every need attended to by the ridiculous number of footmen stationed about, he could almost envision himself as head of the household. One day, very soon, he vowed, all that he surveyed would be his.

The door opened and the butler entered, stiff and unfriendly as usual. When he was in charge, Riggs would be the first to go, Charles decided.

"A package has arrived for you, Mr. Balfour," the butler intoned and placed the small parcel on the table for him.

Charles eyed the package for a moment, and then the butler who still loomed. "That will be all, Riggs."

When he was alone again, Charles snapped the twine that bound the package. It was a paper, a printed copy of that worthless gossip rag, the *London Ladies' Gazette*. But it was the headline which immediately caught his eye. *'Missing Marquess' Cousin and Heir Apparent Guilty of Treason.*

He'd done it. Marcus had gone to the press, or at least one small portion of it, with his suspicions. Charles felt the clawing panic building inside him. If people began to look too closely, everything they had constructed would fall down about their ears.

Folding the paper to conceal the headline, he wrapped it once more in the waxed cloth it had been delivered in and set off to find Cassandra. It was time to cut their losses and run or risk the noose. He'd no more than stepped into the foyer than Riggs was answering the front door. He paused on the bottom step as Marcus entered, Jane Barrett at his side.

"Well, Cousin, you've certainly stirred the pot of scandal broth," he said with false easiness. "And you, Miss Barrett. You've turned out to be an unexpected surprise. Who would have ever guessed such a mousy countenance hid the heart of an adventuress!"

"You're addressing my wife, Charles. She is now Lady Althorn," Marcus answered reproachfully. "You will not disparage her so!"

"For the time being, she is Lady Althorn," Charles offered with a cold smile. "That is, until her father sees it annulled. I understand a certain amount of discord with the in-laws is to be expected, but you've far and away exceed that, Cousin."

There was a commotion at the top of the stairs as the man in question, Mr. Barrett, appeared. He took one look at the couple and his face purpled with rage.

"I'll see you dead for this, Althorn! We'll have pistols at dawn!" the man shouted.

Charles used the confusion to make his escape. Heading up the stairs and past the still ranting Barrett, he made directly for Cassandra's chamber. No doubt the servants would be glued to the rather loud and nasty scene unfolding in the foyer. With that, there was little chance of them being discovered.

"We have to go," he said, entering her room, and putting the heavily-wrapped paper down on her breakfast tray. "It's too late to salvage anything here."

She perused the headlines after removing the wrapping. "This is nothing."

"It is something, Cassandra! If I'm accused of treason, we'll be outcasts. Between this, the suspicious demise of my entire family and our very unorthodox relationship, we will be absolute pariahs here."

"We have to stay here, Charles, just long enough to get the money... then we can go anywhere. Spain, Portugal... even to the Americas!" she insisted. "But we cannot run out now... not yet. We can't give up everything we've been working toward! I will not be poor! I didn't marry that disgusting, wrinkled, old sot and let him rut on me every night for months just so I could leave here empty-handed!"

"We will find another way to make our fortunes," he said. "This isn't just about money! I could hang for this. And they might well hang you with me."

"It would take months for them to build a case. And in that time, we could make off with everything we need," Cassandra insisted. "How long would our love last in poverty? No, Charles. We ride it out here! At least for now… and we proceed with our plan. I assume the turmoil below stairs is the return of our errant bride and groom?"

"Yes," he answered.

"Let Marcus and Barrett reach an understanding. Then when things are calm, we'll plan a celebration, family only, of course, in light of the duke's failing health. And it is failing. I took your advice. He had another seizure during the night. His valet should find him shortly, drooling and unconscious."

"You are devious," he said, awed with equal parts admiration and fear. Cassandra, in spite of her outward appearance of being vapid and insipid, always had a plan for every eventuality. No doubt, there was one that outlined precisely how to be rid of him should the need arise. Her slow poisoning of the duke had been self-serving at first, a way to end his abuse of her nubile, young body. But Charles come to realize that there was a part of her that enjoyed looking at the broken down wreck of her husband and knowing that she was the cause.

"It's all for us, my darling. I don't even care about the title. I just want as much of her lovely money as we can get our hands on. I imagine that with my beauty and your charm, we could take the courts of Europe by storm. Could we not?"

Knowing, as always, that it was in his best interest to agree with her, Charles said, "We will, my darling." But in that moment, for the first time, he was envisioning a future without Cassandra. It was too late to cut and run. It likely had been long before Marcus and his new bride arrived. But once the duke was dead, and if Cassandra was to be believed that was only minutes away, Marcus would ascend to the title. It was all coming to a head too quickly and the time they needed to make an escape had dwindled at an alarming rate. Still, they stood there, Cassandra deeply in denial and all but enslaved by her own greed.

Slowly, with dawning realization of just how impossibly flawed her logic was and how epically their plans had failed, Charles reached another conclusion. It was too late to leave, too late to cut his losses and run. But that didn't mean he would have the perfect amount of time left to exact his revenge on those who had either denied or cost him everything. He might not have what he wanted, but neither would they.

IN THE STUDY, having finally convinced her father that they should retire there rather than continue shouting at one another in the foyer, Jane held her hand to her head in an attempt to ward off the looming megrim. "Father, please! You are being unreasonable!"

"Unreasonable? You married a damned imposter!" He shouted so loudly the windows rattled. "He's not even the Marquess of Althorn!"

Jane knew that there was only one course of action left open to her. It was time to confess all of her sins. "I wrote that article. I wrote it out of spite and desperation to prolong our engagement long enough to make my escape. I thought, erroneously, obviously, at that time that Marcus was the last man on earth I wanted to be married to!"

"You did no such thing! That article was written by that same fool who has been spreading malicious gossip through the *ton* for years!"

"Yes… and I have been. I can show you my account books where I've been paid well for every column and article written," she said. "I did this. Furthermore, you cannot have our marriage annulled as it has already been consummated."

"You were just wed not even an hour ago!"

"And I've spent the past two nights alone with my husband without the benefit of a chaperone," she added, ignoring the heated blush that colored her cheeks. "An annulment is impossible. There are no grounds for it. And you can pretend all you want, but I know both you and Charles had a hand in the kidnapping that resulted in my being so compromised. Waiting to marry ceased to be an option by your own design."

Her father blinked at her in stunned surprise. "Now, see here, Jane—"

"Now, see here, Father... I know how you work. I know how you think. Charles might have suggested it for his own selfish reasons, but you eagerly accepted. And unless you want me to tell the entire world via my column in the *London Ladies' Gazette* that you engineered your own daughter's abduction to force a marriage, you'll stand down now."

"You wouldn't dare!" he shouted.

"I would. Furthermore, I already have. The article has been written and entrusted to a dear friend. The moment you appeal for an annulment, that will be sent to the publisher," she lied. "For decades, you've been attempting to pawn me off on poor Marcus. Now that we're married, you're fighting tooth and nail to keep us apart. You've gotten what you initially wanted, so take it and be happy."

"I don't care about the scandal!"

"You do," she said firmly. "You wanted to have a connection to the aristocracy because it would open doors for you in business. It would give you new opportunities for investment and it would increase your social cache. You have that now. Do not ruin it out of spite!"

The door opened and her stepmother entered. She had clearly been listening for some time. "William, you will cease at once," she said. "They are married, albeit in a very shabby fashion. It is done and we will all move on now!"

"Yes, you will," Marcus said. "I cannot deny you the use of my name and title as entree into society, and I would not, though it may afford you less entree than you once hoped. But I will not have either of you in my home... ever again. Your treatment of Jane, for the entirety of her life it seems, has been nothing short of cruel and barbaric. That ends today. You will both leave at first light in the morning. If you wish to visit with my father after we have retired to our country home you may, but we will never again share the same roof."

William Barrett drew himself up to his full height. "Is this the kind of husband you want then, Daughter? One who would cut ties with your family and keep you from us?"

"Yes," she answered evenly. "He is the husband I want. And everything he said was uttered with my full and eager blessing."

Her father turned then and stormed out, leaving Mrs. Barrett behind. The woman looked Jane over, from head to toe, with disdain. "You were an always embarrassment to him. He doesn't realize it now, but being cut off from you is a blessing. When he and I are blessed with children of our own, they will be all that you are not."

Jane said nothing further as her stepmother turned on her heel and followed her husband out of the room. To Marcus, she said, "That was unpleasant, but I had expected it to be far worse."

He crossed the room to her. "It's for the best, Jane. I know you're hurt by your father and your stepmother—"

"I'm not," she said. "Not really. I think I stopped letting their words hurt me a very long time ago. I attempted to follow her edicts more to keep the peace than because I was seeking her approval. I always knew that no matter what I did or what I became, that would be withheld."

"All that's left is dealing with Charles and Cassandra," he said.

As if in challenge to his statement, Riggs entered the library. "Forgive me, Lord Althorn, your father has had an episode. He's gravely ill, my lord."

Chapter Eighteen

M ARCUS FELT THE muscles of his stomach tighten defensively at the butler's pronouncement. "Has his physician been sent for?"

"Yes, my lord. But I fear he will not survive until the man arrives."

That statement spurred Marcus to action. He was practically running as he left the library and climbed the stairs, taking them two at a time. He didn't knock or wait to be bid entrance to his father's chamber, but simply burst inside.

Owlsley, his father's valet and loyal servant for decades, was crying silently in the corner. On the bed, his father lay heaped beneath a mound of sheets and blankets. Even then, his lips appeared to have a bluish cast.

Marcus approached the bed and knelt beside his father.

"It's done," the old man whispered. "You married the girl?"

"Yes, Father."

He nodded though the gesture cost him precious energy. "Good… good then. Your stepmother poisoned me," he said.

"You're certain?"

"I had suspected it for some time. But after last night, I was sure. She poured me a brandy, but when I refused it, she forced it down my throat. I'd have died already had I not forced myself to cast up my accounts," he said. "As it is, I'm dying anyway. You'll see to it she's punished?"

"I will," Marcus promised.

"You were a better son than I was a father," the old man admitted. "But I'm not sorry for what I did. You're set up for a fine future now."

Marcus didn't answer. The old man was taken by a coughing fit and when it had passed, his lips were speckled with blood. His breath wheezed in and out of his lungs in such a manner that it was plain he had a very limited number of them left.

"I love you, Father, and I forgive you for anything that has passed between us that was not as it should be."

The old man simply nodded again and then closed his eyes. After a moment, his chest stilled entirely and the valet fell into fits of weeping. "Did you hear his confession, Owlsley? What he said about the duchess?"

"I did," the valet confessed.

"Say nothing until you are told otherwise. It's best if she has no warning that we are aware of her misdeeds. Is that understood? And see to it that bottle is well hidden. I don't want her to destroying the evidence."

The man nodded again, still weeping bitterly.

"You'll be fine, Owlsley," Marcus said, getting to his feet. "You'll not be turned out. See to having his body prepared. I've no notion who to call first in this situation."

"Yes, your grace," the valet said tearfully.

Your grace. The mantle had already been passed, he thought bitterly. Exiting the chamber, Marcus found Jane standing in the hall surrounded by a bevy of servants. "The fifth Duke of Elsingham has passed away," he stated. "You will offer any assistance necessary to his valet in making the necessary preparations for his burial."

There was a flurry of bows and curtsies as they all murmured in a subdued fashion, "Yes, your grace."

When they had gone to see to their duties, Marcus met Jane's gaze. "It hurts far more than I imagined it would."

"He loved you," she said. "He was maddening, tyrannical, obsessed with wealth and appearances, but he did still love you... even if he failed at showing it."

Marcus nodded. It was true enough. But more profound was what she did not say. His father, in spite of being notoriously difficult, had loved him. Her own father did not.

"We need to talk privately," he said.

He led her once more to the small gallery, the same place where they had shared their first kiss and where the trajectory of their dealings with one another had shifted so perfectly. "Cassandra poisoned him. He admitted that she forced poison-laced brandy down his throat last night after he refused it. Owlsley has been instructed to hide the remaining brandy before Cassandra can destroy the evidence."

"We need to call in someone from Bow Street," she urged. "Let them deal with both Charles and Cassandra. I do not like this, Marcus. They are clearly feeling desperate or they would not have sped up their course of action to such a degree."

"She's quite right. And I'm afraid your discovery of Cassandra's little exploit last night will be your undoing."

Neither of them had heard Charles approach. He'd been concealed in the gallery all along, likely to observe what was taking place near the duke's chamber.

"Charles," Marcus said. "Whatever you're about, it's far too late. Surely, you see that? This can still end in a dignified manner for you."

"Why should I care about dignity now?" the other man snapped. "My entire life has been devoid of it! I've been a beggar at your table for as long as I can remember! Do you honestly believe Thomas Carter is your only bastard brother? Did you not know the old man had been rutting with my own whore of a mother even before my father wed her?"

Marcus hadn't known, but it certainly explained Charles' animosity. "There is no need for this. If you wish to be acknowledged—"

"I do not wish to be acknowledged!" Charles exploded as he pulled a pistol from within his coat. "I'm done taking scraps when the lot of should have been mine!"

"Charles," Marcus began, but Charles was having none of it. He lifted the pistol and aimed it directly at Jane. Marcus fell silent instantly.

"I am the elder brother you see... by a full year," Charles explained. His tone was sing-song, like a child with a secret. He waved the pistol wildly as he spoke. "The title, had our late father been a more honest and honorable man, would have been mine! He'd have married my mother and now I would be the Duke of Elsingham! Instead, I'm just a poor relation... scrounging and begging like a dog!"

The soft hum of the servants doing their work had stopped. There was little doubt that Charles' exclamation had been heard throughout the house. The sound of a pin dropping would have echoed for days in the still quiet.

"And now the world knows you are not only a traitor but a bastard, as well," Marcus said softly. "If you want to see me dead, so be it, but know you're signing your own death warrant. You'll hang for it, Charles. That is a certainty."

Charles smiled. "I had thought to kill you, but then I thought better of it. You have eternally been the good son, the one whose conscience always led him down the proper path. Until now—until your lovely bride here. Tell me, Brother... did you ruin her in name only or did you manage to actually do the deed? If not, I'm afraid you've missed your opportunity. She'll leave this world as innocent as when she entered it." With that statement, Charles leveled the weapon once more, pointing it directly at Jane, at a distance that could be nothing less than fatal.

As he pulled back the hammer, he said, "I decided that killing you would end your misery too quickly. I'll kill her instead, and leave you to live with the guilt of failing to save her... the same way you failed to save our worthless father!"

JANE HAD SLIPPED her hand into the pocket of her borrowed pelisse. After her father had set upon them the instant they entered the house, she hadn't yet had the opportunity to remove it. In that moment, she was infinitely relieved to have been waylaid by her father's ill temper and accusations. It meant the Lord Highcliff's gift to her was still close at hand.

Her fingers closed about the small muff pistol that he'd offered her as a wedding gift. The man's timing and foresight were uncanny.

She waited, biding her time for Charles to step closer.

"Come here," he demanded. "I want him to have a better view when I put this pistol ball right between your passably pretty eyes."

"No," she answered. "I'm not leaving Marcus' side."

"You will or so help me I will put a pistol ball in him now the way I should have done at Corunna! I was too greedy then... wanting to see him carted off to work as slave labor for the French!"

"If you want me at your side, Charles," she said challengingly, "then you'll simply have to come here and get me."

"I will," he said. And casually, without a care, he fired the pistol.

Marcus slumped to the floor, his hands grasping his thigh as blood seeped from the wound. "Run, Jane. He only had the one pistol ball. You can escape him before he reloads."

"I don't have to," she said. As Charles neared her, she raised her hand, never even removing the gun from her pocket, and pulled the trigger. The ball discharged with a deafening bang, her small gun much louder than Charles' larger one had been. The sound was still reverberating throughout the gallery as he stumbled toward the railing. Blood seeped from behind the dark cloth of his waistcoat, staining his fawn breeches and lacy cuffs. He fell, tumbling over the railing to the floor below, landing on the heavy marble with a sickening thud.

Jane didn't bother to look. She had no desire to see the carnage that waited below. Instead, she lifted her skirts, tore at the hem of her petticoat until a long strip of fabric gave way. Kneeling next to Marcus, she tied it out about his leg. "I didn't think he would actually shoot you."

"I don't think anyone has ever been able to accurately predict Charles' behavior," he said with a grimace. "It's clear to me now that it was envy that drove him mad."

A brace of footmen rushed in, led by Riggs, who offered immediate apologies, "Forgive me, your grace. We didn't know whether to wait for him to make his move or rush in. It seems the duchess had a better understanding of the situation than we did."

"There is nothing to forgive," Marcus said, as the footmen helped him to stand. With one arm about each of them, they helped him limp toward his room, Jane behind them. "If you'd rushed in, Riggs, the outcome may have been far worse. We need to see to it that my stepmother does not escape this house. She's guilty of poisoning my father."

"It's been taken care of, your grace," Riggs said. "I took the liberty of setting several footmen to guard her door after Owlsley told me what the late Duke of Elsingham had confessed to you. The physician should be here to attend you shortly. I haven't sent anyone to fetch the lads from Bow Street yet. I thought, perhaps, you might want it handled more discreetly."

"My goodness, Riggs. If they'd had you at the front, I daresay Napoleon would have been defeated more quickly," Marcus joked. He needed a moment of levity, something to break the terrible tension that had settled over the house.

"What shall we say about this unfortunate end to Mr. Balfour, sir? I daresay it would not be well thought of for the new duchess to be guilty of manslaughter... even if it was well deserved."

"I will say that I shot him in self-defense," Marcus insisted, "We quarreled because—I can't think of why we should have quarreled."

Her father had been listening from the hall along with the servants. "Because he'd been harboring a secret affection for my daughter, of course. When she chose to go through with the wedding to you, your grace, he was quite overcome. Driven mad by unrequited love. It's at least a more sympathetic reason than being jealous of his legitimate sibling or, infinitely worse, facing the hangman for treason."

"It's utterly ridiculous, and no one who sees me would ever believe it. But it is a better option than the truth," Jane agreed.

"What about the duchess?" Mr. Barrett asked.

"You mean Cassandra? Jane is the duchess now," Marcus corrected, grimacing as he laid back on the bed. The cloth she'd tied about his leg was already soaked through with blood.

"Will she hang?" Barrett asked. "The scandal—"

"I'm more concerned with the fact that my husband is bleeding profusely, Father," Jane snapped. "Cassandra's fate can be decided later!"

"She will not hang," Marcus said through gritted teeth. "As much as it pains me to say so, we are better off if the nature of my father's demise remains unknown." He looked pointedly at the servants gathered and at Mr. Barrett.

"There is a convent in Scotland, near one of our estates," he continued, "Cassandra will live out the remainder of her days there, or the truth will win out and she will pay the ultimate price for her crimes."

"She will never consent to that," Jane insisted. "That would be tantamount to death for her regardless."

Marcus offered a casual shrug. "I hadn't planned on offering her a choice."

Jane noted how pale his face had become. It was obvious to Jane that he was in a significant amount of pain. She'd seen the scars on his legs, knew that he'd been injured in battle before. That Charles had taken such precise aim led her to believe he'd been aware, as well.

"Get bandages and bring me a pair of shears to cut away his clothing. He's losing blood very quickly and we need to staunch that wound or calling for the physician will have been a pointless endeavor," she ordered.

"Speaking of Napoleon," Marcus said as Jane went about issuing orders like a general, "I believe you may be something of a tyrant yourself."

"Hush. This is no time to be flippant. You always do that at the worst possible moments!" she snapped as she cut away his clothes with the scissors that had appeared as if by magic. Without the bunched cloth in the way, she tied another tourniquet about his leg, much tighter than before. When the task was done, her hands were coated in blood.

He smiled much like a drunkard. It was clear the loss of blood was impacting him and he would not be conscious for much longer. "I will endeavor to do better, Wife."

Jane watched his eyes flutter closed and her heart stuttered in her chest. Only that morning, she had wondered if perhaps what she felt for him was love. With the very real possibility of losing him forever staring back at her, she could finally freely admit that it was. She loved her husband.

"He can't die, Riggs. Don't let him."

"Begging your pardon, your grace, but I fear that isn't up to me," the butler answered.

"Of course, it is," she said. "You rule this house with an iron fist. You only have to forbid it and then it will not be." Then, for the second time in her life, Jane fainted.

Chapter Nineteen

THE GROUNDS AT Thornwood Hall were bare and desolate. Winter on the moors was harsh and yet strangely beautiful. As Jane walked through the dreary garden, the skirt of her black mourning dress snagged on a rose bush, the thorns tugging at the fabric. She leaned down to try and extricate the dress without doing more damage, but a hand on her arm stopped her.

"Let me," Marcus said. "You'll prick yourself."

She looked at him, still leaning heavily on his cane. "If you bend over here, then we'll have to call the footmen to pick you up off the cold, hard ground. I can weather the sting of a few thorns," she assured.

"You should not have to," he said softly. "You've weathered enough already."

Jane rose, her dress freed and only a few minor scratches for her troubles. They'd fled London, seeking solace in the country away from the gossipmongers. J.E. for the *London Ladies' Gazette* had been curiously quiet on the front of the scandal-ridden Elsinghams. Jane had, in fact, retired her pseudonym but had allowed Lord Highcliff to have use of it should he ever need to flush out another criminal in the upper ranks of society. The former duchess had not gone quietly into the convent. She'd attempted to flee and Bow Street had been called after all. She'd been caught with jewels and silver taken from the family home.

She looked at the letter clutched in Marcus' free hand. "I take it that is from Highcliff?"

"It is. There was no trial for Cassandra. He saw to it. By what means, I cannot say. Regardless, she has been committed to an asylum for the remainder of her days. No doubt, the convent looks infinitely better to her now. Pity she could not have had the foresight of her namesake."

Jane shuddered at the thought. "They are horrible places, and she is a horrible person. I cannot feel sorry for her even though I know that if I were a better person, I would."

"You are the best person I know," Marcus offered. "You've certainly been unwaveringly kind and sympathetic with me when I have been the worst patient one could possibly have."

She smiled at that. "You haven't been so bad... of late. The first week, when you had to remain abed—well, it's a thousand wonders I'm not in an asylum next to Cassandra."

As she walked on ahead, he caught her hand and pulled her back. "Let's stay here a moment longer," he urged. They were hidden from the house by the tangled branches that comprised the maze. The house was barely visible over top of it.

"You are not up to whatever it is you have in mind," she stated. "It's too cold out here by far!"

He laughed. "You'd be surprised what I'm up for, my darling. There is something I need to say to you, Jane, and I'd prefer to say it in a garden. It seems many of our most meaningful conversations have taken place there."

"Or in galleries," she retorted.

"Yes, but our conversations in galleries tend more toward the wicked side of things," he replied. "Do you recall the night of my return and our conversation in the garden?"

"I do. You asked to court me," she said, "for us to get to know one another and then decide if we should wed."

He grinned. "So, I did. Things did not work out quite that way, did they? We resolved your initial animosity to me but, sadly, my ability to offer you the time you had asked for to make a decision fled in the face of our families' machinations was compromised."

She nodded. "So it was... and so was I. What are you getting at,

Marcus?"

"I only wish to ask... do you regret it?" He uttered the question softly, with far more hesitation than she typically saw from him. "Given that we shall forever be so scandalized we can do nothing more than rusticate in the country with only one another for company, I feel I ought to ask."

Jane stepped closer to him and wrapped her arms about his middle, pressing close to his side. "I've many things to regret... my father's unfortunate temper and even more unfortunate choice of bride, the sad circumstances that led to your inheritance of the title, the fact that Charles actually shot you at my refusal to do his bidding... but I do not regret that our courtship was interrupted by marriage. In truth, I feel I have the best of both worlds."

It was true. He was forever making unexpected and romantic gestures toward her. Only the day before, he'd gifted her with a beautiful writing box of dark mahogany inlaid with mother of pearl. She had yet to confess to him her true ambition of writing a novel, but suspected that he was already aware.

"I should have said something sooner," he whispered. "I offered to make a declaration of affections to you once, in exchange for your cooperation in going to a more secure location. You refused me. I would make that declaration now."

Her heart was pounding. He'd shown her in a dozen ways the depth of his feelings. But neither of them had ever made a proclamation to one another of just where their hearts lay.

"And I would not stop you from doing so. Indeed, I am waiting with bated breath," she murmured.

"There here it is, Jane, and it matters not if you feel you cannot yet say it in return. I believe that, in time, this marriage between us will offer us both the greatest of happiness. It's already given it to me. I love you, Jane, and I'm content to wait forever until you feel inclined to return the sentiment."

Jane laid her head against his shoulder, her ear pressed just above his heart. "You are the most foolish of men, Marcus. On the morning of our wedding, I questioned myself. Even then, I suspected that I had fallen in love with you. It would not have taken much as I'd spent the better part of my life quietly worshipping you from afar. But when Charles shot you, when I saw you bleeding so profusely and had to accept the possibility that I might very well lose you, then I was certain."

"Certain that I am a foolish man or certain that I am the foolish man that you love?" he teased.

She laughed in spite of the serious nature of their exchange. She would always laugh with him, Jane realized. Their lives might never be perfect, but they would always be joyous. "I am hopelessly in love with you. And lord willing, I will remain that way until I die."

His arms tightened about her, pulling her even closer. "Is that the book you'll write then? A sweeping tale of love and romance? Will it be dashing?"

She looked him then and playfully smacked his arm. "You've been snooping!"

"Only a little. That was why I bought you the writing box. I found some of your discarded drafts tossed about the library in a fit of artistic pique," he said. "Do you miss writing for the Gazette?"

"No. I do not miss having to bribe servants for gossip, having to conceal my identity and sneaking about in the mews to ferret out what I could from other households. I never liked gossip. It was simply the easiest thing to earn a decent wage at," she muttered. "All in my ill-fated bid for freedom."

"Would you really have run away on your own?"

"Yes," she said. "I was imagining some little cottage on a cliff in Cornwall where I could stand against the wind and watch the angry sea. I thought it would be rather romantic. Now, I see it would only have been lonely. I'm far happier right where I am."

"With me," he finished.

"Always, my darling."

The End

Reviews are tremendously helpful to authors as they can increase advertising opportunities for them and boost the visibility of their book at retailers. If you enjoyed The Missing Marquess of Althorn, please consider leaving a review to let other readers know.

Also by Chasity Bowlin

Don't miss the other books in the Lost Lords Series from
Chasity Bowlin and Dragonblade Publishing:

The Lost Lord of Castle Black
The Vanishing of Lord Vale

Coming Soon in this exciting series:
The Resurrection of Lady Ramsleigh
The Mystery of Miss Mason
The Awakening of Lord Ambrose

Other historical romances from Chasity Bowlin:
The Haunting of a Duke
The Redemption of a Rogue
The Enticement of an Earl
A Love So Dark
A Passion So Strong
A Heart So Wicked
The Beast of Bath
The Last Offer
Worth the Wait

About the Author

Chasity Bowlin lives in central Kentucky with her husband and their menagerie of animals. She loves writing, loves traveling and enjoys incorporating tidbits of her actual vacations into her books. She is an avid Anglophile, loving all things British, but specifically all things Regency.

Growing up in Tennessee, spending as much time as possible with her doting grandparents, soap operas were a part of her daily existence, followed by back to back episodes of Scooby-Doo. Her path to becoming a romance novelist was set when, rather than simply have her Barbie dolls cruise around in a pink convertible, they time traveled, hosted lavish dinner parties and one even had an evil twin locked in the attic.

If you'd like to know more, please sign up for Chasity's newsletter by going here.
http://eepurl.com/b9B7lL